I0690297

# SACRED WOMAN

# SACRED WOMAN

## CYNTHIA E. KAZALIA

**BALBOA.**
PRESS

A DIVISION OF HAY HOUSE

Copyright © 2011 Cynthia E. Kazalia

All rights reserved. No part of this book may be used or reproduced by any means, graphic, electronic, or mechanical, including photocopying, recording, taping or by any information storage retrieval system without the written permission of the publisher except in the case of brief quotations embodied in critical articles and reviews.

Balboa Press books may be ordered through booksellers or by contacting:

Balboa Press
A Division of Hay House
1663 Liberty Drive
Bloomington, IN 47403
www.balboapress.com
1-(877) 407-4847

Because of the dynamic nature of the Internet, any web addresses or links contained in this book may have changed since publication and may no longer be valid. The views expressed in this work are solely those of the author and do not necessarily reflect the views of the publisher, and the publisher hereby disclaims any responsibility for them.

The author of this book does not dispense medical advice or prescribe the use of any technique as a form of treatment for physical, emotional, or medical problems without the advice of a physician, either directly or indirectly. The intent of the author is only to offer information of a general nature to help you in your quest for emotional and spiritual well-being. In the event you use any of the information in this book for yourself, which is your constitutional right, the author and the publisher assume no responsibility for your actions.

Any people depicted in stock imagery provided by Thinkstock are models, and such images are being used for illustrative purposes only.
Certain stock imagery © Thinkstock.

ISBN: 978-1-4525-3272-1 (sc)
ISBN: 978-1-4525-3274-5 (hc)
ISBN: 978-1-4525-3273-8 (e)

Library of Congress Control Number: 2011902410

Printed in the United States of America

Balboa Press rev. date: 3/1/2011

*To John*

# PREFACE

People often ask if a fictional piece reflects the author's actual experiences. In truth, much of the work contained herein is sheer, unadulterated fantasy. Yet this is *my* story even as it is *every* woman's story. We all journey markedly different paths but, ultimately, divergent roads merge, bringing us home to our authentic selves. *Sacred Woman* represents every woman's ageless struggle to discover and celebrate the gifts within. The *Sacred Woman* principles manifest eternal wisdom infused with potent, transformative powers.

Thank you to each of you, my companions who walk this earth with me. You are my wise teachers and I honor you. I am forever indebted to John, my loving, gentle giant. He accepts who I am, flaws and all, and encourages me to fully live as the eccentric, marvelous person the Universe created me to be. I also appreciate the many masters, past and present, including Sandra J. Burkeen. Blessings continually flow from close family, intimate friends, and complete strangers. It is a distinct privilege to share this life with all of you, especially my remarkable father, Lawrence J. Frank. Dad, an Eagle Scout and United States Air Force veteran, consciously chooses to live an inspiring existence as an exceptional, exemplary man.

A project of this magnitude requires time and expertise from innumerable sources. I am thankful to the enormously talented professionals at Balboa Press, a subsidiary of Hay House, Incorporated. This book would not have been possible without their on-going support and guidance. I also value the skilled photography of Ken Forrester of Imagine . . . E3:20 Photography. Ken and his wife, Amy, enrich this world.

Finally, I thank God, for all things – including infinite love, grace, patience, humor, and guidance. My greatest desire is to dwell in alignment with the Divine.

# PROLOGUE

Mighty. Eternal. Omnipotent. In a place of light and love, beyond all space and time, the spiritual elders communed in unified purpose around the sacred circle. Their garb, their manner of speech and movement, reflected diverse tribes, various traditions, and unfathomable gifts. Lakshmi, the raven-haired, breathtakingly beautiful Hindu goddess, her sari ornamented with shimmering rubies as well as precious stones of every hue, positioned herself next to Soma, an equally resplendent Zulu princess. Male and female, the twelve enlightened spirits represented the Most Holy. Together, they worked to prepare the innocent being, now reverently kneeling before them, for the time of transition.

The twelve were of one mind yet it was Aine, the Celtic goddess who translated shared images into soft, audible words. Finally, the task at hand completed, she gently inquired, "Are you ready, my child?"

"Yes, I am ready," responded the Beloved, her unfaltering voice clear, without a trace of perceptible fear.

"And so, it begins," commanded Banchewa. The medicine man, his muscular, finely toned body covered in sacred animal skins, gestured to the others with his exquisite, ornately carved staff.

The twelve rose from their exalted positions and ceremoniously encompassed the Beloved. These powerful spirits, eternally joined, physically intertwined, clasp each others' hands as they raised their arms, their indivisible souls, up to the heavens. Then the chant, a sound with no discernable beginning or end, electrified the cavernous chamber. Muted at first, the timeless voices rose like an enveloping crescendo - perfect in pitch and harmony.

Child of the Universe
Begin this day your journey.
Celebrate the virgin path,
Rich, consecrated Earth hold holy.
Seek Wisdom not in stars above,
Nor mortal man below.
For the Great Creator whispers truth
To quiet, listening souls.
Honor sacred contracts entered,
Before your birth of flesh.
Sit humbly at each master's feet
And teach the lessons you know best
Embrace thyself - a glorious being,
Adorned in gifts of divine imperfection,
Creation's power dwells within,
Forever radiant, your guiding light
Child of the Universe
Sing! Dance! Laugh! Play!
Angels herald your precious presence -
Awake to this new day!

# PART I

# THE ARRIVAL

# CHAPTER 1

*"I can't do it, Grandmother," the petulant, discouraged, voice exclaimed. "I can't please anyone! I don't even know why I bother to try. Everyone thinks that I am but an impulsive child. I don't think that I even make a difference in this world. "*

*The old woman, her face bearing the lines of many lifetimes, peered curiously at the girl. Something in the heartfelt words resonated within the ancient's soul. Ageless eyes, clear and brilliant in color, bore into the eleven year old that shared her bloodline. The girl, her own fruit not yet ripe, felt as if this one, this being who walked the earth long before her own birth, penetrated her very being.*

*Finally, the old woman spoke, her voice barely more than a raw, raspy whisper, as the sound of crinkled, fallen leaves underfoot. "Once upon a time, I knew a girl who felt as you now do." And, as her eyes stared off into another time, a different place, the normally quivering voice steadied as she began to tell a story with no beginning or end. A story of long ago - meant for all eternity.*

The child entered this world on the wings of a hawk. Its feathered form cut silently through the darkness of night with the precision of a hunter's knife. Land and water, a delicate mix of shadow and light, merged beneath his powerful, relentless form. Effortlessly, he crossed mountains and deserts and plains. Stars, incandescent threads against an ebony tapestry, illuminated the celestial journey as if aware of the importance of their friend's fluid, ceaseless movement.

Neither hunger beat at his belly nor thirst threatened to ground him. The spiritual elders provided for even this, the most basic of needs. Regardless, the Winged One understood that this moment's was not the time for physical nourishment. He flew on, intent on his spiritual mission - the Beloved with whom he had been so carefully entrusted.

Atop a voluminous pile of downy feathers, a baby rested contentedly on the hawk's broad mid-section. Peaceful slumber gently caressed this holy passenger as she entertained visions laced with the wisdom of the ages. All knowledge and truth flowed deep within the rivers of her subconscious. Yet she slept - unaware of either the earth below or the heaven that was, and always would be, within her grasp.

On that ground so far below, a lone wolf ran. Running Wolf, as he appropriately came to be called, instinctively followed the path that the Beloved traveled. It mattered not that she journeyed now on the wings of a hawk. For, like the Winged One, Running Wolf served as an animal spirit, an anointed entity summoned to guide and protect this child as she walked the great Earth. Neither time nor space, things seen or unseen, could separate either animal from his charge.

Night leisurely revealed its infinite mysteries before conceding to the pristine brilliance of an untouched dawn. Cloaked in dense fog, as protective wrap swaddling a newborn, the Winged One crossed the final mountain peak just as the fiery orb rose unceremoniously over the horizon. The regal bird then exited the evaporating mist, skimmed the translucent, azure lake with his wings, and landed softly in an iridescent field.

This was the Valley of Lilies. Ringed by majestic mountains melting into crystal waters, the meadow boasted a breathtaking array of lilies. White and pink. Orange and yellow. Waxy, elegant crowns stretched upward, greeting the ever-expanding sunlight as golden trumpets heralding revered royalty.

The hawk, too, lifted a talon in greeting - if only to acknowledge Running Wolf's presence. The wolf inexplicably materialized in a natural clearing not long after the bird ceased its eternal flight. The carnivorous animal returned the simple gesture, stretching out his front paws, lowering his head to honor this kindred, winged spirit.

Then the four-legged one skillfully closed the distance between them and expertly lifted the Beloved off the Winged One's back. He moved rapidly, carrying her in his powerful, steeled jaws as a coveted gift, its contents yet unwrapped. The trio proceeded without hesitation in the direction of the Beloved's future.

A single cabin populated the thick, densely wooded area by the lakeshore. Its rough hewn walls bordered a dirt floor, offering the two occupants shelter from the chill still lingering in the dew-laden spring air. Smoke trailed lazily out of the stone chimney. Nothing stirred.

Running Wolf arrived at the weathered front door of the cabin and gently lowered then released the baby upon the flagstone doorstep. He positioned himself, with intention, next to the precious bundle, eyes darting, alert yet still, like a palace sentry. The Winged One adjusted the Beloved's coverings with his mighty beak then soared to the top of a tall pine tree. Waiting. Watching. A glint of silver flashed among the sleeping child's soft cashmere blankets as the brightness of the yet rising sun enveloped them.

Inside the shelter, Elu pulled himself up from the pallet that he shared with Mahwah and stood erect, his back straight, muscular body lean. Long hair, grey for more than ten winters, lay tamed in two intricately beaded, braids. His physical movements revealed no indication of advancing age as this man silently moved to the hearth. Elu reached for the fire stick to poke the still warm embers. Then he knelt at a crudely constructed altar, opening his expansive arms and, with true humility, giving thanks to the Great Spirit for yet another day.

Across the modest room's expanse, still enjoying the morning glow under the warmth of a bearskin covering, Mahwah, her body rejuvenated from the hours of rest, observed her husband with deep affection. He was, without question, a good, decent man who had served the Great Spirit well during their long walk together on this earth. It seemed like only yesterday that Elu and Mahwah played as children on the banks of Swollen River or stole kisses behind Red Rock. Yet they both knew, were acutely aware, that they had little more than twelve summers remaining before the time of final transition.

Mahwah rose and joined her husband in morning prayers. Their chants suggested one voice, one spirit, one soul. The room swirled faster and faster around them like a vibrant, rotating dervish as their bodies merged and transformed. They became one with the fire's smoke as it curled up the chimney and assumed the form of doves, flying across the ever-widening sky.

Then, without warning, it was finished. The chanting stopped and, finally, Elu spoke, "It is time to fulfill our sacred contracts."

"Yes," said Mahwah quietly. She remembered another time and place. Long ago. A time not of this world. Both Elu and Mahwah had entered into a holy agreement with the Beloved - an arrangement to teach and learn from one another at this specific moment. Her heart filled with unparalleled joy as she recognized the long-awaited gift manifesting in their lives.

Insistent scratching at the entryway prevented further thought. Elu opened the weighty, cumbersome door and directed his attention downward until it rested upon the wolf still guarding his charge. "Go now," the man commanded and the animal complied, at least in theory, trotting but a few feet away. The Winged One remained vigilant upon his perch in the needle-filled branches of the high-reaching pine.

With indescribable emotion, Mahwah brushed past her husband to encircle the Beloved in her open, aching arms.

"She is her father's daughter - Adanya" the old woman proclaimed.

The baby awoke, her long lashes fluttering, at the utterance of her true name. Adanya opened her eyes, small pools the color of robin's eggs, and gazed up at the couple who would be her parents. Charming wisps of ebony ringlets delicately framed the fair, smiling, heart-shaped face.

But Elu heard neither the words of his ecstatic wife nor the proclamation of his daughter's name. Rather, his focus was drawn to a long chain of fine, liquid silver around the baby's neck. At the necklace's midpoint hung a vessel, a pendant. Symbols of this universe - the moon, sun, and stars - were expertly carved into the unique, intricate design gracing its surface. Precious stones - rubies, emeralds, diamonds, and sapphires - encrusted it.

Like no other jewel, its barrel shape fascinated Elu. He estimated the pendant's size approximately four inches long and, perhaps, two inches wide. A perfectly formed ridge ran along the circumference of its mid-point. Could there be two sections to the artisan's expertly crafted piece?

Elu cradled the vessel in his expansive, calloused hands. Then, after careful thought, he attempted to separate the jewel's top from its bottom, rotating it over and over, appreciating its fine craftsmanship, and, finally, pulling gently at either end.

Blue sparks emanated from the silver pendant and Mahwah gasped in horror, her mouth agape, as her mountainous, six foot, four inch, husband was thrown across the room like a limp, seemingly lifeless, ragdoll.

# CHAPTER II

*"Elu and Mahwah never again touched the necklace," said the old woman. Misshapen hands, twisted by the passage of time, consciously fingered the jeweled cylinder prominently displayed between supple, albeit sagging, breasts. "In fact, they warned the Beloved never to separate its pieces."*

*"Grandmother," exclaimed the girl. "Is this is your story?"*

*The woman smiled a secret smile. "Morning Dove, that is not easy to answer. This is my story even as it belongs to every woman."*

*Then she continued. "A fortnight after the baby's arrival three visitors rather unconventionally appeared."*

At the stroke of midnight, their actual identities shrouded by heavy, velvet-hooded cloaks, the women entered the dwelling, their unheralded presence wresting neither Elu nor Mahwah from dreamless sleep. The Winged One, alert in his chosen post, failed to issue an alarm. Likewise, Running Wolf, in his usual position at the foot of the cradle, remained watchful yet motionless.

Dagmar led the trio. Costumed in shades of magenta, her sleeves and skirt hem trimmed in fine gold, she bent over the white birch bed that Elu lovingly crafted for his daughter, gently lifting the awakening babe. Adanya observed an aura of light radiating from Dagmar's countenance. Yet the helpless, trusting infant uttered no sound, felt no fear, as a deep sense of peace and contentment radiated within her being.

Diella and Samara, as Adanya grew to know them, followed Dagmar, the babe nestled in the crook of her arm, out into the beckoning night. Stars shone brightly against the celestial ceiling as the unusual procession made its way across dew-laden fields to the enormous, waiting oak tree.

The *Tree of Life* stood apart from the forest surrounding the Valley of Lilies, about a stone's throw from the water's edge. Its branches, gnarled over thousands of years, shot up more than a hundred feet to brush the ever-changing sky. Its roots pressed downward, deep through the earth's abundant soil to the inner core from which sprang all life. And the tree grew, as it had through all eternity, as a living testament to the force which connects all living things.

The women knelt reverently as they came to the *Tree of Life*. The tree, one with all that is holy and good, breathed in their presence. Then Dagmar placed the infant in the tree's protective branches. And Samara uttered the spell, speaking charmed words to bring forth fire, "Ignectium. Protecta. Illumina."

Fire danced, immediately igniting, ringing the massive circumference of the oak tree's broad trunk. The women, feminine spirits cloaked in human form, now stood under the tree's canopy of delicately scalloped leaves, encircled in flame. Diella gently embraced the child, lifting her graceful arms to hold the Beloved high over the women's respective heads. In turn, with all the pomp and circumstance befitting the occasion, she majestically passed the bundle on to both Samara and Dagmar who repeated the centuries-old ritual.

The guides, for that was indeed the mystics' true calling, blessed the Beloved - the one who had received all blessings since the beginning of time. Then Dagmar spoke, "This is the child for whom heaven and earth has waited."

"This is the child who will altar the Universe for all time and for all living things," continued Diella.

"This is Adanya. The holy, most chosen, Beloved," finished Samara. "May her path, this sacred journey, open every beating heart even as it celebrates her own soul."

The infant watched, mesmerized, her speech limited to unintelligible, untranslatable gurgles, as the women performed mysterious acts and moved to internal rhythms until just before dawn. The fire continued to blaze, to dance and leap in the moonlight, without any known origin. Finally, it was time for the emissaries to give the baby their chosen offerings.

From the voluminous folds of her taffeta skirt, Dagmar produced a leather journal. On the front cover, tooled in the dark mahogany grain, was the *Tree of Life*. Dagmar lovingly ran her hand over the image before proclaiming, "Write the wisdom of your soul upon the pages of this book. Call forth your inner self even as you call upon the Almighty."

Then Diella knelt next to the swaddled infant. In her hand was a masterfully crafted fiddle. The stringed instrument emitted a sound that reverberated throughout the most expansive regions of the Universe.

"This fiddle plays the eternal song," said Diella. "Celebrate its music within your heart. Sing and dance as you bring forth its timeless melodies."

"And," said Samara, as she revealed an amethyst box made of the finest crystal, its glittering lid adorned with a porcelain butterfly knob, "this is the Box of Intentions. It holds your innermost dreams and wishes. Use this gift wisely. The power of the Universe lies within."

Then it was over. Dagmar forcefully clapped her hands once and the encircling flames instantaneously vanished. Underfoot, mature grass covered fertile ground, showing no sign of either ash or ember. The trio again bowed, paying homage to the *Tree of Life*, before returning the Beloved to her resting place within the cabin.

Adanya neither forgot - nor consciously remembered - the events of this night for many years.

# CHAPTER III

The bountiful seasons brought joy to the loving, close-knit family. Elu and Mahwah watched with delight as Adanya grew from infant to toddler and beyond. They marveled at the two animal guides who traveled the forest glen, accompanying their child as she played with carefree abandon among the towering fir trees. The beasts, especially Running Wolf, proved particularly gentle. Yet the pair fiercely protected their charge from harm.

Once, as the Beloved contentedly picked wild blackberries in a particularly thorny thicket at the edge of the woods, an openly hostile black bear, with an intense dislike of visitors in his perceived territory, emerged like a whirling, unpredictable windstorm. Having spent less than seven summers on the earth, the astounded girl froze in abject terror, dropping the half-filled, woven basket she clutched in her hand. Berries tumbled like unexpected raindrops scattering upon dry ground. The bear, his belly empty, hungrily eyed the plump, succulent fruit, originally intended for one of Mahwah's mouthwatering pies, and ferociously growled, standing to full height on his hind legs. Everything moved in slow motion.

Without warning, Running Wolf howled, baring his teeth and thrusting himself between the aggressive threat and Adanya's diminutive, paralyzed body. Snarling, lunging, mirroring the bear's every move, this fearless protector, at least temporarily, prevented the ravenous, menacing animal from advancing. That is, until the enraged bear took a powerful swipe at Running Wolf with his left claw. Still, the wolf, who at first offered no visible sign of injury, refused to retreat from his defensive position. Soon, however, like crashing sea waves, crimson flooded the surface of his grey and white fur coat. Raw skin hung loose. Running Wolf briefly faltered as the bear turned his undivided attention to Adanya.

A screech pierced the afternoon sky as the Winged One swooped down upon the bear's head. The bear cried out in a mixture of uncontrolled rage and raw pain as the bird's sharp beak penetrated, again and again, the soft tissues of his left eye. The eight foot, five hundred pound animal flailed frantically, unsuccessfully, as the hawk called upon other creatures of flight to join in the attack. Hundreds of previously airborne birds answered the echoing call. Finally, the partially blinded bear, confused, humiliated, and in excruciating pain, conceded defeat, stumbling off into a protective covering of trees. Where there had once been an eye, only a bloody, empty cavern remained.

That evening, Elu enjoyed the tantalizing pleasures of Mahwah's, particularly satisfying, blackberry pie while his daughter chattered excitedly. Adanya, adrenaline pulsating like an over-primed pump through her tiny body, told the story again and again.

"Running Wolf saved me," she exclaimed with the enthusiastic innocence of a six year old. "And the Winged One attacked the bear again and again." Adanya rounded the table with outstretched arms, rising and flapping, as she reenacted the bird's heroic feat.

Through it all, Running Wolf lay still in the corner of the cabin, breathing low, shallow breaths. His wounds were, by any known medical standard, severe. Elu had expertly halted the bleeding and bandaged the injured area. The gaping wound required more than one hundred stitches but Running Wolf emitted not even a whimper as Elu skillfully guided the needle and thread through the animal's savagely torn, ravaged body.

Elu, experienced with the nature and scope of bodily injury, recognized the severity of the attack and wondered if this loyal, selfless animal might have knowingly sacrificed his own life to save Adyana. It appeared less and less unlikely that the noble animal would survive the night.

When the sun rose the next morning, however, Running Wolf, quite miraculously, showed no sign of prior injury. His magnificent coat, which only the previous day matted in clumps, entire patches of fur missing, his skin bearing the inevitable brown stain of dried blood, presented as full and whole again. Running Wolf bore no visible physical evidence of the encounter with the bear.

Elu and Mahwah stood in awe of this incomprehensible sight. But, in their time on this earth, they had learned to trust the Great Spirit's hand, his indescribable works in their life. There was an intoxicating rhythm, a benevolent flow, to the Universe yet much remained beyond their understanding. That's why the couple registered only moderate surprise when three gifts - a journal, fiddle and glass box - mysteriously appeared, years ago, in Adanya's cradle.

At the time, Adanya, the infant recipient of these generous offerings, possessed neither language skills nor sufficient memory rendering her unable to explain their origin. Like the animals, though, these sacred offerings were never far from the child's touch as she grew from baby to toddler to young girl. Every night after dinner, Elu and Adanya played a private concert for Mahwah and the four-legged forest dwellers. Elu gently blew sweet breath through the cylinder of a handmade flute while his daughter's own, seemingly enchanted, fingers gave the fiddle life. The melodic sounds, hauntingly beautiful, filled the Valley of Lilies causing its inhabitants, creatures great and small, to pause and listen. Every living spirit appeared mesmerized by the enchanting innocence, the pure magic, of the father and daughter's musical interludes.

By Adanya's eighth birthday, the young girl adopted a habit of journeying deep into the forest upon full completion of her daily chores. Elu and Mahwah sensed that their only child needed the time to fully discover life, to explore the world within. Adanya would, in preparation, attentively wrap her journal and fiddle, along with the Box of Intentions, in a bit of cloth, securing them tightly with rawhide straps. Then she walked a solitary path - except for the company of her constant companions.

On one particularly steamy June day, Adanya enjoyed a private excursion to Tranquility Falls, a wonder that rose more than two hundred feet above the mirrored surface of the placid water below. Its fluid, tumbling forces, graceful, ever-changing as the seasoned body of a magnificent woman, fell majestically, rolling playfully into the azure lake. Ageless rocks at the top of the falls, their smooth, weathered surfaces marbled in tones of rust and slate gray, formed a natural slope into the lake.

Carefully setting her package of gifts on the water's bank, Adanya undertook the rocky climb to the pinnacle, diving fearlessly, without hesitation, from the top of the falls and cutting the surface of the waiting water below like a precise, sharpened blade. Then she swam, happily bobbing in and out of the cascading pool. Meanwhile, a butterfly, signaling personal transformation, played around her - skimming the water then fluttering off to drink the heady pollen of nearby wildflowers.

Drying off on a smooth rock warmed by the mid-day sun, Adanya lazily watched the graceful butterfly's flitting wings. She considered with awe its path from fuzzy caterpillar to soaring beauty. Then she opened her journal and wrote:

*Beauty gliding on the breeze,*
*Utter magic in my garden.*
*Tempting me with fluttering wings,*
*Telling me to come out and play.*
*Ever graceful . . .*
*Regal in a monarch's robes.*
*Flying by my spirit soars,*
*Living in the sun's warm glow*
*Yet a mystery to us all.*

"Transformation," she wrote. "How wonderful to become something new and different and beautiful. I wish that something magical lay deep within me."

Adanya put down her feather quill and curiously picked up the fragile Box of Intentions. The vessel, glistening like a polished gem, puzzled her. Intuitively, she understood that it possessed the power to manifest dreams. But she did not yet understand how it worked. Quite frankly, it baffled her young mind. Each day, the girl tested the box's powers. Sometimes she would put a ladybug or a blade of grass in it.

Hours later, Adanya would eagerly lift the lid to view its contents. Uncertain of what to expect, she felt dismayed to discover its contents virtually unchanged. Oh, perhaps the lady bug looked a bit perplexed or the grass a tad wilted, but, alas, nothing more.

On this day, however, almost as an afterthought, Adanya intentionally tore a page from her journal and wrote hastily on its pulp surface, "I want to see a deer." Then she determinedly folded the paper, creasing it over and over again, and placed it in the box.

As the sun dropped low behind the mountain range, Adanya recognized that the time necessitated a return to Elu and Mahwah. For the young girl spent almost a full day in rapturous adventure and, undoubtedly, her parents anticipated a safe return - soon. Nonetheless, Adanya felt defeated. All afternoon she painstakingly searched for a deer within the forest glen, straining her eyes with eager anticipation. Nothing. Frustration mounted. How hard could it be to spot a deer in this natural habitat?

Eventually Andaya returned home, albeit more than a little disappointed. Mahwah, her maternal instincts guiding her, sensed her daughter's sunken spirit. In fact, the palatable, depleted energy reverberated throughout the entire dwelling. Yet the girl adamantly refused to share her thoughts with the older woman.

It wasn't that the daughter held her mother in contempt. In fact, Adanya possessed a deep, abiding love for both Elu and Mahwah. But this all seemed so silly. How could she possibly give her confused thoughts voice?

Adanya, silently dutiful, aided her mother as the two prepared hearty portions of homegrown food for the evening meal. Cornbread and venison as well as leeks garnished the marked surface of the sturdy, functional table. Then the hardworking pair greeted Elu as he arrived home from his work in the adjoining fields. Elu, too, sensed his daughter's discontent.

As the meal commenced, Mahwah asked Adanya to fetch the lentil soup from the outside fire. The girl obligingly responded to her mother's biding and, struggling under the combined weight of the massive, cast iron pot as well as the hearty nourishment within it, brought it into the cabin, sloshing a substantial portion of its contents onto the dirt floor. Mahwah quickly relived her daughter of the weighty pot, placing it on the hearthstone, and then retrieved the oversized serving bowl from its storage place.

The serving bowl, pottery comprised of fired red clay, stood as a cherished family heirloom, of little material value, crafted generations before by Elu's ancestors. The bowl, speckled with fine cracks as well as deep crevices signifying extensive use, reflected years of unfailing service. Yet the image decorating its curved sides remained bold, completely intact. The long forgotten, long deceased artist had crudely depicted a sleek, four-footed animal boasting a full rack of horns.

Adanya, sullen from the day's apparent disappointment, absentmindedly fingered the pendant around her neck. She looked at the bowl with unseeing eyes.

# CHAPTER IV

By her twelfth summer, butterflies followed Adanya. They flew, merrily flitting in and out of the Beloved's path. Translucent wings, painted a breathtaking assortment of colors and patterns, delighted the girl. Yet, while Adanya celebrated the caterpillar's breathtaking transformation - its obvious grace and majesty - marveling at the inescapable sight, she did not fully comprehend the airborne insects' presence.

Elu and Mahwah also marveled. They marveled at each plentiful year's rapid pace as well as the immeasurable beauty that grew within their daughter. Like many parents, they marveled at the inescapable fact that their only child would soon be a young woman. For it seemed like only yesterday that the Great Spirit, by means of hawk and wolf, delivered Adanya, a small, contented baby, to their door.

But no longer was Adanya that small, contented baby. Her waist-length hair and round, maturing breasts served as a visual testament to the passage of time. Additionally, an unmistakable, untamed restlessness, pounded incessantly, demanding satisfaction, with every beat of her heart. Like the horses that ran wild throughout the valley, their thundering hooves echoing off the mountains as the distant drums of long forgotten tribes, Adanya railed against the fates that tied her to this land.

No longer did the Beloved enjoy the simplistic peace within the Valley of Lilies. There had to be more to this earth – a life beyond the pure, unpolluted waters, perhaps even beyond its snow-capped mountains. This life here was far too simple, too basic. Adanya instinctively knew that greatness awaited her.

The girl explored herself – experimenting more and more with the three gifts that she'd been given. For, while the potter's deer of four summers ago escaped notice, Adanya observed with increasing frequency that requests placed in the Box of Intentions did, in fact, come to pass.

Experiences with the box played as an entertaining parlor game to Adanya. She'd relax with Running Wolf on the emerald, moss-covered forest floor, skirts spread out around her as the reflective crystal box rested on her lap. The Winged One flew in ever widening circles above their heads.

"What should I wish for, Running Wolf?" the half-grown girl would ask rhetorically. "Perhaps some pretty beads to decorate the new skirt that Mahwah is soon to sew for me?" She wrote the word "beads" on a journal page, tore it out, folded it, and placed it in the box.

Whatever the request, Adanya often spend the next night, sometimes days or weeks, anticipating the item's arrival. In the case of the requested beads, however, the girl expended minimal energy in the wait.

First, Peddler Cratch, stopped by the cabin. Grizzled, his face twisted like the gnomes Adanya imagined to live in the deepest, darkest, most uninhabitable regions of the forest, Cratch forged a friendship with Elu and Mahwah long before Adanya's entry into their lives. He visited the Valley of Lilies every full moon to swap stories and indulge in a plate of Mahwah's enviable cooking. Cornbread and a shank of lamb certainly sat better on the belly than possum or squirrel.

Cratch, or more specifically, his goods, fascinated Adanya. His ox-drawn wagon held a wealth of tonics and trinkets, pelts and household goods, from distant lands. There was bright fabric and scented soap - even a fine comb made of ivory. And, on this particular trip, Adanya discovered, tucked away in a box decorated with exotic, fire-breathing dragons, an assortment of beads that the trader explained, in overly elaborate detail, a merchant bartered in exchange for some fine grain whiskey.

But the story of the beads doesn't end there. Later that week, long after the family bid farewell to Cratch, Elu simply decided, without any discernible prodding, to remove the beads from the braids that he had worn his gray hair in for so long. He offhandedly asked Adanya if she would like to add these beads to the collection that the peddler so eagerly traded for Mahwah's handspun wool. Now Adanya possessed an abundance of beads, enough to adorn many skirts.

Adanya never told Elu and Mahwah about these manifested wishes. In truth, she still had not yet figured out how the Box of Intentions operated. Certainly, it gave her thoughts life. But, once received, the materialized objects rarely appeared in the originally envisioned form. And some wishes never came true at all — at least not in Adanya's estimation. Therefore, it seemed prudent not to mention the box's abilities - inconsistent or otherwise - to her parents. They might, fearful of its power, forbid its use.

If the secrets contained within the Box of Intentions eluded her, Adanya discovered other essential truths in the surrounding world. Mahwah, whose very name meant, "Mother Earth", passionately taught the young girl to revel in nature's mysteries. The woman imparted wisdom to the Beloved regarding the sanctity of every spirit, every plant and animal.

Mahwah revealed to Adanya the miracle of spider webs and rising suns. For, limited in sight, the spider spins her intricate web in virtual darkness, never visually witnessing its full magnificence. Nonetheless, the spider works tirelessly, trusting that every movement, even the slightest effort, ultimately produces a uniquely designed, divinely inspired pattern of spectacular proportion.

Likewise, explained Mahwah, comes the sunrise. Often darkness floods the evening sky, voiding it of even the stars necessary to light one's journey. "But always," said Mahwah, "a glorious, new dawn follows the blackest of nights."

She also taught Adanya how to understand an animal's thoughts, the mental images with which every beast communicates. Soon Adanya, to her parents' amazement, could literally talk with the creatures of the earth, sky and water. These creatures connected with this compassionate human in a manner normally reserved exclusively for their own kind. Yet, the girl herself reserved her own most private thoughts for her journal.

Mahwah spoke to Adanya with increasing frequency about the changing seasons – spring, summer, fall and winter. From planting to harvest, each played a particular, irreplaceable role. Even bitter winter, with its harsh winds and innumerable snowfalls, served Great Spirit. For, as Mahwah pointed out, from the dead of winter comes the long-anticipated birth of spring.

It seemed crucial to the now bent, exceptional woman, advancing in years, that her child fully understand, or at least embrace, the known and unknown purpose behind every whispered breeze.

"The Universe is unfolding perfectly," she explained to her daughter. "You must speak these words every day in your thoughts, words and deeds. Your heart must know this to be true."

"But how can this be when there is death and disease?" challenged Adanya. "What of the tribes in faraway lands that war against one another? Surely these things must be bad, imperfect even."

Mahwah smiled. "The Great Spirit names neither birth nor death. Nothing is either good or bad – merely an opportunity to learn the great truths. All things that pass through our lives are invaluable gifts. For each event, even those that taste like bitter fruit, provides wisdom, a portal to grow closer to the spirit within us."

Adanya spoke not in reply.

Elu, a man of fewer words, spoke even less. In fact, as he and Mahwah drew closer to the time of their own transition, his physical presence was but a shell. No longer did he fill a room with his once hearty spirit. He detached from daily interactions, barely articulating either needs or observations to those around him. But what Elu did utter proved of infinite importance.

"You will always be a child," he said one night to Adanya as they harvested the autumn crops under the illumination of the full moon.

Adanya laughed and danced about, her skirt swirling, its beads gleaming in the steady rays of bouncing moonbeams. "I am your daughter, yes. But I am almost full-grown," she proclaimed proudly.

Elu watched Adanya – half-woman, half-child – as she whirled among the earth's bounty. Then he touched her arm with sudden urgency, his full strength surging through her. She ceased to dance almost immediately, looking up at the creased, much loved face, puzzled. Then she searched the eyes that she had come to know so well.

"What is it, Father?" she asked gently.

Suddenly, she knew not what his heart held. It was if Elu journeyed to a far away place - listened to a voice that only he could hear.

Adanya grew increasingly alarmed. She put her hand over the much larger one that Elu still rested on her arm. Again she asked, this time with great insistency, "Father, what is it? What is wrong?"

Hearing her fear, Elu returned from his solitary journey. Then he cupped one hand to her face and, stroking his daughter's silken cheek, said, "Come. Let us go sit by the tree."

Elu took his daughter's hand, leading her past the crops, out of the fields. This troubled Adanya for, while the family always planted and harvested by the cycles of the moon, they never once left the earth's return with harvesting incomplete.

The pair walked. Adanya moved silently, without question, for, though many trees stood in the forest, she instinctively knew Elu's intended destination. It was the old gnarled one. The one that stood alone by the lake, the tree whose branches swayed for all eternity.

When they reached this predetermined destination, Elu dropped to one knee as he always did, bowing his head. Adanya, who had observed this private ritual throughout her life, did not question it. Instead, she merely waited, reserving comment, until Elu raised his head and motioned for her to sit beside him.

Adanya complied, sitting as he had beckoned, and the butterflies that trailed her, even at this late hour, glided upward, becoming one with the leaves overhead.

Elu looked at his daughter. At first, the man, once so invincible, seemed to falter, uncertain as to what to say. Then, as if guided by some unknown force, his tenor changed. There was an unmistakable resonance to his voice, a meaning to his words, noticeably absent in recent months.

"I have loved you like a daughter yet you are not my child," he finally said. Adanya started to laugh, opening her mouth in protest, but Elu silenced her with a raised hand.

He gestured around them. "You belong to all heaven and earth. You are a child of the Universe. You are without beginning or end. All power, that which is seen and unseen, lives within you. This is your rightful inheritance."

Observing the open confusion on Adanya's face, Elu smiled reassuringly. "It is alright, my child. One day you will understand. You are not yet ready."

Adanya's mind raced uncontrollably, images colliding. She sputtered, struggling to organize her jumbled reaction, put ponderous fragmented thought into words. "But, but . . . how . . ."

Elu interrupted her utterance. "Fear not," he said quietly. "For you cannot forget that which is already written upon your heart."

Adanya shook her head slowly, bewildered. "But Father, I know not of what you speak," she said. "Of course I am your daughter. How can it be otherwise?"

Elu did not immediately answer. Instead, he rose, resolute, moving with purposeful strides in the direction of the fields. Then he abruptly stopped, turning back to gaze once more upon Adanya. Even from a distance, Elu saw unbidden tears shining in her blue eyes.

"Only love is real, my child. Nothing else matters," he reassured her. "The Great Spirit's life force connects all living things."

Then softly, almost inaudibly, he added, "I am always with you. Neither time nor death can change this."

That night, the crops uprooted and placed in the harvesting barn, Adanya slept fitfully. Elu's words troubled her. Not his daughter? What did this mean?

# CHAPTER V

Into Adanya's fitful slumber floated three women. Regally attired, the Beloved recognized her spirit guides instantaneously. For the trio, this visiting procession of heavenly dignitaries, entered her subconscious, dreamlike state with increasing frequency. Adanya happily welcomed their familiar, comforting presence.

As in previous appearances, the spirit guides solemnly beckoned Adanya to join them beyond the cabin's physical confines, with neither hawk nor wolf, in the splendor of night. The girl rose without thought, her bare feet gliding effortlessly across the unyielding, frost-tipped ground, watching as the others, encircled in flame, danced with rapturous abandon around the branched deity that Elu honored only hours before. Adanya, who had not entered the sacred circle since Dagmar first cradled her, stood alone on the outmost parameter of the flaming circumference.

"It is time," proclaimed Dagmar. "Come. Join us, Adanya."

Adanya surveyed the imposing circle of fire, noting neither beginning nor end. Crackling flame shot up as an impenetrable, insurmountable barrier, twenty-five or more feet, lapping the expansive ebony sky.

"But, Enlightened One, I cannot walk through fire," she despondently replied. "The flames will surely engulf my skin, destroy my flesh, for I am but a mere mortal."

"Nonsense," responded Dagmar. "Tonight you must walk through fire. Nothing can destroy you."

"Come," encouraged Samara and Diella in eerily synchronized unison. The erratic, ever-heightening flames framed their hauntingly, disembodied faces in the imposing wall of fire.

Fearful of displeasing her spirit guides, Adanya ignored her own considerable reservation, moving hesitantly forward.

"Stop," Dagmar imperiously ordered. "My child, you must never do anything out of fear, especially fear of displeasing others," she explained. "Rather, you must embrace the very circumstance that you fear - for you - with faith. That is courage."

The spirit guide allowed Adanya to absorb her words, continuing after but a brief pause. "Stand and breath deeply, inhaling and exhaling the life force, until your soul is balanced. Only then must you leap into the unknown."

Adanya complied with Dagmar's unsettling instruction. The Beloved slowly, with intention, breathed in the pure, crisp air inhaling all that is good and pure while deliberately exhaling toxic thought. She called upon the gods to protect her with the unparalleled earnestness of a sacrificial lamb before the slaughter. Then Adanya walked, unflinching, through raging flames, her single-minded destination the coveted safety of the inner circle.

Then it was finished. Once in the sacred space, the three spirit guides, with notable fanfare, offered congratulatory salutations, commending Adanya's demonstrated courage. Adanya, briefly numbed by successful completion of the death-defying feat, shook off any temporary paralysis, quickly inventorying her midsection and appendages from head to toe. Miraculously, she appeared virtually untouched. Her clothes, her body, showed neither indication of smoke nor the anticipated ravages of intense heat.

Yet something indeed changed. The pendant that Adanya proudly wore since birth now inexplicably glowed. Its pure silver barrel emitted a shimmering amber coloration. The very sight frightened the Beloved who struggled desperately, clawing urgently, to pull the chain from her neck.

"No, my child," said Dagmar. She insistently corralled Adanya's flailing hands, preventing further assault on the vulnerable, fine chain. "There's nothing wrong. The color signifies that it is time for the Great Spirit to reveal your destiny. Open the vessel."

"But, Enlightened One," exclaimed Adanya in disbelief. "Elu and Mahwah repeatedly warned me never to force the locket open."

Samara smiled. "It was not their destiny to open the pendant. That is your right alone, your inheritance, as a Child of the Universe, for it is your destiny that resides within."

Adanya cradled the bejeweled vessel, watching incredulously as it mysteriously restored to its original coloration. Then, rather timidly, holding the pendant's base firmly with her left hand, she rotated her right hand over its jeweled surface, gingerly turning the top piece counter-clockwise. Almost immediately, the encrusted pieces fell apart, a single content spilling out.

The girl, uncertain as to what to expect, registered surprise at the simple piece of parchment on her lap. The paper, yellowed with age, was meticulously rolled like an old scroll. Small black ribbons secured both ends.

Adanya looked up at the Enlightened Ones. Her face mirrored the disappointment that filled her being.

"What is it?" she asked.

"Open it," prompted Diella.

Slowly, carefully, Adanya untied the ribbons. Then she unfurled the ancient, cracked scroll.

Written in an unfamiliar script, were these words:

"You will find your gift within the goddess."

Astonished, Adanya looked up into the faces of her spirit guides.

"But what does it mean?" she asked for yet a second time that night.

# CHAPTER VI

Adanya dozed soundly on her pallet in the pre-dawn hours. Still, she acutely smelled acrid smoke, presumably lingering from the circle of fire, stagnant and suffocating in the stale, heavy air. In fact, the fire's intense heat now, without known reason, singed her skin. Where were the Enlightened Ones? They appeared to have vanished.

Something tugged at her urgently, incessantly demanding attention. Adanya's eyes flew open. This was not a dream! Fire engulfed the cabin, consuming the structure as a ravenous beast with its cruel, insatiable appetite. Running Wolf, as in times past, ignored his personal well-being, pulling at her left upper arm with his razor sharp teeth. The Beloved heard the Winged One's frantic cries in the now moonless sky.

Adanya brushed Running Wolf away. "Elu, Mahwah, where are you?" she screamed in uncontrolled terror over the deafening, ear-shattering roar of the fire. Timbers, weakened by the continual onslaught of merciless flame, dropped one by one as once proud, mortally wounded soldiers felled in enemy attack. Ash and debris licked Adanya's face like an evil seducer, tempting her to succumb to the overpowering carbon monoxide filling every square inch of the home. Fear rose as poisonous bile in her throat. There was no opening in the flames that imprisoned her. This is how she would die.

Then Adanya heard a voice within speak. "Tonight you must walk through fire. You must do the very thing that you fear – for you – with faith."

As in her earlier dream, Adanya calmed her breathing, called upon the gods and the Great Spirit they faithfully served, to protect her, then, wrapping herself in bed linens as a, albeit meager, measure of protection, lowered her head and moved through hell's inferno.

She awoke, hours later, to the morning sun warming her face. Running Wolf lay next to her, his fur providing immeasurable warmth in the crisp fall air. In her sleepy haze, Adanya recalled the horrible nightmare that previously filled unconscious slumber. What an awful dream!

But when Adanya forced open her eyes, a nearly impossible feat as fire and smoke quite successfully swelled the lids nearly shut, she realized that last night's horror had, sadly, been quite real. The cabin once shared with Elu and Mahwah, the cabin that Elu painstakingly built, log by log, with his own hands, was now, heart-wrenchingly, reduced to little more than worthless rubble. Only glowing embers, still producing notable smoke in the cool morning air, remained.

Realization flooded Adanya's being. Frantically, she scrambled to her feet. Where were Elu and Mahwah? Why had they let her sleep when everything lay in absolute ruin? She called for them, over and over, her throat raw from the effects of noxious gas, but only the consolatory whisper of the massive fir trees answered her.

Adanya collapsed as the truth filled her soul. Sobs racked her body. How could this be? What god would let this happen? Where was the Great Spirit?

Time stood still as the hours ticked by slowly. Exhausted, Adanya's sobs gave way, first to whimpers, then to quiet, inconsolable despair. She gasped for elusive breath until, eventually, the rhythm grew more even, less shallow. There, in the silence, Adanya heard, "The Universe is unfolding perfectly."

# CHAPTER VII

*"But, Grandmother," cried Morning Dove. "How can that be? How can the Universe be perfect when it took away everyone that Adanya loves?"*

*The old woman seemed not to hear her young granddaughter. Only silence filled the space between them. Then the elder spoke. "Love can never be destroyed, my child. And all that happens on this Earth is for a divine Purpose. Nothing is ever really good or bad. It simply is. All things come from the Creator that loves us. The fire, real or imagined, merely burns our human consciousness so that we might consciously ignite the glorious fire within."*

*Morning Dove allowed the words to soak into her consciousness, speaking no more, as the Ancient continued to weave the story of long ago.*

In the days that followed, Adanya moved as a sleepwalker, a spiritless zombie roaming aimlessly, devoid of either passion or purpose. It would have been easy surrender, to relinquish her own breath as a means of reuniting with her parents in sweet death. Elu had once shown his daughter, purely as a precautionary measure, which forest plants and berries quickly, irreversibly, ceased a man's breath. But both Elu and Mahwah's lovingly engrained lessons also taught Adanya to trust in the Great Spirit as well as the Universe's plan for her young life. Something in the heartbroken girl's inner being recognized this ageless covenant between man and his Creator, and, despite unimaginable despair, clung desperately to this unspoken promise.

Adayna, with Running Wolf's tireless, unfailing assistance, sorted through the charred remains of the once happy homestead. It was a grueling, gut-wrenching task as nothing survived the ferocious blaze that so mercilessly consumed her parents' lives. Or so Adanya thought.

On the second day, after sifting endlessly through soot covered debris, Adanya moved a charred timber. The task was not easy for such a small girl.

Adanya weighed substantially less, by hundreds of pounds, than the fallen structure's support. Yet she summoned amazing strength, hoping to find Elu or Mahwah under the weighty, burnt oak. Nothing. But, though exhausted, fatigue rolling over her like blows from an enemy's unceasing battering ram, her eye caught a glint of in the afternoon sun. There, under the protection of the fallen timber was the Box of Intentions. Beside the container sat Adanya's precious fiddle and journal – unmarred by the fiery, life-altering event.

Adanya never located the bodies of Elu and Mahwah. They appeared to have become one with the smoke which silently rose like ascending doves to kiss the sky. No grave needed dug. No body required burial.

Still, on the third day, Adanya went to the *Tree of Life* and, under the comforting embrace of its eternal branches, gave thanks to the Great Spirit for her parents. She remembered their sacred teachings, their role in her life. Then the Beloved sang and danced around the branched deity – her fluid movements honoring the never ending cycle of life and death.

Through it all, the Winged One and Running Wolf remained still, stoic at the grieving daughter's side, as honored guests at a burial mass. They listened, absorbing the soulful music Adanya passionately played on her fiddle, a reverent, mournful tribute to Elu and Mahkah. Finally, at sunset, when hushed silence enveloped the Valley of Lilies, neither bird nor beast calling out, Elu's unmistakable voice, perfect in pitch and tenor, echoed throughout the mountains. "I am always with you. Neither time nor death can change this."

Adanya lay down her instrument and wept.

Time passed in its own, almost unnatural, rhythm. Every day Adanya poured feelings of grief and despair onto the pages of her journal. Like a mantra, Adanya repeated Mahwah's words, "The Universe is unfolding perfectly." Again and again. Over and over.

In truth, the effort proved more rote than representative of personal belief, but still she repeated it. "The Universe is unfolding perfectly." The words resonated as a single life preserver in stormy, life-threatening seas.

Adanya created temporary living quarters in the harvest barn. The barn, untouched by natural destruction, sat filled to its rafters with the labor of that last night. Corn, squash and potatoes adorned the tree bark that served as a makeshift plate at mealtime. In addition to this bounty, fish from the lake as well as milk from the cow comprised most meals, though the bounty often spoiled, uneaten by the grief-stricken child.

At night, while Running Wolf and the Winged One stood vigilant guard, Adanya sought refuge with the livestock. Ox, cow and sheep welcomed her gentle presence. The Beloved felt less alone, perhaps more alive, surrounded by the frequent stirring, the company of beating hearts.

Still, though warmed by the beasts' heat, Adanya wondered. What happens when fall turns to winter? How would she survive? One night, in desperation, she wished upon a shooting star, a luminous paintbrush dipped in gold, streaking brilliantly across an otherwise dark sky, for help - any kind of assistance. Then, to be sure, she placed her wish for help in the Box of Intentions. Oh, if only Elu and Mahkah were still alive.

On the eve of the full moon, Cratch, the peddler, made his way to Elu and Mahwah's land. He eagerly anticipated good company – and hearty servings of home cooked food. This time the grizzled traveler carried a new hunting knife as a token of friendship for his long-time friend. The journeyman who traded Cratch the piece for a supply of chewing tobacco insisted that its honed blade once rested in royalty's hand, protecting the crowned owner from unexpected fate. Into its one-of-a-kind handle, the original maker painstakingly carved celestial symbols - moon, sun, stars, and other orbs.

Horror filled Cratch as his aging, nearsighted ox pulled the rickety, overflowing cart onto Elu and Mahwah's property, his unbelieving eyes opening wide as he absorbed the devastating scene before him. Nothing of the, once sturdy, family shelter remained. What tragedy befell his good friends? Quickly, Cratch scanned the area for signs of life. No human form came forth. Then he bade his ox to stop as he slowly, reluctantly, jumped down from the wagon's high seat.

Cratch explored the forever altered site, compelled to search for non-existent remains, then, begrudgingly admitting defeat, sorrowfully set up camp by the lake. There, on the second day, as he bathed in frigid waters, the pure, clear lake where he and Elu so often fished, the peddler observed a lone figure emerge from the forest. Uncertain as to friend or foe, Cratch cautiously moved toward the shoreline, intent on grabbing his hatchet as well as something to cover his god-given nakedness. The peddler, though not particularly modest, saw no good reason to expose his nether regions to potential harm.

Slowly, the blurred, distant image came into full focus, the peddler finally recognizing Adanya, butterflies about, a hawk perched regally on her right forearm. At her side, already sizing up the uninvited guest, was that ever-present wolf. Adanya raced to the family friend, one foot faster than the other, as if the goal line, this campsite destination, brought her back to Elu and Mahwah and the cherished life they once shared. Then, at the finish, she collapsed, the enormity of her loss too great to bear.

As night approached, revived, freshly clothed in a new top, skirt, and leggings generously gifted by Cratch, Adanya recounted the painful, forever remembered events of recent weeks. Her hands worked unconsciously as she talked, tying a silk scarf, patterned with butterflies, around her waist. The dull, flat voice provided but a glimpse of the girl's exhausted body, her shattered heart.

Uncomfortable with emotion, uncertain as to how to offer comfort, Cratch self-consciously, a bit off-handedly, presented Adanya with the knife originally intended for Elu. It seemed fitting that the father's only child inherit it. Touched, Adanya thanked the peddler, then, without further comment, tied the weapon to her waist.

Cratch listened throughout supper, toothlessly gumming the campfire cornbread that Adanya whipped up for him. When words gave way to comfortable silence, Cratch noticed that the girl's physical demeanor suggested relief at sharing her tremendous burden with another human. To this outside observer, the pain felt unbearable. He could not comprehend the unimaginable grief within her. But Adanya shed no tears for, like a well that stands for forty years in an arid land, none remained.

Finally, running his arm across his mouth to wipe off the excessive food remnants from his scraggly, peppered beard, he commented, "Ain't good for a young girl to live in the woods. Can't survive without no kin."

Adanya said nothing. Something in the depths of soul welled up, railing against the fate that was to come. Yet she remained silent.

"Gots family over in the next village. A sister. None too friendly but she might take you – in exchange for the food in the harvest barn," he continued. "No, ain't good for a young girl to live in these woods." His twisted face, misshapen with age, seemed more final, increasingly resolute with every word.

Still, Adanya said nothing. And the silence sealed her fate.

Within two-day's time, Adanya and Cratch loaded the harvest into Elu's wagon and harnessed Elu's ox to it. They released the chickens and the other animals into the wilderness, tying only the cow to the back of the wagon.

As the wagon wheels creaked, groaning under the cargo's excess, pulling away from the empty foundation where the cabin once stood, Adanya felt an unspeakable sadness wash over her like cleansing, purifying bathwater. She grieved one last time for Elu and Mahkah, the life they once shared.

Adanya anxiously fingered the pendant around her neck. And, throughout her being, the words rang out, **"You will find your gift within the goddess."**

# PART II
# THE QUEST

# CHAPTER VIII

*"But, Grandmother, how can silence seal one's fate? Grown-ups are always telling me to be quiet," said Morning Dove.*

*"Silence is good as an opening to the soul. But Adanya remained mute even when she sensed that this was not the right path. In her silence, she chose to walk it," explained the Ancient.*

*Morning Dove tilted her head, her brow furrowed, as she considered these words then rejected their merit. "But, Grandmother, Adanya was but a child. She didn't have any choice."*

*"Ah . . . ," smiled the elder knowingly. "But of course she had a choice. It matters not the age for the Universe always presents each of us with choices. And we do what we wish."*

*"Ha!, " Morning Dove retorted scornfully. "I don't do as I wish.*

*The Ancient's piercing look bore into her granddaughter's core as the elder's words rang out to the corners of the earth. "We all walk the path of our own choosing. Sometimes our acts are in accordance with the Great Creator. Sometimes, however, we are unwilling to pay the initial price of listening to the soul."*

*Then the woman finished, "It is at those times, the moments when we fail to listen, that we pay the highest price of all."*

Cratch's sister, Brumledi, as the peddler accurately predicted, begrudgingly took the orphaned girl into her home. The gesture, however, came not without considerable cost. In fact, the cost proved far greater than the earth's plenty and the single milk cow that Adanya originally offered - very great indeed.

Brumledi and her silent, long-suffering husband, Ohan, resided in a six-room, cobblestone house in the seafaring town of Ambilen. Adanya, who never before ventured beyond the Valley of Lilies, marveled at the sights and sounds of the costal village. Merchants hawked their wares while children played tag in the bustling, overcrowded streets. Every day the newcomer explored quaint shops and traveled the short distance to the town's pier. Never before had she seen the vast waters that rolled unending before her eyes.

Adanya envied the women's more refined style of dress with gaily feathered hats and long, luxurious skirts. Mahwah's beautifully beaded skirt, her leggings and embroidered top, now seemed terribly simple, certainly unfashionable. Ambilen exuded a sophistication previously lacking in the Beloved's former life by the lake.

But if Adanya's dress reflected simplicity, the relationships within that cobblestone home proved far more complex. Certainly the building itself was exceedingly finer than the modest, rough hewn cabin that the girl once shared with Elu and Mahwah. The lavish furnishings, including a golden harp, originated from exotic places and far off lands. Magnificent, intricately woven, tapestries draped the walls. Handcrafted with premium silk threads, expertly constructed, the coverings depicted gentile images of gods and goddesses. Zeus and Apollo. Hermes and Aphrodite. Could this be a sign? Is this what the scroll meant with it said, **"You will find your gift within the goddess"?**

No answer immediately emerged. But, while the enviable structure provided shelter from the outside elements, it did little to shield its inhabitants from the turbulence within. This was not the peaceful sanctuary of Adanya's short-lived youth. Every day a tempest brewed within the restrictive, suffocating confines of its stone walls.

Adanya, lively and talkative in her days with Elu and Mahwah, grew reserved, astoundingly mute, as she first observed the household. For the polarizing relationship between Ohan and Brumledi both fascinated and repulsed her.

Every morning, Ohan, a dutiful, dedicated husband, patiently listened, unperturbed, to a laundry list of grievances, less real than imagined, from his overbearing, ill-tempered wife.

"Ohan, you don't make enough money as a shopkeeper," railed Brumledi. "If you made more money then I could trade that lazy, good-for-nothing Adanya for a proper servant."

"Yes, dear," replied Ohan. "You're right. I need to make more money."

"Ohan, you don't speak your mind often enough. Why can't you be bolder with your thoughts?"

"Yes, dear," came the oft repeated refrain.

But, as Adanya soon discovered, the real issue, neither money nor words, resided naught in Ohan's behavior. For when he deferentially complied with Brumledi's stated requests, the demands suddenly, without warning, changed.

Once, in an attempt to secure more money, Ohan undertook extra night work herding sheep at an outlying farm. The work itself, which came only after completing twelve or fourteen grueling hours at the mercantile, was not inherently difficult. But Ohan, more suited to a gentleman's life, rarely indulged in physical labor. His small frame, his keen mind, was not designed for the rigors of outdoor work. And the storekeeper found it frustrating, physically taxing, to shepherd the stubborn, sometimes willful, creatures in the treacherous, unforgiving hillside surrounding Ambilen.

Nonetheless, a weary but rightfully proud Ohan eagerly presented his precious hard-earned coins to his wife as a token of undying affection. Brumledi, after ordering Adanya to clear the supper table of its unclean dishes, peered dismissively at the shiny tender in the black velvet coin bag, her angular face registering disgust.

"Why do you work so many hours, Ohan? Lettia's man comes home before the sun's last light. He helps her with the day's chores," she sniffed indignantly before greedily gathering the coin bag in her boney fingers and depositing it in the deep pockets of her skirt.

It was never enough.

Furthermore, in the few instances when Ohan actually spoke his mind, the home's ever-brewing storm exploded into an electrifying show of thunder and lightening bolts. Brumledi only respected the bold sharing of ideas when uttered thoughts mirrored her very own.

It is important to note, however, that Brumledi's tirades, these emotional tsunamis, wreaked havoc with others residing in the household as well. The couple's three children, Braun, Mietta and Petro, though slightly younger than Adanya, often encountered the full undiluted force of the woman's uncontrolled wrath, her endless discontent. The daily discourse varied but the children gingerly tiptoed through each tense hour like frightened, vulnerable townspeople fearful of awakening a sleeping giant.

When the giant unpredictably wakened, however, each child dealt with the resulting onslaught differently. The two older children, Braun and Mietta, following Ohan's passive example, retreated silently. Braun spent time, exerted understandable frustration, in his father's workshop pounding boards like a man possessed. Mietta, on the other hand, weathered unpredictable storms camped out in the room that she now, quite unhappily, shared with Adanya. Petro, the youngest, a cunning, likeable boy of nine years, followed a markedly dissimilar path than his siblings. He combated the giant's advance with an armory of wiles and thinly veiled flattery.

Surprisingly, Brumledi favored Petro. Perhaps the affection compensated, in some small way, for the vile reaction the woman demonstrated more than nine years earlier when advised by the Healer that a third, unexpected child resided in her womb. Brumledi's violent outcry rocked the already unstable home. She permanently threw Ohan out of their marriage bed, hitting him with his own bedding as she chastised him, berating her husband repeatedly with unspeakable curses, for carelessly planting his seed, once again, in her womanhood.

Every day, as the months passed, Brumledi secretly hoped to turn out the growing fetus. This mother of two young children completed necessary chores with an unprecedented vengeance. She, rather theatrically, threw herself down the winding, spiral staircase, an effort that failed to prematurely induce labor but did little for her previously damaged spine. Undeterred, the spiteful, headstrong woman consumed plant roots reputed to possess poisonous fluid in the hopes of eradicating the unborn child.

Yet, even though she doted on Petro, perhaps out of unassuaged guilt, Brumledi staunchly refused to permit her youngest son to play with the village boys. She lectured Petro that his peers, dirty sorts in her estimation, spawn from filth, bore little prestige and certainly proved unworthy of association with her noble son. Petro listened attentively to his mother's words, often nodding his head affirmatively in somber agreement.

"Yes, Mother. You speak with great wisdom. I understand," said the young boy. He gave the woman a perfunctory kiss on her cheek and left the room.

Following these exchanges, Adanya often caught sight of Petro's plum cotton britches as he scampered down the weeping willow tree which grew, tall and strong, alongside his bedroom window. The youngster disappeared into the streets, playing yantri, a game of chance more than any remarkable skill, with the village boys until afternoon's elongated shadows signaled his return. Petro then effortlessly ascended the willowy branches, entered an open second story window, descended the home's staircase, and assumed his rightful place at the dinner table - his sainted mother none the wiser.

Yet, despite its vibration of continual unrest, for Adanya, life in her new home was not entirely without merit. If the increasingly hostile surroundings left emotional needs unfulfilled, there was certainly no physical lack. The girl had food in her belly and a roof over her head. Furthermore, Ohan and Brumledi made no discernable distinction between their own children's material needs and their unanticipated border's desires. For this, Adanya felt eternally grateful.

In fact, the contrast between the home's material abundance and its emotional void, the contaminated atmosphere, confused Adanya. Many folks might suggest, perhaps rightfully so, that she endured little to complain about. Nonetheless, Adanya never quite understood Brumledi or felt comfortable surrounded by the women's irrational, self-induced misery.

For a considerable period, Adanya thought the unrest normal. Perhaps this is how people actually lived outside of the Valley of Lilies. Her only real examples prior to this experience had been her own parents. Maybe this was how most people interacted.

Or, perhaps, the fates were merely guiding Brumledi through a challenging period. Brumledi obviously possessed redeemable traits. In fact, on the rare occasion when storm clouds subsided, the conflicted woman could actually be quite humorous. Furthermore, few matriarchs would consent to board a twelve year old girl, especially one not of their own clan's blood. This remarkable act alone, while not entirely selfless, deserved respect.

That said, as Adanya grew more accustomed to her environment, she relinquished any initial feelings of trepidation, once again finding her voice. The girl spoke out with increasing frequency against the cruel, unwarranted attacks that assailed not only the family members but Adanya as well. The enraged giant, while terrifying, welcomed these escalating sparring matches. It was as if Adanya represented an opportunity to prove her superiority and Brumledi baited the unsuspecting girl, time and time again, as mere sport.

Adanya, however, detested the senseless, verbal warfare. Venomous emotions welled up, twisting her stomach while causing her head to throb in intense pain. Truly, it was never the girl's intent to enter into heated exchanges but even innocent, seemingly harmless statements easily ignited the emotionally charged atmosphere. Adanya mistakenly believed that logic, coupled with sincere, carefully chosen words, would eventually calm Brumledi's obviously troubled soul.

It never worked. Logic culled illogic. There was always some reason that Adanya's suggestions didn't apply. The girl didn't understand. Brumledi railed against the gods and her own bad luck. She lashed out at her husband, her children and, even, herself. She attacked Adanya as an ungrateful cur. Not once, however, did Brumledi take responsibility for erecting the steel bars in her own, self-created prisons.

But, if Brumledi failed to change, Adanya certainly did. Anger, a sense of futility, replaced the girl's inherently peaceful nature. Why wouldn't

Brumledi see the wisdom in Adanya's words? Why couldn't Brumledi love her? Negative thoughts consumed every waking hour. Despair filled the dark, hopeless nights.

Finally, fueled by Brumledi's unkind words, her unfounded accusations, the contentious exchanges between Adanya and the older female reached their zenith. At the conclusion of one particularly brutal conflict, Ohan knocked respectfully, insistently, on the girl's shared bedroom door.

Adanya, angry tears still lining her red, blotchy face, bid him entrance. "What brings you here, Ohan? Do you also want to throw out lies for my ears?" Adanya spoke sullenly, without restraint.

Ohan sank down on the corner of the bed. His stooped shoulders revealed the heavy burden within his soul. "You must be more patient with Brumledi, Adanya. She is a good person who tries to do the right thing."

Adanya snorted indignantly. "She is sick in the head, Ohan. Surely you must see this."

"Yes, my wife is sometimes agitated but she means well. You must not antagonize her."

"But, Ohan," Adanya cried. "She turns the truth to serve her own twisted thoughts. How can you defend her when she treats you so shamelessly? Must I allow her to treat me as nothing but a bastard child? Does not even a bastard deserve respect?"

Ohan sighed. There was truth in the girl's words. Too long had he tried, unsuccessfully, to understand his angry, disconsolate spouse. But the hour of their union was long past. The deed was done. Too much would have to change, to be addressed. Ohan's only solace hinged on the family's self-built illusions steadfastly masqueraded as truth. Adanya's presence, her reality based thought, threatened to demolish the carefully constructed charade of their lives.

The man reluctantly stood, distractedly straightening his pants, his apparent resolve unflappable. Then he looked at the girl that he had inexplicably grown to love like his own daughter. Yet he was not her father.

"It matters not. If further problems arise, Brumledi and I plan to send you to live with the Sisters of the Sacred Covenant. Maybe they can give you what you need." Not able to bear a response, Ohan abruptly turned and exited the room, leaving the speechless girl.

Adanya wrote less and less in her leather journal. She sought only the company of Running Wolf and the Winged One. And the Enlightened Ones no longer crept into her dreams.

The long winter began.

# CHAPTER IX

*"It makes no sense, Grandmother," commented Morning Dove. "Why wouldn't Ohan listen to Adanya? The girl spoke the truth, even if she was but a child."*

*"Yes, my granddaughter. Sometimes our wisest teachers come in the form of an innocent child. But it is not the gardener's place to force the flower's bud. For each flower must choose the time of its own blossoming."*

*"But, Grandmother, if Spirit's lesson falls on deaf, unhearing ears, what is the point?"*

*"Perhaps the lesson was not intended for either Ohan or Brumledi but another, Little One."*

*Morning Dove searched the Ancient One's face in amazement. "But, Grandmother, if not them, whose lesson was it?"*

Spectacularly ruthless snowstorms relentlessly pelted Ambilen in the months that followed, feeling more like the wrath of vengeful, overly zealous gods than the renewing, seasonal handiwork of Mother Nature. Ice repeatedly encased the seafaring village rendering it inescapably paralyzed, hazardous for townspeople to venture out, much less earn a proper wage. Snowfalls reached unprecedented heights, drifting across walkways, closing roads for transport, and imprisoning the helpless, albeit resilient, inhabitants.

Through it all, Adanya endured the prescribed hibernation in the comfortable room shared rather uncomfortably with Mietta. It proved an indescribably lonely, a decidedly solitary existence as Brumledi, without warning, impulsively banned both Running Wolf and the Winged One from the residence. Adanya knew not how the creatures survived in the frigid, life-threatening temperatures - or if their bodies even still held breath. She feared that, like Elu and Mahwah, her precious companions no longer walked this earth. Or perhaps, feeling abandoned, they, in turn, abandoned her. What if they no longer loved her?

This fear, this belief that no one in the Universe loved her, heightened Adanya's already intense feelings of despair and isolation. She wept uncontrollably at Brumledi's frequent tongue lashings, no longer offering churlish retorts or staunchly defending her actions. The heartless woman watched with undisguised contempt as pools overflowing with notable pain filled the injured girl's eyes.

"Adanya, one who spills tears as you must house demons in her soul! I don't know why the Great Spirit cursed me with such an unstable ward," the unfeeling woman proclaimed.

In truth, Adanya thought with increasing frequency about the Creator. Why had he brought her to this place? What was the point? Why didn't anyone love her? Was there even a purpose to the interminable hours between sunrise and sunset? Adanya nervously, unconsciously, fingered her pendant as of in answer to an unspoken prayer.

One day, as the bitter wind howled like a banshee wailing unheeded warnings of impending death, Adanya sat unaware, cross-legged on the wide, wood planked floor of her room, a warm blanket, spun of lamb's wool, tucked around her gently curved shoulders. She commiserated on her plight alone, as Mietta competitively played board games with her family in the downstairs parlor, except for the company of a long-legged spider seeking refuge from winter's far-reaching, icy grasp. The Beloved never felt more removed from the world - and the isolation slowly suffocated her very existence.

Adanya, quizzically observed the eight-legged creature as it determinedly scurried up the clammy, moisture-glazed stone wall. Her eyes followed the spider ever upward, studying the higher and higher pursuit until he reached his intended destination, a web, the insect's glorious creation, woven skillfully in the upper right corner of the window. Interestingly, despite the glorious overall effect, the individual strands of the web, when considered independently, held no immediately discernable wonder or significant meaning. One thin, spongy strand intersected, seemingly at random, with another and another.

Nonetheless, the resulting design instantly captured one's attention as a miraculous sight to behold - especially when the sun's brilliance shone through the fine, silken threads. Single, seemingly unrelated, threads divinely ordered to form absolute, unduplicated magnificence.

What had Mahwah told her so long ago? "The Universe is unfolding perfectly."

Adanya took out the Box of Intentions, reverently wiping a thin layer of dust from its crystal surface. Much time passed since she called upon its mysterious powers.

"I don't understand how this works. But, if you can hear me, Great Spirit, I desperately need your help. Please send someone to love me."

She tore a piece of parchment from her journal. "This is my last hope," she said to no one in particular. Then she picked up a quill and dipped it into the dark, fluid ink. On the page, she wrote a single word, **"Love"**.

A voice not her own spoke in the silence. "You will find your gift within the goddess."

Adanya, as if hearing this revelation for the first time, suddenly understood precisely what she had to do. She would search for the goddess in the spring!

# CHAPTER X

Spring arrived in the third year. The harbinger heralding the emergence of this long-anticipated season never warbled a sweeter, more long-awaited song. Nor had the celestial ceiling, appropriately painted a cornflower blue, ever looked so expansive. From the rich, fertile earth sprang fresh, celebrated life.

Adanya, now fifteen, walked the streets of the costal town as a virtual stranger. Few people recognized the stunningly beautiful woman who traveled in the company, once again, of wolf and hawk. Perhaps that's because, like the butterflies merrily trailing her, Adanya experienced significant transformation.

No longer a child, the blood that is a woman's crown visited regularly without invitation. Full, ruby lips, intoxicatingly complimented by firm, inviting breasts, gave way to an enticing hourglass form. Adanya's physical appointments hinted of tantalizing mysteries, as of yet, undiscovered.

But it was Adanya's delicate, porcelain face that captured exclusive attention, mesmerized those souls whose unsuspecting gaze fell upon it. Her fiery eyes, once the color of robin's eggs, deepened over the extended winter to a brilliant sapphire. Surrounded by luminously vibrant, wildly spiral tresses, Adanya's countenance brought even right thinking men to their knees. The woman, quite unknowingly, was a temptress.

Yet no matchmaker darkened Ohan and Brumledi's door. Girls notably younger than Adanya, by three, even four years, eagerly sought Yeti's renowned matchmaking services. Adanya, however, little more than a servant girl, brought neither noble name nor gold coin to the marriage bed. She intrinsically understood, as Brumledi emphatically, rather gleefully, told her, that no worthy man would extend his hand.

Nor would the most unworthy of men hungrily pursue her. There was something unsettling about Adanya - something that abruptly halted even testosterone imbued males from gracing her presence. Men, wary of the wolf and hawk who maintained vigilant watch over the lass, rarely lingered to smell the heady, aromatic perfume anointing her body. And the butterflies, those creatures with gossamer wings, proved problematic. They wove, in and out of the Beloved's flowing, raven-hued locks, encircling her aura, leaving hardy, confident men unmistakably perplexed, decidedly flummoxed.

Then there was Adanya's unusual manner of dress and speech. No refined woman wore shorter, colorfully beaded skirts, intentionally exposing her calves. Was she a harlot? And, while the Beloved spoke to no man, animals readily understand the girl's tongue. Goats, oxen, horses - it mattered not. All creatures bowed low in the presence of Adanya.

But if animals communicated with Adanya, the townspeople most certainly did not. Mothers herded their children across the street if the girl's shadow darkened their path. Covert whispers, inadequately muffled by gentile hands, replaced normal greetings. Was the woman a sorceress?

"Mark my word," implored one stout woman in hushed tones, loud enough to be heard and oft repeated. "There's many a spell cast on the eve of the full moon. And that dark one knows more about the world below than many a maiden."

"Aye," said another. "I hear that she sacrifices goats to appease the infidel who has fallen from the Great Spirit's favor. She curses all god-fearing mortals that cross her path."

Adanya ignored these cruel, stupid comments. But the rumblings, the immense pain within her soul, cemented her resolve. It was time to find the goddess. It was time to find the abundant riches, the gifts missing from her life.

At the spring equinox, the girl slipped stealthily from her bed chamber, journeying deep within the forest. Barefoot, her swift feet barely touching the velvet, moss-covered ground, she closed a great distance long before the owls hooted. Adanya paused for breath only when the round moon shone brightly on a clearing in the forest glen. There, the Winged One kept watch from the tallest tree while Running Wolf remained, ever-alert, at his charge's side.

Gathering twigs into a moderately high pile then expertly rubbing sticks together, demonstrating skill known only to seasoned woodsmen, Adanya lit a blazing bonfire and proceeded to pull her fiddle from the belongings carefully selected, attentively compiled, for this auspicious occasion. She caressed the finely tuned, highly polished instrument like an old, dear friend. This gift that played the eternal song had remained untouched, silent for many a season. Adanya lovingly picked up its bow, leisurely caressing the taut string. Then she moved the bow rhythmically, back and forth, weaving an eerie, hypnotic tune, drifting in and out of the trees.

At the stroke of midnight, the melodic, lonesome serenade ceased. The girl lay down her fiddle now drawing out the knife that Cratch once gave her. Pressing its blade in the dirt, Adanya outlined a sacred circle.

Blessing it with the pendant around her neck, she placed a goddess figure, carved of fine oak, into the Box of Intentions and reverently set both the box and its contents inside the circle. Adanya laughed and spoke to Running Wolf. "I am so alone. I would take anyone, even the blackest of hearts, to love me."

With intent, she lifted her outstretched arms to the night sky, invoking the goddess.

*"By the Earth from which all life springs,*
*By the Air that gives mortal man breath,*
*By the Fire that burns the sacred soul,*
*And by the blessed water that knows your pull,*
*I beseech thee, Moon Goddess, to appear."*

Adanya held her breath until the count of five. Then she opened her eyes, anxious, quickly scanning, but, alas, nothing. No movement or change of any kind. Her heart slowly sank with overwhelming disappointment. Reluctantly, the Beloved lowered her limbs, bending over to collect her scattered belongings. Only a few seconds later, however, still absorbed in thought, Adanya bolted in fright as a great flash, light of unknown origin, illuminated the four corners of the earth. Too terrified to scream, Adanya sought immediate refuge behind an enormous boulder.

Smoke filled the forest glen and out of the thick haze a lone female materialized. Strikingly beautiful, dressed in black, head to foot, the curious visitor adorned herself with no jewelry save for a six point star hanging at her neck.

"Moon Goddess?" asked a frightened Adanya, slowing inching out from her protective shield.

"If you wish it so, my dear. Did you not call for the Moon Goddess to appear?" replied the imposing figure.

"Why, yes," Adanya stammered as she stepped out from behind the rock's refuge. "It says, 'You will find your gift within the goddess.'"

"What does?" the visitor asked.

"My pendant," replied Adanya. "That's what the sacred writing inside it says."

For the first time, the woman seemed to take notice of the glittering pendant that lay between Adanya's breasts.

The woman peered at it. "Ah, yes, the scroll of all eternity," she acknowledged as she reached out a milky white hand.

At that precise moment, as the hand moved in the direction of the jewel, the Winged One swooped down, seemingly out of nowhere, taking the chain in his beak and flying just out of reach. Simultaneously, Running Wolf placed himself between Adnaya and her intriguing guest.

"Winged One, Running Wolf, stop!" commanded Adanya, embarrassed by the uncivilized action. Then she bowed to the goddess. "Please forgive them. For they know not what they do."

"It matters not," snapped the Moon Goddess. "The hour is late. Perhaps we will meet again." And, with that, the deity simply vanished.

In the deep woods, an uninvited, unobserved guest, witness to the night's events, squelched a muffled gasp of unadulterated horror.

# CHAPTER XI

*"Adanya must be most powerful for the Moon Goddess to appear at her summons," said Morning Dove.*

*The Ancient One was quiet. For a moment, girl feared that her grandmother had fallen asleep. But then the elder replied with a rush of unforgettable words, fueled by fiercely-held conviction.*

*"Adanya has no more power than the beggar on the street. She is no more sacred than the harlot that foolishly sells her body for coin."*

*"But, Grandmother," countered a puzzled Morning Dove, "Adanya summoned the Moon Goddess and the most holy appeared. Surely that must mean the girl is more powerful than a common beggar. Certainly she is more pure than woman that sells her body only for the tender of a longing, misguided man."*

*Anger flashed in sapphire eyes. "Adanya, the beggar, a harlot - they are all the same. The Great Spirit makes no distinction between them. They are all most sacred," said the Ancient. "And I tell you this. The foolish child got exactly what she asked for."*

Like a finely tuned orchestra, spring played an exhilarating overture ushering in a glorious, initially melodious, summer. There was little hint of the impending false cord, fatally struck. Adanya, content yet exhausted from her nights in the forest, executed her numerous chores lethargically, without complaint. But there was a secretive air about the girl that failed to escape Brumledi's intense scrutiny.

"Adanya, you move like a man that has been out all night drinking firewater. What ails you?"

"Nothing ails me, Brumledi. Perhaps it is the hot sun that drains my life force. Still, I have completed my chores and can help you with dinner, if you please."

"Ha! An anchor only serves to slow the ship. But, if you insist, prepare the cooking fire and chop the vegetables."

Suddenly a third presence in the summer kitchen revealed itself. "Adanya is very good at starting fires," the high-pitched voice commented. The two women whirled in succession, astonished by the unexpected interjection.

Petro perched leisurely the table. His legs, unable to fully reach the floor, swung in synchronized rhythm. Adanya noted that his perpetually innocent face held the most peculiar expression. He looked as a satisfied Cheshire cat, full of cupboard cream and untold mischief. It was as if the boy knew something.

"Whatever do you mean, Petro?" questioned his impatient mother.

"Oh, nothing. But I think that Adanya is very talented, very talented indeed. Few people can start a fire for guests the way that she can," replied the boy. He shot the wary, shocked girl a meaningful look, raising one eyebrow for emphasis.

"But we are having no guests tonight. What is this foolishness?" Brumledi, puzzled and more than a little exasperated, looked first at Petro and then at a notably mute Adanya. The girl's face blanched as white as the crisp, newly starched apron she wore. "What is going on?"

Adanya feared the worst. Her heart raced uncontrollably. She felt faint as the room swirled around her. This was the end. Petro would tell Brumledi and ruin everything. Adanya felt as a vulnerable row boat, inadequately prepared to endure the perfect storm on already choppy seas. Quite unexpectedly, however, Petro, with a magician's slight of hand, expertly turned the tide of the conversation.

"Why, Mother. I merely compliment Adanya's ability with fire because she will never cook with your skill. You are indeed magnificent in the culinary arts. All Adanya can do is conjure flame. Isn't that right, Adanya?" Petro sent another electrifying glance at the anxious girl.

He then kissed his mother on the cheek, exaggeratedly bowing to both women. "I trust that we will consume a feast yet again, Mother. But, truly, all things pale in comparison to your great beauty." Without another word, Petro practically skipped out of the room.

Brumledi placed an aging hand on her cheek and gently touched the spot brushed by her youngest son's lips. "My land, that boy is a charmer!"

"Yes, most charming," Adanya flatly agreed. She trembled despite the intense heat in the summer kitchen. What did Petro know?

Adanya soon forgot about the household's youngest resident, however.

She continued her undiscovered nightly liaisons with the Moon Goddess in the heart of the forest. The Beloved found comfort in this newfound friend, that is, if a deity could be appropriately titled, "friend". Certainly the goddess taught her interesting rituals and never before seen practices.

The only element marring these welcome escapes was the consistently odd behavior of Running Wolf and the Winged One. While the beasts did not prevent her from traveling into the forest, their behavior still provoked concern. The animals often blocked the outside door when Adanya sought passage for her midnight excursions. Still, ever obedient, these companions reluctantly stepped aside as the Beloved commanded.

But, perhaps most perplexing, was the beasts' disrespectful behavior towards the Moon Goddess. The animals refused the deity's bidding. And, as that first night, Running Wolf frequently placed himself directly between the Beloved and the Moon Goddess.

Adanya had never previously observed such odd behavior - or had she? Something tugged at her brain. What was it? She couldn't remember. Then, one night, long past the bewitching hour, into her dreams came a peculiar vision . . . a one-eyed bear. The ferocious beast lunged at the Beloved with a railing, outstretched claw. The pendant around her neck glowed like fire. She heard the Winged One's cries in the skies above and instinctively felt Running Wolf's presence.

Just before the fleeting imagines faded into the morning sun, Adanya saw it. The bear wore a six point star.

# CHAPTER XII

*"That's the bear that threatened Adanya's life more than ten summers ago,"
exclaimed Morning Dove. "But dreams make no sense. Why would he wear the
same star as the Moon Goddess?"*

*"Why, indeed? Things are not always what they appear - either in our
dreams or on this earth. But the soul is our inner eye. And it sees all things in
the pure light of truth. That's why Adanya dreamed this particular dream," said
the Ancient.*

*"It wasn't a coincidence?" asked her incredulous granddaughter.*

*"There are no coincidences, Little One. All things happen for a reason
according to a divine plan. And, often, unexplained happenings are messages
from the inner self. It sends us signs.*

*"Listen to your inner voice, Morning Dove. It always speaks what you most
need to hear."*

The signs continued - the dreams, the animals' strange behavior. Yet
Adanya adamantly refused to acknowledge that nagging, unsettled feeling
which haunted her. In fact, as if to spite herself, she visited the forest glen
with increasing frequency. There, under the shadow of darkness, she learned
about power - all kinds of power.

The woman in black introduced Adanya to complicated spells, conjuring
innumerable potent potions. The student initially questioned these complex,
multi-layered lessons of curious incantations. Wasn't this the magic of the
underworld – dedication spells and love potions? Alarm filled Adanya's
being.

But the Moon Goddess treated the Beloved's questions with disregard,
singlehandedly dismissing the hesitant girl's fears. "Didn't the ancient scroll
tell you that you would find your gifts within the goddess? I am revealing

to you the mysteries and powers of the Universe. This world will one day be yours."

Still, something didn't feel quite right. The angst within grew. But Adanya remained silent. After all, wasn't it impudent for a mere mortal to challenge the superior ways of the gods? Besides, she had much to learn.

The spells themselves, at least on the surface, appeared harmless. For instance, the love potion simply fated the addled tailor, Macan, with Lottie, an overweight, overbearing spinster. Certainly love was a good thing. Didn't everyone seek it?

It never occurred to the mixed-up girl to consider whether love actually existed in the absence of willing hearts. Likewise, did the spell to help Widow Lockshine locate her knitting needles serve the aging mistress' highest purpose? Or did it merely delay the old woman from seeking necessary help in her advancing years? The questions went unasked.

Furthermore, with increasing frequency, the incantations assumed more sinister purposes. Once, after a particularly frustrating day with Brumledi, the Moon Goddess encouraged Adanya to cast a spell to bring on back pain.

"It's just a harmless prank, my child. A bit of sweet revenge," smiled the deity encouragingly. "A little pain for all the anguish that the bitter woman's caused seems fair."

Adanya, however, remained uncertain. For, while she certainly resented Brumledi's behavior, she wished no harm to her already troubled guardian.

"It feels wrong," ventured the girl.

"Wrong," scoffed the Moon Goddess. "Wrong is the unfair manner in which she behaves. Wrong is the tyranny she brings upon the household."

In the end, Adanya relented. She reasoned, rationalizing to herself, that a small break from Brumledi's daily tirades might indeed do the family good. Ohan could behave as he pleased without the always present threat of retribution. The children might play free, unrestrained by the constant criticism normally surrounding them.

The spell was cast. Brumledi's back, her already injured spine, deteriorated at an unprecedented rapid pace. The pain, so intense that the local Healer announced his patient permanently infirmed, prompted the wailing women to retreat to her bed. Every night, Ohan and the children sat helplessly in Brumledi's chambers, a kind of informal vigil, watching as their wife and mother writhed in unimaginably heightened pain.

Adanya's guilt grew intense, consuming every waking moment. She begged the Moon Goddess to relieve Brumledi of the curse. Certainly Brumledi could be unkind, even cruel, but Adanya desired no hand in this woman's misery. For the first time, as she absorbed the family's distraught reactions, Adanya understood how much the family relied on Brumledi.

Simply put, the household failed to function without Brumledi's controlling oversight. Ohan spent his hours dazed, his face buried inconsolably in his hands, neither eating nor sleeping. When the children sought guidance, he unintelligibly mumbled, non-responsively. Braun and Mietta adamantly refused to leave their mother's bedside.

Petro, however, reacted entirely differently. He gave Adanya cold, hard looks. One day, he struck out at her, landing a sound punch on her arm. "What have you done to my mother?" he shouted.

Caught off-guard, Adanya could find no words.

"You take that spell off my mother, you witch, or I will tell the town counsel about you!"

Adanya, bursting into tears, fled into the deep forest, seeking refuge in its towering trees until the sun gave way to darkness. Then, inching out from her hiding place, she beseeched the Moon Goddess to come.

Surprisingly, when the goddess finally materialized, after hours of desperate appeals, she appeared unmoved by the girl's obvious distress. "You are weak but, as you are merely mortal, I expect no less."

"But you don't understand, Moon Goddess," Adanya cried. "Brumledi is near death! And the household cannot function without her."

With a disgusted wave of the hand, the deity ultimately conceded to Adanya's repeated requests for the spell's removal. The Moon Goddess uttered words, dispensed phrases unknown to the girl. Then, the goddess' mouth contorted as if she consumed bitter herbs, the deity provided a dismissive nod.

"Go home. It is done. Brumledi is healed."

After that harmful, unforgettable experience, something in Adanya's soul cautioned her not to return to the deep woods. But she did, one more time. Oh, it wasn't that she didn't now know that this type of black magic was wrong. Certainly she understood that. For the most powerful of gods focus their unlimited resources for the ultimate good of the earth and its inhabitants - not destruction.

But somewhere in her mind, twisted by the years in Brumledi's home, Adanya felt that she herself was to blame. Maybe she somehow enticed the Moon Goddess to inappropriately use her powers. Maybe she was the one who had caused all this to happen. And, in a very real sense, she was right.

Adanya ventured back into the forest for one final rendezvous with the Moon Goddess. She felt compelled to apologize for being weak and human and unworthy. She sought to beg the deity's forgiveness. She wanted the Moon Goddess to love her.

The Moon Goddess, seemingly touched by Adanya's deep emotion, soothed away the girl's fears. "There, there," she said as she massaged Adanya's sobbing shoulders. "You are indeed a worthy subject. Let me give you one chance to redeem yourself in the eyes of the Almighty."

"Oh, Moon Goddess," choked the grateful girl. "I would do anything to show you how much I am devoted to you."

"Good! Then bring the trespasser from his hiding place."

"What?"

"Get the one who betrays me," commanded the Moon Goddess her voice, its timber, suddenly as cold as a mountain stream in mid-winter. "Find him . . . now!"

When, in obvious confusion, Adanya failed to move, the goddess herself disappeared behind a cluster of brambly bushes, re-appearing with an iron, unfailing grip on the alleged betrayer. Petro, decidedly unhappy at this unexpected turn of events, squirmed, crying out, unable to break free from the woman's grasp.

Adanya gasped. "Moon Goddess, this is no betrayer. This is, Petro, the youngest son of the family that took me in when I had no one in this world. He means you no harm."

"He spied on us and betrayed me. We will sacrifice him tonight to appease the gods."

"But he is a child," pleaded a frantic Adanya, her heart racing. "He has spent naught but a handful of summers on this good earth."

The pleas fell on deaf ears. The Moon Goddess expertly tied the squirming Petro to a spit that hung over the fire. When Adanya tried to rescue the boy from imminent demise, the Moon Goddess roughly shoved her to the ground, rapidly securing her hands and feet with leather straps as well.

"Apparently, we will have two sacrifices tonight. The god of the underworld will be well-pleased."

"But, Moon Goddess . . ."

"'Moon Goddess' - how I tire of that unworthy name. I am not the Moon Goddess."

Adanya looked stunned, confused. "But you said . . . I mean, when I called you 'Moon Goddess' . . ."

The emissary of the underworld haughtily laughed. "I merely said, 'If it pleases you', but that is not who I am."

Upon seeing Adanya's horrified expression, the woman gave another ill-tempered chuckle. "Don't look so surprised, my child. You asked for me. Don't you remember?"

Adanya, her brain darting uncontrollably as she frantically endeavored to recall, offered no immediate reply.

"You said that you would take even the blackest of hearts to love you. Well, be careful what you wish for. I, my dear, innocent Adanya, am Aeracura, Goddess of the Underworld. I proudly wear the black cloak of eternal death."

Her hands and feet bound, Adanya helplessly watched as Aeracura prepared a dedication spell over the spit bearing a terrified, hog-tied Petro. Running Wolf, however, silently appeared from his spot in the trees and now crouched low behind his charge. His razor sharp incisors began to carefully, yet furiously, chew through the leather ties binding her hands.

Adanya lay still and watched, motionless, too scared to breathe, as the witch gathered the spell's necessary ingredients: an egg, a cow's tongue, the powder of a ground goat's hoof. The witch continued to pull essential materials out of thin air — except for one.

One necessary component stopped Aeracura dead in her tracks. "I need an amulet," she stated yet unable to instantaneously materialize one. Her dull, lifeless eyes further narrowed as they fell on the jewel Adanya wore. "Ah, yes, I will rip the powers from that stupid child's neck. I will use the pendant which holds the ancient scroll."

The witch, now fully transformed, bore no resemblance to the Great Spirit's elder. The beauty Adanya once imagined evaporated, melting away as puddles of wax to reveal the woman's true identity. And no sight in Adanya's young life had ever looked more terrifying.

Aeracura closed the distance between the fire and Adanya. Then, with nary a whimper from either Running Wolf or the Winged One, the witch snatched the pendant from around the Beloved's neck.

Her twisted, gnarled fingers shook as she tried to separate the two sides of the pendant. But hard as she tried, the pieces failed to fall open. Suddenly, however, the earth trembled and opened up. Then, just as it had for Elu years ago, lightening emanated from the pendant. The electrifying bolt threw the stunned witch more than fifty feet away into an overgrown, prickly thicket.

In that moment, Adanya, whose hands had been loosed by the wolf, quickly drew her hunting knife and cut the ties from her legs. Then she sprang up, somersaulting towards the spit, and rapidly released a whimpering, rather warm, Petro.

Adanya raised her blade, creeping soundlessly toward the thicket. But what she saw only caused her to rub her eyes, shake her head in disbelief. The Winged One, sitting on growth in the thicket, held Adanya's pendant in his beak. The witch, however, had vanished!

# CHAPTER XIII

*"Adanya saved Petro," exclaimed Morning Dove. "She's a hero."*

*"It is true, Adanya called forth her highest self in those final, critical moments. But she is also solely responsible for setting those fateful events into motion. That truth, she must forever own."*

*Morning Dove remained unconvinced. "But the witch lied to her. Adanya was an unwilling victim as much as Petro. She didn't know the woman was a witch."*

*"It is possible to be victimized yet no one is an 'unwilling victim', Morning Dove. We all choose our path, our different roles. If we choose to be a victim it is because that role is more comfortable to us in that moment than asserting our own personal power."*

*"On some level," said the Ancient One, "Adanya always knew the truth about the Goddess of the Underworld. The inner self is very wise. Sometimes, however, we mortals simply fail - or refuse - to listen."*

*Then she added, "And, make no mistake, Adanya did get exactly what she asked for."*

The ocean waves that hurled the ship back and forth mirrored the turbulence in Adanya's troubled soul. She spent her days in the windowless bottom of the hull with the steerage - cows, mules, chickens. The smell, the vile, odorous mixture of both human and animal waste, proved pungent. Nausea, the never-ending sort that stems from a combination of seasickness, bad food, and poor living conditions, served as her constant companion.

For the past three months, the girl had called the crude yet seaworthy craft her "home". But there was actually no place on earth that Adanya felt at home. Her spirit, not unlike the ship, drifted aimlessly, literally unbalanced. It was as if she sailed on a voyage with neither a known destination nor designated port. Long days gave way to endless misery as she relived her last days in Amblien.

The memories evoked deep pain, greater than the rise and fall of bile in her throat, as well as overwhelming remorse. Over and over again, Adanya replayed the tragic events of the summer in her mind. The initially beautiful vision of the Moon Goddess transformed into the repulsive creature that was the Goddess of the Underworld. Petro tied to a spit and left to roast, rotating around and around over open flame.

But the worst images stemmed from the scenes that played out with Brumledi after both Adanya and Petro returned to the house. Petro ran, screaming, running recklessly through the sleeping forest, bounding up the front steps, shrieking his mother's name. Brumledi flung open the door, prepared to battle yet unseen demons.

In the agonizing minutes that followed, Petro recounted, not just the happenings of those last few hours, but the days that culminated in one horrifying night. He talked of how, from the very first full moon, he had tracked Adanya into the forest, watching, unobserved, as the girl played the fiddle then placed a carved figure into the Box of Intentions. He meticulously regurgitated all that followed - from the appearance of the Goddess of the Underworld to the chants, spells, and incantations Adanya uttered.

The boy left nothing to the imagination - the love potion, the knitting needles, and Brumledi's back pain. He concluded his rambling, unimaginable tale with a fictionalized account of that fateful, final bonfire. In Petro's adapted ending, the boy told his mother, using colorful imagery highlighted with maximum embellishment, how he heroically freed himself from the spit and rescued the cowering Adanya.

Brumledi listened with horror, making no sound save for the occasional gasp or unintelligible guttural noise. Then, finally, when fatigue silenced Petro, she turned her blind, uncontrollable rage upon the girl still standing in the open doorway.

"What evil have you done, girl? What shame have you brought upon this family?" demanded Brumledi.

Adanya hung her head as she dropped, tearfully, to her knees. "It was an accident. I didn't mean for all this to happen, Brumledi. You must believe me! I am so very sorry."

"Sorry? You ungrateful cur! I fed you and clothed you. Treated you like one of my own. And this is how you repay me?"

Adanya, sobbing so hard that hiccups racked her convulsing body, begged Brumledi's forgiveness. "I am truly sorry. Please forgive me. Please don't hate me."

Brumledi spat on the girl now rolled in a miserable ball at her feet. Then she sneered, "You are nothing to me. This world would be better off if you had never been born. To me, you are dead."

Where was the goddess of the scroll now?

# CHAPTER XIV

*"Adanya destroyed her life. She failed, didn't she?"*

*The old woman looked at her granddaughter. "Adanya indeed caused pain for both herself and others by not listening to her own inner voice. Nothing, however, can destroy us."*

*"Grandmother, that makes no sense. People kill each other with increasing frequency. There are floods and fires. The earth moves and swallows up those that once lived on it. Of course, humans can be destroyed."*

*The Ancient One thought carefully about Morning Dove's words. Then, finally, she spoke. "It is true. The body can be destroyed. Yet nothing in either heaven or earth destroys the spirit - and that is our true essence."*

*"As for failing . . ." her words drifted off, unfinished.*

The cargo ship, its sails billowing with a warm, south of the equator breeze, finally arrived at the island of Moricea. It had been more than three months since its crew and passengers, two-legged as well as four-legged, had eyed dry land. Still, the vessel's seasoned captain opted not to sail dangerously near the sandy, welcoming coastline. Deceptively alluring, the surrounding reefs, with shimmering pink coral and exotic tropical fish, possessed a well-earned reputation for exceedingly treacherous navigational hazards. More than a few overly confident seafaring men, experienced or not, unintentionally dug watery graves in the tranquil setting. This ship's crew prudently dropped anchor more than a mile off shore.

Adanya, emerging topside after months of self-imposed imprisonment, shielded her eyes against the brilliance of full sunlight. She stumbled clumsily, unsteadily on wobbly limbs inadequate to carry even her own weight. Before Adanya regained her bearings on the main deck, Running Wolf left her side, leaping effortlessly and disappearing over the side of the ship into the turquoise waters far below. The heartsick girl, frantically crying his name into the wind, strained to see her cherished beast in the rise and fall of the ocean.

It was then that she saw them. Copper-skinned men with almond eyes, the likes of which Adanya had never seen, paddled handcrafted canoes, expertly hallowed out, toward the ship. The synchronized motion, muscled, glistening arms rotating in an enthralling show of physical prowess, fascinated the young girl.

So did the boats. These vessels, like miniature toys on the vast, unending sea, positioned themselves alongside the three story ship, waves lifting them precariously upward as if to meet their honored guest, then, quite abruptly, down again.

"What are they doing here?" asked Adanya of the wretched, unclean man who stood to her right.

Without either warning or reply, the bearded sailor's rough, calloused hand reached out, secured a rope with a double loop bowline knot around Adanya's small waist and lowered the terrified girl, kicking and screaming, over the side of the ship. There the Beloved dangled, suspended in mid-air until, eventually, she felt her body steadied by strong, capable arms. Inexplicably, she found herself seated in a small, violently rocking craft, her few, meager possessions precariously positioned next to her.

As Adanya righted herself uncertainly in the canoe, her eyes wide with terror, the natives expertly turned the vessels. For the first time, Adanya fully surveyed the incredible landscape before her. Its resplendent beauty, the likes of which she had never seen, literally stopped her breath. Dolphins, creatures of remarkable grace and majesty, jumped joyously, in jewel-tone waters adorned with lacy white foam. Colorful birds - combinations of red, green, yellow, and blue - flew through the air, swooping in geometric patterns, as if to greet her.

Her heart leaped as she spotted the Winged One, his own feathers regally spread wide, looking decidedly drab among the many hues. The warm, glorious, sun beat down upon her pale, drawn face as an elixir prescribed to a long ill patient. Could this be paradise?

Bare-chested natives, dressed in patterned sarongs, pulled the boat to shore and assisted Adanya out of its confines. Waves lapped at the girl's ankles playfully as she tried to stand upright in the fine sand. But, as the Beloved tentatively attempted the first walk on dry land in months, her legs collapsed. She fell in a heap, like a beached whale caught inland after a torrential storm.

"I'm sorry . . ." stammered Adanya, quickly working to gather herself. "I haven't walked on land for a long time."

Running Wolf emerged like the god Poseidon from the sea, shook the remaining saltwater from his coat, showering his delighted charge. Adanya laughed, dissolving into tears, relieved that her cherished friend was alright. The emotion of the last several months threatened to overwhelm her. Finally, however, she grabbed onto Running Wolf's wet, matted fur and pulled herself upright.

Subsequent attempts to walk, however, produced similar results. The ever-shifting sand offered no firm base, no sturdy support, for the girl's rubbery legs. Finally, the leader of the landing party, a short man with a thick middle and legs the circumference of mighty oaks, uttered words unfamiliar to Adanya's ears. Almost immediately, rather ceremoniously, she found herself lifted onto the broad shoulders of the men.

This is how, despite her initial protests, Adanya first toured the Polynesian village - atop bare-chested men with Running Wolf majestically leading the procession. The Winged One, content with an aerial view, soared high above them.

This world, a world like none other, appeared as a fairy tale. It was as if characters came to life out of stories that men, men with too much whiskey in overextended bellies, told around late night campfires. Thatched huts sat on the dazzling white beach. Exquisite women, with long blue-black hair, came out of the doorways, or away from cooking fires, to greet the new arrival. Babies suckled at exposed breasts, toddlers hiding shyly in the folds of their mothers' immodest skirts.

As the procession continued, its destination still unclear, young children approached bearing gifts. They repeatedly called out a word unfamiliar to the young girl.

"Namaste", said the children. "Namaste." Adanya, uncertain as to its meaning, decided that the word must stand for "hello" in the lyrical native tongue. She hesitantly repeated it back to them.

Again and again, the men stopped, kneeling so that the heralded visitor could lower her head as the islanders encircled her neck with magnificent flowering blooms. The necklaces, their sweet, heady fragrance, a combination of lotus as well as other mystical blossoms, caused Adanya to swoon. For a moment, she barely believed her good fortune. Then her thoughts unexpectedly darkened. If only they knew the shame carried within her heart.

Adanya's unconventional transport continued, past the village, up a steep, mountainous terrain. She marveled at the enticing, ever-changing landscape, the spectacular visions surrounding her. Trees, vastly different than those rooted in Ambilen, swayed lazily in the gentle, sea breeze. Flowering plants and bushes seemed to blossom in honor of Adanya's procession. It was as if the earth itself rose to greet her. Butterflies, absent during the long voyage, swarmed Adanya once again.

Finally, Adanya's eyes fell on what she assumed to be the final destination. An imposing wall rose up before them. Twelve or fifteen feet high, it surrounded a compound, a small cluster of approximately fifteen buildings built of a sand and clay composite. High from a stone bell tower, shimmering in the intense afternoon heat, a deep, rich sound drifted through the air, filling the island paradise. The bells rang out, again and again, in celebration of the party's arrival.

"Oh," Adanya thought sadly. "If only they knew how unworthy I am of such honor. Surely, they will discover my flawed soul and refuse entry."

But, much to Adanya's amazement, the impressive wood gates opened. The men, who had carried the girl without complaint, gently deposited their precious cargo at the entrance. A woman, dressed in a white, flowing robe, her head covered with a cap of identical fabric, strolled with measured purposefulness towards the girl.

"Welcome, Adanya," the smiling woman said. "I am Sister Angelica." Deep lines creased the holy one's face but there was an unmistakable aura of peace and love about her. "We are honored that you have chosen to visit the Sisters of the Sacred of the Covenant."

Adanya collapsed at her feet, sobbing at the compassionate greeting. The undeserved, unanticipated kindness proved too much for her fragile heart to bear. "Sister, I am not worthy of your hospitality." The girl's anguished sounds grew louder as years of pain and misery washed over her yet again. "I am evil. I am nothing."

The sister bent down and tenderly enfolded Adanya in a comforting embrace. Then she whispered in the distraught girl's ear. "Hush, my child. The Universe is unfolding perfectly. You *will* find your gift within the goddess."

# CHAPTER XV

*Morning Dove gasped. "How did Sister Angelica know? How could she have possibly known what Mahwah said so long ago? How did she know about the pendant with the ancient scroll?"*

*"These things I cannot say, my child. For, as old as I am, there is much in Heaven and Earth that even I do not understand."*

*"Was it a coincidence?" Morning Dove stopped short as another thought entered her consciousness. "But you said that there are no coincidences, no things that happen merely by chance. Do you think that this was part of a divine plan?"*

*The Ancient One chuckled. "You have learned well, Morning Dove. That's right, there are no coincidences."*

Untouched by man, the Sisters of the Sacred Covenant lived as a tight-knit cluster of women who, with intention, dedicated their simplistic lives to the Great Spirit. They spent every waking hour in reverent, single-minded worship. They understood, better than many a pious, richly compensated priest, the sanctity of breath as well as each God-given moment on this earth. Rather than pompous ritual, worship at the convent consisted merely of daily living, celebrating a bona fide, progressive relationship with the Most Holy. The sisters observed the sacred in the everyday - whether mucking animal stalls or breaking bread together. It mattered not. All life, all material goods, came from the Creator to which they were eternally connected.

The sisters vigorously farmed the land and fished the sea, cooking their own food, responsible for their own sustenance. The daily fare, albeit basic, consisted primarily of rice, fish, and bread as well as the many fruits that grew plentifully on the island. They studied the teachings of the Most Holy, as well as those elders that served him. Additionally, for more than one hundred years, the founding women, as well as those who came after them, lived harmoniously with their island neighbors, the Moriceans.

The two groups shared the earth's bounty even as they jointly embraced the gifts of the Almighty. The natives entrusted the religious sect to introduce their brown-skinned children to the Creator, to teach his generous, loving ways to them. Each day, children as small as three or four years of age clambered up the steep mountain, which had arisen from the ocean before the beginning of time, to sit eagerly in the bamboo shelter that the sisters erected exclusively for this purpose.

The lessons learned, however, differed significantly from the schools on the mainland. For most schools, like the overcrowded, single room schoolhouse in Ambilen, taught children how to read and write and count. These traditional educational centers, overseen mostly by men with beady, off-putting stares, magnified a thousand fold by off-center, wire-rimmed spectacles, taught curriculum primarily rooted in the village's economy.

In fact, the Ambilen school lessons instructed students on only the most practical of matters. Boys, mostly aspiring merchants or farmers, learned essential skills. The headmaster, Master Langford, drilled his young charges in market day practices. It was imperative that these youngsters, inexperienced in the less than ethical market exchanges, sell their produce, livestock, and other wares without being duped. That's why, by their third year, male pupils expertly counted tender and balanced books.

Young girls, on the other hand, if they attended school at all, most certainly needed to know how to manage the household accounts and other matters. For, one day, they would marry fine, upstanding men. It reflected poorly on their respective families if new wives proved ineffective in managing the silver coins with which their hardworking spouses entrusted them.

In stark contrast, the Sisters of the Sacred Covenant promoted an entirely different curriculum. The island children, sitting in a circle on plush, silk pillows, first learned, from an early age, how to breathe. Masters taught their students how to, with full awareness, expand their belly, then their entire body, with the life force. Once inhalation was successfully mastered, they learned how to exhale. Teachers spent entire days, even weeks, focused exclusively on the art of breathing - breathe in . . . 1, 2, 3. . . breathe out . . . 1, 2, 3.

"Breathing in, I embrace my highest purpose," instructed Sister Angelica. "Breathing out, I release all that does not serve me." Breathing centers and grounds each person, the sister explained. Conscious breathing brings each person, regardless of his or her age, back to the true self.

Adanya now joined the children in daily lessons. After the group excelled at conscious breathing, they advanced to the spiritual practice of eating. The students, including Adanya, learned to honor the essence of each food - corn or fish, squash or pineapple - as well as the land or water in which it flourished. Students even acknowledged the planter and fisherman who brought the bounty to the table. They learned to prepare food as well as to eat or drink, with full awareness. The depth of these spiritual teachings resonated within Adanya's very soul.

As the many lessons continued, Adanya proved a willing, earnest pupil. The unparalleled attentiveness stemmed, in part, because her neglected spirit thrived in this atmosphere of love and acceptance. But it was more than that. Adanya, not long after her arrival, heard unsubstantiated rumors that advanced students learned the wisdom of the gods. Adanya desired to quickly master the lower levels. Maybe then the goddess, her goddess, would deem the Beloved worthy of an audience.

Outside of school, Adanya's living quarters, shared with Running Wolf and the Winged One, were, by any standards, minimalistic. The 8x8 foot space, supplied with only a wash bowl atop a crude table as well as a straw pallet, seemed spacious, however, compared to the cramped quarters of recent months. Neat and clean, it offered Adanya something never before experienced - private space.

Privacy extended outside the room's walls as well. No one ever asked Adanya about the circumstances which brought her, quite alone, to the covenant's doorstep. In fact, any inquiry would have gone unanswered. Not long after Adanya's arrival, Sister Angelica instructed the girl to take a vow of silence. According to the sister, Adanya's time was to be spent in commune with the gods.

"It is impossible to know your soul, if you do not quiet yourself," explained Sister Angelica on the third day of Adanya's arrival. "You must tune out senseless noise and turn inward. Listen only to Spirit's whisperings."

"Oh, Sister Angelica. If only that were possible," Adanya cried, heartsick. "But you have no idea what I've done."

"Hush, child," said the sister. "The past is no more. Only the present moment is real."

With these words, Sister Angelica silenced Adanya for a period of no less than six months. The girl walked the halls, attended classes and ate with the Sisters of the Sacred Covenant yet no one spoke directly to her.

The sisters passed the novice, acknowledging her presence with little more than gentle smiles and congenial nods.

Initially, the lack of language, the deafening silence, felt uncomfortable. But in the quiet moments, Adanya began to find her way home, back to the spirit forgotten long ago.

The path did not come easily. Yet, in some ways, the process was remarkably pure and rudimentary. For Sister Angelica and the other residents supported Adanya. These gentle teachers reminded Adanya of her own great wisdom. The girl needed only to ask her inner self to reveal what was already written on her heart.

Four months into the healing process, Adanya, once again, turned to the blank pages of her journal. The last entry, written more than three years earlier, not long after her arrival in Ambilen, seemed like a lifetime ago. Who was that girl? More importantly, who was the woman that walked with her now? Adanya resumed her journaling, pouring out her very soul.

> *As I begin a new phase in my life, there is a renewed sense of purpose for my place in this world. In this moment lies a magical day yet untouched by the painter within me. What will I paint? Will my strokes be bold and vibrant or quiet and delicate? What gifts will I call forth from the divine soul deep within? How will I choose to impact the lives around me? The canvas is mine to create.*

Then Adanya knelt and humbly prayed as never before. "Oh, Great Spirit, speak to my heart your purpose for this life which I dedicate to you. Let me enter this year with a renewed sense of wonder at the magnificence of your creation. For this world, its people, even my very spirit, are indeed divine. Work through me to fulfill my mission here on this earth."

More often than naught, the words on the page reflected Adanya's jumbled mixture of thoughts and feelings. One day, the words indicated hope, the promise of new beginnings. The next day's writings, though, suggested a sad, troubled girl. Adanya felt as a prisoner, trapped in the weighty, unforgiving shackles of yesterday's choices.

But still, every day, she wrote. If negative thoughts or feelings overwhelmed her, she calmed her breathing, lowering her heart rate, by returning to the lesson of conscious breathing.

"Breathing in . . . 1, 2, 3 . . . I embrace my highest purpose," Adanya repeated Sister Angelica's words. "Breathing out . . . 1, 2, 3 . . . I release all that does not serve me."

*Hope is a remarkable gift. For it is hope that drives us from the comfort of a warm bed on a cold January morning. It is hope that gives the grieving parent the desire to live one more day in a world that no longer holds a beloved child in its grasp. And it is hope that prompts the seemingly hopeless to continue on the journey - just one more day.*

*Where does hope come from? Hope comes from deep within me. Hope stems from an internal knowingness that there is a plan for my life. It rises up within me, seemingly unbidden, when all seems lost and meaningless. For even in the midst of great despair, I know that I am a beloved child of the Creator. And, while I may not understand all that is happening in each moment, the Omnipotent does. That gives me great hope.*

The words that Mahwah had spoken so long ago came back to her - again and again. Like a personal mantra, the girl spoke the words silently. "The Universe is unfolding perfectly." Adanya truly didn't fully understand the truth of these words. But, as in those lonely, desolate days following the deaths of Elu and Mahwah, she desperately clung to them.

Sister Angelica, in the moments before imposing the vow of silence, encouraged Adanya to write the lessons that life's experiences, including the black period in Ambilen, taught her. The sister advised the girl that she could alter the list, making additions or corrections throughout her journey as she acquired broader insight, greater wisdom. Adanya, uncertain of what else to do, regularly recorded and revised a list of lessons in her leather journal.

Thus, the healing process began. Still, devastatingly harsh memories haunted Adanya. She verbally flogged herself, again and again, for the choices made in the forest glen. One day, however, in the midst of yet another tedious mental review of past sins, Adanya heard a distinct voice in the silence of her private space.

"Stop!" The commanding tenor, neither male nor female in origin, echoed in the chamber.

Startled, Adanya quickly glanced around her room, eyes rapidly scanning back and forth - nothing. She peered out the oval window but observed only a patch of blue, open sky reflecting a mild, tropical winter. The old, heavy door to her chamber creaked as she pulled on it yet the interior hall revealed no one.

The Beloved sat, virtually stunned, on the cool dirt floor of her room. Where had the voice come from? Had she gone mad? If not, there was only one other possibility. Adanya picked up her journal and wrote:

*In this world, everyone goes through periods of darkness, times of doubt, fear and grief. No one escapes personal anguish as we travel on this journey. The question is: Once it has passed, must I choose to relive it? Do I have to roll it over in the recesses of my mind and examine its many shapes? Am I, lessons learned, destined to hold it in my heart as I enter new phases of my life?*

*No! The past robs me of the here and now. Once enlightened, I let go of anything that no longer serves me. Yes, I acknowledge that the blackness, the internal fire, once existed but it acted only as a tool to further shape me. I rise from the ashes into the light that is now me. I let go of anything inauthentic.*

A prayer then rose up within her.

"Dear Being of Light," began Adanya, "help me to live, fully present in the world of today. Let me speak not of the blackness that once was but of the light that shines around me now. Darkness matters not. Teach me to embrace the person I am and the circumstances that surround me today. Let me fully live in this divine moment. Amen"

As she silently finished the inaudible prayer, Adanya felt a quiet, almost imperceptible, rush of physical relief. It was as if a great burden mysteriously, quite miraculously, lifted from her petite shoulders. Her spirit, markedly lightened, rejoiced in the inconceivable glory of the present moment. Adanya permitted the feeling to flood her being. From somewhere inside the girl's body, a thought nudged at her brain.

"I am safe. I am happy. I am whole," thought Adanya. She hugged herself. "That's the beauty of living fully in this moment." She returned to her journal and added another line to the list of lessons learned. Still, she guarded these revelations, sharing the incomplete list with no one.

As the days wore on, however, Adanya recognized a return of uncomfortable, suffocating anger, bubbling beneath her outwardly calm exterior. She experienced an undeniable rage towards herself. How could she be so stupid as to engage the black powers? She also felt overwhelming anger for Brumledi. Why didn't the woman love me? And she felt anger for the Goddess of the Underworld. How could this entity pretend to be my friend? The enumeration went on and on.

Hostility threatened to overtake the Beloved. Yet she spoke to no one - for the vow of silence continued. Finally, however, when the poison boiled over, venom encroaching on her life blood, Adanya broke down. She begged the Universe's forgiveness. Then the Beloved wrote long, excruciatingly raw, letters to both Petro and Brumledi, detailing her transgressions, seeking their forgiveness as well.

Letters finished, posted for delivery on the next outgoing ship, Adanya turned her undivided attention to recording her many sins, real and imagined, on a loose sheet of parchment. Over and over she wrote, "I forgive myself for . . ." Finally, energy expended, sins exhaustively penned, the Beloved brought flame to the page, watching as fire consumed her flawed acts, leaving behind only fine, black ash.

Over the months of healing, Adanya repeated the cathartic process, at times writing the names of individuals who caused grievous injury to her. Again, over and over, she wrote, "I forgive you for . . ." and completed each sentence with the offense. Then, fiery process repeated, Adanya blew the ashen remains out onto the wind, returning it unto the earth. It was finished.

# CHAPTER XVI

That night, three regally dressed women crept silently into Adanya's contented dreams. The girl, recognizing her honored guests, immediately knelt before them and wept.

"My Holy Ones, where have you been?" she cried. "Did your love which once nurtured me, filled my very being, cease because of my unworthy soul?" Tears fell rapidly as a flowing waterfall without beginning or end.

Dagmar bent down, cupping Adanya's heart-shaped face in her hands. "Look at me, child," the spirit guide said. Adanya raised her watery eyes and gazed into the face of pure love. "Nothing will ever stop the gods from loving you. We are always with you."

Adanya struggled, her chest rising and compressing at a quickening rate, to regain composure. "But you didn't come to me," she announced accusingly, with such stripped bare emotion that the Winged One stirred on his chamber perch.

"In the Valley of Lilies, you visited me at the rising of each new moon. But, then, you stopped. After the deaths of Elu and Mahwah, after I went to Ambilen, you never again came to me in slumber. Why? Did my sinful nature offend you?"

Samara, her mahogany skin aglow in the illuminating rays of the moon, responded. "Adanya, nothing in heaven or earth can ever separate you from the Creator. We will never leave you for we have known you through all eternity."

The Enlightened One continued to speak, her tone rich and thick as poured molasses, in a cadence that soothed Adanya's spirit. "We have always been here. But your very own soul, cloaked in shadow, could neither see nor feel our presence."

The impact of the words, their true meaning, silenced Adanya. Was that possible? Did she prevent the Enlightened Ones from reaching her?

Suddenly, the truth of this realization emanated through her being, radiating an intense heat.

"I was the one who put up the wall," Adanya murmured the words, half astonished, even as she knew them true. "I was the one who couldn't hear you. But it seems impossible. I was so sad and lonely."

"My child," said Dagmar, "your bitter state, your confused, erratic thoughts shut out the light. Only now can we, once again, make ourselves known to you because you have permitted it. You've calmed your mind, made peace with the war that raged inside you.

"But," continued Diella, "no matter what was happening in your life, we always surrounded you with the life force that connects all of us."

Could this be true? The intense, very real, feelings that enveloped her like a shrouding fog - the anger and despair - was it all of her own making? How could this be? Was she always loved? How could she feel so incredibly alone when love and light surrounded her?

Samara, telepathically reading her thoughts, replied. "The light is always there even if a haze of emotional or physical upset temporarily obscures it. Like the sun that continues to emit its warmth, its brilliant rays, even though storm clouds block the orb from view."

Adanya was not alone. Nor would she ever be. She was always loved. The power, the light, of all heaven and earth surrounded her - today, tomorrow and always. Everything else was but an illusion.

"Come." Dagmar redirected the women with unmasked urgency. "The full moon is waning. We must go to the water's edge."

The spirit guides hurriedly led Adanya down to the pure, white sand. Adanya felt the velvet grains, cooled by the evening breeze, beneath her bare feet. She heard the roar of the ocean as it moved rhythmically in and out of the shoreline. Brilliant stars shone like rare diamonds against the black canvas of the nighttime sky.

Adanya's white, flowing robe clung to her youthfully appointed body as a sultry, unexpected wind suddenly whipped 'round, caressing her being with a touch as soft as exquisitely spun silk. Dagmar's right hand, adorned in emeralds and rubies, drew a sacred symbol in the air about an inch from Adanya's face and the girl, reverently, involuntarily, closed her eyes. Then Diella plucked a handful of seaweed from the waters, draping it on the Beloved like a crown.

Their voices chanted as hands moved up and down Adanya's energy field, never actually touching her physical vessel, slowing at certain points as if to tune or adjust an unseen element. Then the Enlightened Ones anointed her head with aromatic oils, dipping the girl's trusting body into the sea – once, twice, three times. The third time Adanya found herself fully submerged in salty, churning water.

All noise stopped. It felt as if time itself stood still. Adanya no longer heard the ocean's waves as they crashed onto the shore. No longer did the Enlightened Ones chants fill her soul.

Adanya opened her eyes. She stood not on the beach but, rather, suspended deep within the sea. Miraculous visions filled her mind's eye in the crystal underwater regions. Her body, now remarkably light, moved with graceful fluidity, a sort of languid motion. Starfish and seahorses greeted her, nudging the Beloved gently with long tentacles and blunt, friendly noses.

Dolphins serenely encircled the newcomer, inviting the Beloved to join in their playful late night swim. Adanya, whose breathing adapted easily to the creatures' world, felt no fear, only an all-encompassing peace. Her spirit soared with a freedom, a euphoric pleasure, never before experienced, as she glided and jumped through the waters, holding onto arched grey fins, riding with abandon, straddling upon the smooth, curved backs of the mammals.

Adanya witnessed unimaginable splendor. Rarified objects, treasures far more precious than gold or silver, lay strewn along the ocean floor. Coral reefs, feathery foliage. Creatures never before encountered ventured out of the deep's oblique murkiness. Mermaids, with luxurious, flowing hair, their scaled bodies sporting iridescent flippers of every hue, called out to her, "Namaste."

Adanya returned the familiar greeting. "Namaste." Then she briefly closed her eyes.

When she opened her eyes again, Adanya observed golden particles of sunlight streaming through the chamber window. She lay again on her own straw pallet at the Sisters of the Sacred Covenant. Was it all a dream?

Adanya contemplated the vision a bit longer before noticing a large, oblong stain on the dirt floor. Water? It had not rained last night. Puzzled, she ran her hand through her tangled locks in amazement. As the Beloved gestured, she encountered something wet and decidedly slimy. The girl abruptly pulled her hand down, opening her palm to discover a green leaf, a form of plant, perhaps. Seaweed?

Then she heard Dagmar's unmistakable voice, "Adanya, do not limit the gods. The power of the Universe dwells within."

# CHAPTER XVII

*"Grandmother," asked Morning Dove, "are the Enlightened Ones real? I mean, are they actually emissaries of the Divine?"*

*The Ancient One remained silent for a moment. Then she quietly asked. "Does it matter?"*

*Morning Dove, annoyed at the non-responsive question, gave an exasperated sigh. "Of course it matters. If it was just a dream then it's not real."*

*"Eternal wisdom comes in many forms, Morning Dove," said her grandmother. "As the Holy Ones said, it is a grave mistake to limit the Creator."*

*Then, without another word of explanation, the elder continued weaving the story.*

The six months of silence ended. Adanya emerged feeling healthy, with a renewed sense of purpose. As Sister Angelica anticipated, the imposed period served to center, to ground the once reeling girl. Adanya, her emotions now firmly balanced, remembered the sacred mission of the ancient scroll. Surely, she could find the goddess on these holy grounds. For the Beloved had already developed an extensive list of spiritual truths in her journal.

The journal, after months of revisions, read:

**In this moment, this is what I believe. It might change.** What followed was a listing of Adanya's personal beliefs about the world and her place in it. Some phrases were written boldly while other passages were crossed out as the writer worked to carefully refine her thoughts. Certain sentiments were underlined for emphasis. Like Adanya herself, the effort was obviously a work in progress, a piece that the girl would re-visit and edit throughout her life.

But the greatest accomplishment to date, the healing of Adanya's troubled soul, brought the searching young girl to a very specific conclusion. She desired to become one with the Sisters of the Sacred Covenant, to join the prestigious order. Her highest thought in this moment centered on discovering her gift, dedicating her soul, under the watchful protection of the Sisters of the Sacred Covenant.

One day, as Adanya tended errant growth rampaging within an otherwise stunning garden, she broached this topic with Sister Angelica. "Sister, I would like to devote my heart to serving the Divine. Is my cleansed soul worthy enough to join the sacred convent?" Adanya, paused, fervently praying that Sister Angelica deemed her valuable enough to join the order. "Do you think that I could humbly serve the Creator?"

A benevolent, thoughtful smile spread across Sister Angelica's face. "There are many ways to serve the Divine, my child. Why do you wish to commit yourself to this life?"

Adanya hesitated, struggling to find the right words. "Because it is peaceful here and the work that you do is sacred. The outside world spews so much chaos and hatred and confusion. I feel certain that the goddess does not, could not, live beyond these walls."

The sister didn't answer Adanya immediately. Instead, she turned her undivided attention to a gardener's bed that, though once quite beautiful, showed signs of extensive neglect. Weeds sprouted everywhere. Tangled, creeping, vines choked budding life out of hopeful vegetation. Yet in the middle of unimaginable disorder, a single, crimson rose grew. It flourished, its blossoms full and untouched, as if oblivious to the vile weeds, the wanton disregard, that surrounded it.

Sister Angelica struggled with the tenacious, uninvited intruders invading the poorly kept garden. Adanya watched, uncertain as to how the woman would respond to her question - or if the revered sister remembered it at all.

Finally, with a handful of weeds successfully uprooted, Sister Angelica wiped her brow, hopelessly drenched in sweat, and switched from her kneeling, bent-over position. Now she sat upright, cross-legged, with her robes squarely tucked under her. She motioned for her companion to do the same.

"Adanya, you cannot hide from the outside world behind these walls. That is not the intent of this convent." She gestured with a crude hand trowel toward the unwieldy garden. "Weeds, like flowers, can grow anywhere."

"But it is so peaceful here," Adanya exclaimed. "I love the holy resonance of this place."

"It is true. Disciples can find peace on an island, such as this, or in a sacred place of worship. But the Divine is also present within the unsettled village of a warring tribe," said Sister Angelica. "It is not these walls that make this convent holy, nor the sun-drenched sands of this ocean paradise. Rather, it is one's very spirit that consecrates, that makes each setting holy.

"But how could I ever find the goddess within a warring tribe?" Adanya did not understand the meaning of Sister Angelica's words. "Surely the goddess cannot exist where hatred and bloodshed flourish. How can the Divine be in such a place?"

Sister Angelica rose from the ground, efficiently brushing the remaining dirt from her robes. Shielding her eyes from the intense glare of the afternoon sun, she looked directly at Adanya.

"That, my child, is a question that you alone must answer."

# CHAPTER XVIII

The question haunted Adanya as she moved through rewarding, spiritually renewing days with the Sisters of the Sacred Covenant. How could the goddess exist in the midst of a warring village? The query rested, never sleeping, at the forefront of her mind.

But days turned into weeks, then months, with no immediate answer. In fact, additional questions confronted Adanya as she pursued spiritual truths with the island children in the Master's classroom. Each day the Master, a woman of no discernable age or ethnicity, brought fresh, markedly different, perspectives to her students lives.

In one class, the pupils sat still, silently for eight hours, perhaps more, merely to observe a graceful lotus blossom. There was no stated purpose to the exercise. No directions given. The Master simply placed the fragrant subject, floating in a clear crystal bowl in the middle of the children's circle, before silently retreating to her own seated position.

The students, Adanya included, stared at the lotus blossom. They honored its pale, delicate color as well as its curved, elegant shape. They observed its flawless surface, creamy as an ageless woman's delicate, flawless skin. It was hard to believe that such a creation grew from the Earth's soil. Was that the purpose of this exercise - to appreciate the life that sprung up in the midst of muck? Adanya wondered as her frustration, not to mention incessant boredom, grew.

After an hour or so, Adanya's mind, quite understandably, wandered. She drifted into the sea visiting gentle dolphins and welcoming mermaids in their aquatic home. Her mind's eye absorbed marvelous sights as she swam, carefree, through turquoise waters.

Suddenly, however, as if prompted by an inner voice, the daydreams ceased. Adanya gently guided her conscious self back to the here and now.

From that point on, she stayed, fully present, in the company of the lotus blossom.

As the hours passed, Adanya transformed the fleeting moments into an elevated state of consciousness. She witnessed the flower's life unfold before her. She embraced the native farmer planting the seed, tenderly tucking it into the inviting, nurturing surface of the Earth. She felt the sun generating warmth upon the plant even as fierce wind and rain cultivated it in the damp mud.

Hours passed. Still the group watched the flower as Adanya's visions continued. The farmer plucked the fully formed blossom, presenting it to his wife as a symbol of deep, abiding love. The old woman's lined face radiated joy as she breathed in the lotus' heady aroma. Eventually, though, the petals fell, one by one, returning to the Earth. The beauty of the lotus blossom, once again in the soil of its birth, dwelled in all things.

Finally, into the silence, came the teacher's tranquil voice. "Who fathered the lotus blossom? Who is the sacred mother of this flower?"

The room, once crushingly silent, erupted in a carrousel of sound as children voiced varying opinions. Some cried out that the farmer fathered the lotus blossom. Others argued that the earth which bore the flower mothered the lotus blossom. Still others claimed that the father was Apollo, the sun god. For more than an hour the boisterous, good-natured debate continued.

Then, a small boy, no more than three or four years, of age spoke. "The father, the sacred mother, of the lotus blossom is the Great Spirit," he said. The other children ceased to speak.

"And where does the Creator, this Great Spirit, reside?" asked the Master.

The child looked solemnly into the elder's eyes, unwavering, answering without hesitation. "The Creator lives within the flower, Teacher."

The other students, mouths agape, stared at the child in disbelief. How could this be? It didn't even make sense. Where could this baby, this senseless child, derive such a witless idea? Certainly Adanya didn't understand.

The Master, however, broke into a broad smile. The room grew silent again as the sacred instructor walked to the innocent child and bowed low before him. "Namaste. You are a wise teacher and I honor you."

# CHAPTER XIX

It was not the long-awaited, much sought after, goddess but, rather, a mere mortal man, whose flesh and blood forever altered the course of Adanya's life on the eve of her eighteenth year. Nothing foretold of the arrival. Neither harkening bird nor celestial messenger marked the occasion. Yet rarely did an event impact the Beloved more than when these two distant worlds collided.

Adanya awoke the day of that fateful first encounter, blissfully unaware of the impending circumstance, working her normal routine with the Sisters of the Sacred Covenant. In final preparation for taking the vow of commitment, a formal rite of acceptance into the order, she single-mindedly studied in the morning and, as befitting advanced spiritual growth, taught lessons to novices that very afternoon. Then, as lengthening shadows grew markedly longer, Adanya prepared the fish and rice that provided sustenance to the members.

Following evening prayer, a time when Adanya always asked, very specifically and, to date, unsuccessfully, for the goddess of light and love, her goddess, to materialize, she descended the mountainside in the watchful company of Running Wolf and the Winged One, picking her way carefully, to the beach. A full moon, its circumference nearly eclipsing, the night time sky, lit the rocky terrain as the young woman moved. Flowers, their mystical blossoms unfolding only after the fiery orb sunk far below the horizon, lined the walk with remarkable, unparalleled fragrance. Adanya stopped, stooping low to bury her nose in their blooms, picking a delicate stem.

Gazing up at the sky, the Beloved opened her journal, pensively looking at the blank page. Then she wrote:

*I am the sister of the Moon. It follows me as I journey on this earth. I play between the moonbeams at the midnight hour. Hide and seek amidst the light and shadow of the night.*

*I am one with everything in this Universe. The moon and the starts speak my name. I fly among the clouds. We call the same Creator, "the Almighty".*

*The Life Force that created the moon and the stars is my Creator. I am one with the heavens and the earth. And I rejoice.*

Her heart uttered a prayer. "Father of the Universe, thank you for the life force that connects all of creation," she began. "I dance in celebration of the energy that comes from the same Divine Source - you. I feel balanced and whole as I recognize that we are all one. May I always honor our holy, indivisible union. Amen."

The balmy spring air possessed an electrifying quality. For awhile, Adanya sat contentedly on the shoreline, listening to the soothing sounds of the ocean, but restlessness stirred within. She strolled, unhurriedly, towards the village, drawn by the tempting mix of music coupled with laughter. Ever closer, Adanya's nostrils filled with tantalizing aromas. Was a sacrificial pig being roasted? Elongated forms played against the light of the fire's flame as joyful, albeit somewhat inebriated, villagers celebrated the much earlier arrival of the spring equinox.

Adanya stood, cloaked in shadow, behind a climbing, leafy grape arbor, its carved rungs heavy laden with fruit. She knew that the Sisters of the Sacred Covenant strictly forbid its members to mingle with the islanders except in the most sacred and practical of matters. But the sights and sounds reminded the girl of another time, a time long ago, when flute and fiddle played harmoniously in the Valley of Lilies.

However, this was a rhythm unlike any other. Drums beat continuously, as if in commune with the gods themselves. Faster and faster, the drummers' massive hands flew like palm trees caught in the relentless fury of a merciless storm. Sound bounced off the heavens, enveloping festive dancers in frenzied rapture.

Adanya's hips swayed unconsciously, uncontrollably, to their beat. Bodies, male and female, mingled with an ever-increasing fervor. Heat, visible in the heavy night air, rose like lava in the belly of an erupting volcano.

"Do you not wish to join the celebration?"

Adanya jumped, startled at the unexpected voice. She turned to find herself staring at a masterfully broad chest ornamented with muscles that rippled like the crest of enormously powerful waves. Thick, black, shoulder length hair framed a chiseled face offset with mesmerizing eyes. Never, in all her life, had Adanya gazed upon anyone, man or woman, with greater intrigue.

Adanya's own eyes slowly traveled upward, meeting his intense stare, her heart skipping a beat. She tried to speak but no sound emanated from her being.

"You do not like to dance?" he inquired.

For a moment, Adanya felt as if she were swimming underwater, the earth whirling, swirling around her. His voice suddenly possessed a distant, disembodied quality. Her skin, her entire body, tingled. She breathed in his scent as his bronze body glistened in the play of shadow and light.

"I . . . I . . . don't know how," Adanya stammered. She watched his thick, sensual lips, her own fingers moving unconsciously to touch the tendrils that fell softly around her face. The movement loosed the forgotten blossom from her grasp. It drifted effortlessly, like a weightless feather, to the ground.

The man, this beautiful specimen of the opposite sex, nobly bent down, retrieving it. Adanya's breath ceased as he drew closer, his body mere inches from hers, and tucked the bloom in her hair. She felt his fingers linger, tracing the outline of her face. He inhaled the lavender which anointed her bath water every day. Adanya shuddered, her body trembling.

For a fleeting moment, the two stood as if alone, the only inhabitants of this island paradise. The sound of the drums, the images of the people, faded away. Adanya felt a tension, a physical reaction, deep within her as the native slowly leaned forward, his hand still resting on her face, and tilted her chin upward.

Suddenly, Adanya snapped out of her trance-like state, breaking free of the stranger's hypnotic spell. Outstretched arms pushed past the tall native as the Beloved ran, her strides faster and faster, down the beach and up the mountain path, heart pounding, running as if her life depended on it, not stopping until she reached the safety of her chamber.

# CHAPTER XX

*Morning Dove's eyes sparkled. "A handsome man appears, Grandmother? Now the story gets interesting."*

*"Yes," said the Ancient. "He was one of the Creator's masterpieces. Tall and strong, his body served as the most glorious instrument."*

*"Does Adanya give her heart to him? Do they fall in love?" Morning Dove urged her grandmother to reveal more.*

*"Love is most sacred, my child. Few mortals truly understand it."*

Certainly Adanya didn't understand it. Nor did she understand what was happening to her. Every morning, the girl woke and, rather than giving thanks for the awakening, she lingered on her pallet, hugging her body, immersed in the most decadent, unimaginable dreams. Her thoughts always returned to the grape arbor, listening to the fading drums, remembering the thrill of this unknown man's touch.

The dreams, which both repulsed and enthralled, left Adanya tingling, aching for something yet undiscovered. She inexplicably sensed him next to her, his breath on her skin. Unconsciously, her hands moved to the cheek he once touched. She replayed the fleeting sensual moments over and over.

What was happening to her? Did Sister Angelica notice? Adanya worried. Just last night, at dinner, the sister's request for Adanya to pass the bread went unanswered. The bemused sister repeated the single appeal, again and again, until the table of dining women erupted in pockets of gentile laughter. Embarrassed, her face flushing a brilliant crimson, Adanya mumbled an apology, quickly passing the oft requested loaf. Sister Angelica said nothing but there was a look, almost a kind of knowingness, in her gaze.

The Beloved felt drawn to this man like waves crashing upon the shore. Who was this stranger that so completely dominated every thought?

Adanya's heart compelled her to seek him out. She strained for non-existent views of him outside her chamber window. It made no sense. She even revisited the beach in the hopes of glimpsing his form, but the deserted sands offered only charred remains within the empty fire pit. Like the long-eaten pig, this mysterious man evaporated with the morning dew.

Nonetheless, the fantasies grew increasingly elaborate, taking on a life of their own. Adanya imagined his full lips pressing hard against hers in a passionate embrace. Her body cried out for him in a way that the girl thought not possible. Was this the love that she had long awaited? Adanya experienced shame tinged with ecstasy. For she knew the members of the Sisters of the Sacred Covenant, an order she hoped to soon join, must remain untouched by mortal man. Surely these impure thoughts would pass.

One afternoon, a full two weeks after the unexpected encounter, Adanya busily hung laundry in the scorching sun until she noticed something quite curious. Island men streamed through the compound gates. A gathering of sisters lined the expansive entryway, bowing as the natives, men of all age and shape, proudly marched stridently past. The images reminded the young woman of a parade she once attended with Petro on the streets of Ambilen.

Adanya finished securing an apron to the line and, uncertain as to the guests' purpose, moved rapidly down the embankment toward the hub of activity. She walked with increasing urgency, butterflies in her wake, down to the main entrance. There she joined the other observers as the men continued to enter the convent.

"What is going on?" Adanya whispered to Sister Nancia. "Why have men entered this holy place?"

"The islanders are to build a new place of worship to honor the Great Spirit," explained a noticeably flushed Sister Nancia. "They will come, each day, until the project is completed."

Adanya and Sister Nancia silently bowed their heads as the formation of men moved in front of them. Adanya, however, could not keep her eyes closed. Her sapphire eyes covertly scanned the faces in the crowd. Was it possible? Was he here?

Her heart leaped. The dark stranger was indeed here - his shoulders stood a full head above most men. His magnificent body, full of youth's strength and promise, moved with the agility of a lion king, his mane full, and his stoic countenance regal and proud. Every sinew of the toned, muscular form stood as a testament to this mortal's obvious prowess.

Now, seeing him for the first time in the light of day, Adanya observed the most curious sight. There was a picture on his arm - as if an artist had used the glorious flesh as his - or her - own personal canvas. What was it?

Something tugged at her brain - a nagging feeling. Finally, Adanya recalled the foretelling of such a drawing - a "tatau". Afaitu, an ancient woman, regaled by the islanders as a seer, once cornered the girl in the open air market. Adanya, who traveled into the village to trade rice for pomegranates, quite literally bumped into the imposing Afaitu, spilling the basket of fruit.

Rolls of wrinkled flesh reached out to steady the girl. The much-desired, sumptuous pomegranates lay bruised, scattered upon the ground.

"Leave them," the old woman imperiously ordered as she spat on the rolling fruit. "Come with me."

Adanya, repulsed by the ruining of the earth's bounty yet trained to obediently follow the bidding of elders, complied. She dutifully trailed behind Afaitu, without speaking, until the woman motioned for her to sit on a crude, driftwood bench.

"You are the girl that seeks the goddess." Afaitu spoke her words not as a question but as a statement of fact.

"Yes," stammered Adanya, suddenly uncomfortable as she noticed the old woman's scarred left eye. It roamed, wandering aimlessly, independent of its counterpart. Uncertain as where to fix her own gaze, the girl averted her own eyes, looking nowhere in particular as she responded, "The ancient scroll foretold that I would find my gift within the goddess."

Afaitu wetted her lips with the thick roll of fleshy tongue. "You will receive many gifts within this lifetime. I speak only of the painted goddess that brings your future."

Confused, Adanya listened as the seer proceeded to explain the island custom of honoring both the Great Spirit and the many gods by injecting dyes, some kind of pigment, under the skin. A tatau - what did this have to do with the goddess?

"The painted one will give you your future." The old woman paused, pointing a fleshy finger topped with a yellowed, dirt-imbedded nail so long that it curved, at Adanya. "But you must always remember who the sacred father is, who the sacred mother is, if you wish to find the goddess."

Then, with a single flick of the wrist, Afaitu ceremoniously released the baffled girl. Adanya, unsure of what to think, dismissed Afaitu's words as the rants of a disturbed mind, a troubled soul. What else could they be?

That was six months ago. Now Sister Nance insistently tugged at

Adanya's sleeve, bringing the girl's full attention to the present moment. The girl gently shrugged off Sister Nance's touch and looked in the direction that the older woman pointed. A tatau. How interesting. Adanya had never seen one. The painting on the stranger's arm boasted a vibrant array of assorted hues. Yet Adanya could not yet make out the outline of the picture. What was it? It looked like an elephant with an exotic woman.

As the procession continued to pass directly in front of Adanya, the man, as if sensing the Beloved's presence, turned his head, locking his eyes with hers. The virgin girl instinctively lowered her head until he was no longer in view. Could he read her thoughts? She felt vulnerable, stripped naked. It was as if he knew her very soul.

As the impromptu welcome concluded, the women slowly dispersed back into the routine of the day. Adanya, however, remained planted firmly in place, rooted to the ground, unable to move. He was here. He was actually here. The thought terrified even as it tantalized the girl. Something, deep in the recesses of her subconscious, knew their paths fated.

Finally, Adanya moved, absent of mindful thought, in the direction of the laundered clothes. And, while she gathered the wet garments, something in her mind surfaced. She knew what the tatau design was.

It was the goddess - Goddess Lakshmi. Adanya stopped, stunned, as a realization spread over her. This was a sign! It must be. The goddess, her goddess, had finally arrived.

# CHAPTER XXI

Adanya struggled, pulling out the dusty, oversized book, *Spiritual Guide to Gods & Goddesses*, from the shelves in the Room of Enlightenment. The room, its walls, covered in scrolls, ancient manuscripts, and priceless artwork, housed knowledge representing every form of religious belief. The Sisters of the Sacred Covenant believed, rightfully so, that spiritual truths existed in every religion whose origins were founded in pure love. The order celebrated all truth with the firm conviction that it stemmed from the Creator.

Adanya turned the creased, yellowed pages of the holy antiquity carefully. One by one, the illustrator's life-like, painstakingly colored, renderings of the deities looked up at her. There was Athena, the goddess who called upon all mortals to trust the whisperings of their souls. Then there was Brigit, of Celtic birth, who protected virgins, mothers and aging women. Page after page, the author meticulously detailed the powers, the special concerns and interests, of these lauded deities.

Finally, Adanya came to the goddess she sought - Lakshmi. The Hindu deity wore an ornate crown atop dark, cascading hair. Her calm, serene countenance reflected an inner peace. A beautiful sari adorned her body. Lotus blossoms surrounded Lakshmi. For a moment, Adanya reflected back to the Master's question, "Who fathered the lotus blossom? Who is the sacred mother of this flower?"

The elephant's presence, however, interrupted Adanya's concentration. Pictured next to Lakshmi, the artist's depiction of the elephant looked uncannily like the image on the native's bronze arm. The majestic animal's long trunk, its massive body, fascinated the girl.

Adanya read the caption underneath the picture. "Lakshmi is a Hindu goddess who reminds mortals to let go of self-imposed darkness and trust in the light of the Great Spirit. All power lies within mortal man as well as his female counterpart. Humans are urged to let go of fear and connect with their God-given gifts. For the source of all power, to which all living things are connected, is the Creator."

"There is nothing to fear," said Adanya aloud. "The goddess is a sign that all is well, that the path ahead is strewn with many gifts."

Surprised at the sound of her own voice, Adanya spun around, quickly looking about the room. Seeing no one, she continued reading aloud. "The elephant god, Ganesh, moves the mountains, including self-created hurdles, from all mortal paths. Invoke these deities to realize your spirit-filled future."

Adanya snapped the book shut. "This is it," she thought adamantly. "This is a sign that the painted one holds my future. He is the gift of which the ancient scroll speaks."

# CHAPTER XXII

*"Grandmother, is the dark stranger the gift that Adanya seeks?" Morning Dove looked imploringly at the Ancient One. "Is he the one?"*

*The old woman smiled at her granddaughter's obvious excitement. "All spirits are gifts, my child. Each person, every plant, animal, and mineral comes to us at a specific time for a sacred purpose. Some stay for a lifetime, others for only a short time. But they all reveal eternal truths to us, teaching us the lessons that we most need to learn."*

*Morning Dove, dissatisfied with the response, grumbled. "But, Grandmother, is he the one?"*

*"It depends on what you mean, my child. It depends on what you mean."*

Spawn on grains of pure white sand amidst frothy bubbles of lithe sea foam, Manutea's birth occurred at the site of a mystical portal - an opening to all things seen and unseen. The celebrated baby held the coveted title of eldest, first-born son, the long-awaited heir to a fishing dynasty dating back hundreds of years. His conception, his watery birth, consecrated the union of Hori, a humble, hardworking fisherman, and Leilani, the strikingly beautiful daughter of tribal medicine man, Ganu. Although the prolific couple birthed other remarkable offspring, Hori entrusted Manutea with the family's future.

Manutea alone, at the appointed time, bore responsibility for continuing the long-held tradition of providing leadership as well as physical and material wealth for his kinsmen. This time-honored role, envied by all tribesmen, proved no easy task. Tribal law required patriarchs to offer up their coin, open their homes, for the common good of the bloodline. Patriarchs extended their bounty to immediate family members as well as their spouses, cousins, aunts and uncles.

This enormous, potentially overwhelming, expectation, along with a sense of inherent entitlement, shaped the ruggedly handsome boy. Manutea studied harder, applied himself more, than other children, even learning how to read, a skill uncommon among the island people. He spoke less than his contemporaries, choosing to remain silent while others spewed idle thoughts fueled by the reckless, misguided abandons of youth.

Indeed, Manutea carried himself differently than other children. He moved among the throng of islanders with ease yet remained separate, somehow distant, from his peers. Young and old unconsciously sought out this first born son, sensing greatness within him.

Now nearing his twentieth year, Manutea fully embraced manhood. He worked, as he had every day since his ninth summer, with his masterful, aging father. Rain or shine, regardless of the ocean's wake, the pair paddled hallowed out canoes far into beckoning sea, casting handmade fishing nets comprised of twine, skillfully fastened, joining one piece to the next. And, like the rise and fall of one's breath, as Apollo's orb ascended to full altitude then descended slowly over the horizon, the men's patience was, without fail, generously rewarded.

The nets consistently overflowed with delectable, squirming fish. In fact, the frantic writhing of innumerable sea creatures often threatened to capsize the narrow, oblong crafts as father and son struggled to haul the weighty catch over the boats' respective sides. This strenuous, never-ending effort tired the once invincible Hori. Soon, with great relief, he would relinquish his life's ambition, the never-ending responsibility, to his eldest son.

Perhaps that's why, with increasing frequency, Manutea contemplated marriage. Long past the age when couples normally mated, the man's sensuality, his brooding good looks, left no shortage of interested maidens. Women unabashedly, quite openly, competed for Manutea like desirous, in heat mares awaiting the thick, milky seed of a prized stallion.

Raven-haired beauties boldly flirted with the bachelor enticing him with scrumptious, edible delicacies, offerings of fine food made by the expectant hands of ever-hopeful mothers. Sometimes, unbeknownst to these mothers, their daughters also offered the ravenous, insatiable fisherman rich, decadent desserts of a different kind. Nonetheless, while Manutea never declined a sweet, he married naught. This noble waited for the flame that burned eternal.

Many of Manutea's friends already possessed eternal flames. These friends, the boys of his youth, more than two summers earlier, exchanged the frivolities of courtship for the responsibility of commitment. They proudly spoke of gentle, supportive wives, bellies already swollen with new life, who dutifully prepared meals and, as their husbands shamelessly boasted, met physical needs without complaint. A handful of friends even parented children old enough to attend the school with the Sisters of the Sacred Covenant.

Manutea remembered his own time at the school. He once climbed the mountain every day to sit upon silk pillows and soak in the Master's teachings. But that was long ago. He no longer remembered his teacher's face for the boy ceased to ascend the steep terrain in order to learn his father's trade. The sisters, however, created an indelible impression on the first nine years of Manutea's life.

That's why, with Hori's blessing, Manutea labored, shoulder to shoulder, beside other men to build a holy place in which to honor the Great Spirit. He instinctively understood that the gods demanded this type of personal sacrifice. And he especially desired to please the gods, to garner the Creator's favor. For, at the end of summer, Hori would formally hand over the fishing nets to his son. Manutea would then reign as the family's patriarch.

If Manutea experienced pressure or internal conflict regarding this long-anticipated change, it did not show on his placid, unflappable surface. The chosen successor continued to move with a languid ease, a confidence, uncommon in men of his age. And why not? The Goddess Lakshmi, long before his birth, sealed Manutea's fate. Therefore, for one final season, Manutea reigned as uncrowned royalty.

# CHAPTER XXIII

In the days that followed, the Moriceans worked tirelessly to erect a structure worthy of the Creator. They employed a durable mixture of sand and clay for the foundation, every square foot carefully measured and constructed. Crude tools assisted with the fashioning of stone for the walls. Teams of men painstakingly cut away rock from various sites along the mountain and carried them to the construction site.

The Sisters of the Sacred Covenant toiled alongside the island men. They hauled smaller stones, utilizing sharpened picks to chip away at the iron-hard, mineral surfaces. Every day the appreciative women gave thanks for the hearty volunteers, as well as the materials, provided for this project. They knew that generous spirits dwelled within these mortals as well as every rock, each grain of sand.

Relegated to kitchen duty, Adanya strenuously prepared the food that the men ate three times a day. The effort exhausted her, especially since the sisters normally numbered far less than these gigantically proportioned construction crews. Sweat poured from every conceivable pore, as she baked bread in the sun's merciless heat. Yet, at the end of each hectic day, a measure of satisfaction existed in her weary bones. Purpose filled Adanya's soul.

Furthermore, though her bones might ache, that secret place within Adanya tingled as she experienced unfamiliar, unidentified feelings. In fact, her acute senses further heightened as she inhaled Manutea's presence at the convent. It was as if he replaced the life force that once filled her.

Adanya became increasingly aware of Manutea's every move, his unspoken thought. At mealtimes, she maneuvered quickly about the crowd generously refilling cups and plates as needed. She uttered no words as Manutea's smoldering eyes watched her. Yet the air, already thick with the oppressive humidity of the tropics, felt infused with a potentially explosive electrical charge.

Stolen glances, an occasional unexpected touch might have continued, unresolved, had fate not intervened. The two lives came together on moonless night as the pull of destiny grew too overwhelming to ignore.

That unplanned yet highly anticipated evening, Adanya, traveled down the mountain to the community well, struggling to fill and carry cumbersome water buckets. Water sloshed about as she struggled on the return trip to maintain her footing on the slippery, uphill slope. She strained, more and more as the grade increased, against the weight of her burden.

Suddenly, without warning, the girl faltered, losing her balance on the treacherous, unforgiving rock. Her torso pitched forward as the unstable foundation disintegrated, bit by bit, under her feet. Unable to right herself, Adanya was about to slide, unsupported, off the side of the mountain path, careening thousands of feet to the ocean below, when a vice-like grip encircled her.

Adanya's heart raced as thoughts, one after another, entered her brain in succession. Elu often spoke of the celestial beings interceding to save careless humans from harm's way. Did the Creator dispense a guardian angel to rescue her? For, unless this was a horrific dream, Adanya recognized that she had been snatched from the unforgiving clutch of certain death.

The shaking girl opened her eyes to see the Goddess Lakshmi. Adanya dropped to her knees, giving thanks, paying homage, to the deity. Over and over again, she repeated, "You are the greatest of all deities. I sing your praises throughout this Universe. You are the greatest of all deities. I sing your praises throughout this Universe."

A deep chuckle filled the night air. "I am indeed quite wonderful but a humble 'thank you' would suffice."

Adanya's eyes flew open and observed the unmistakable legs of a mortal man. The girl jumped to her feet. "You tricked me, sir," Adanya sputtered, embarrassed. "It was a most unkind thing to do."

"Unkind? I think not. Unkind would have been to let you plunge over the side of this great mountain as an unwanted sacrifice to the gods." There was a bemused lilt to the voice. "Alas, however, you are right. I am no god." The stranger then bowed low. "I am Manutea."

Adanya involuntarily sucked in her breath as the introduction sank in. This was the one of who the seer spoke. This was the one who held her future. There was so much to say, to talk about. But the rescued girl found herself inexplicably tongue-tied. Fear of unknown origin gripped her.

"Of course, although I am but a simple fisherman, you are welcome to bow before me," Manutea continued. "Perhaps there are offerings that you can give. What is the appropriate gift when one saves another's life? Would you like to wear the shackle of servitude? I think seven years should repay such a great debt."

Adanya, uncertain of her own ears, said nothing. "Or perhaps," said Manutea, "you choose to offer yourself in sacrifice to the gods. The sisters still require that all converts be untouched by mortal man, do they not? It's been awhile since we've sacrificed so beautiful a virgin."

In a fury, Adanya, now fully recovered, drew herself to full height. "How dare you, sir! You are lower than a snorting boar to suggest that I repay your acts with my own death. No rational person would save me only to have me voluntarily give up that spared life." She spat the words with palpable intensity.

"As you wish," the measured reply came. "Then I understand that you willingly enter seven years of servitude."

"You understand nothing, you arrogant fool! Why would I desire to cook and clean for you?"

The man took obvious pleasure in the girl's range of emotion. "Of course, there are other duties, that you could perform," he said in a suggestive tone. "We will, however, have to address your careless tongue. No self-respecting servant speaks to her master with such familiarity."

Adanya, infuriated beyond words, emitted a strangling noise. "Argh . . . . . .." She reached up, palm open, intent on placing a well-executed slap on the impertinent stranger's cheek. But Manutea, expertly blocking the assault, went on the offensive. He bent down and, drawing Adanya close, passionately kissed his would be attacker.

Initially, Adanya struggled against the stranger's unexpected overtures, attempting to raise her arm, to squirm out of the all-encompassing embrace. But her body, as if disconnected from conscious thought, betrayed her, eagerly responding to Manutea's touch. She wished the moment to last forever, to linger eternally in his arms. But, without warning, the native abruptly released her.

Adanya watched as her future slipped away into the night.

# CHAPTER XXIV

For Adanya, life began on that narrow, rocky mountain path. The love-struck girl credited Manutea with her very breath as she absorbed earth's gifts anew. Never before had emerald grass appeared so lush or the azure sky so vibrant blue. The skylark's solitary song resounded like a joyful chorus of jubilant angels, their harmonious voices lifted to heaven. Indeed, Adanya responded animatedly to mundane, everyday experiences as a storybook princess alive with her prince's first kiss.

> *I am a vibrant, ageless spirit! Every day is an unbelievable adventure. For, though my mind remembers the follies and missteps of my youth, my heart sings that I have come to this new dawn. Sacred is every passing hour.*

> *I open the Universe's gift at this divine time in my life. Love waits for me. Its glorious treasures are stored within my beating heart.*

> *I now choose to dance at the festival. Too long have I stood, hidden behind the grape arbor. This is my time to whirl in the changing rhythms of the mesmerizing music. I move with a passion that shouts out my love for this world and the heavens above me.*

The romantic pair, who spoke naught in the presence of the Sisters of the Sacred Covenant, spent a fortnight secretly sharing sunsets. Each evening, long after the island men bid the sisters farewell, returning to waiting, welcoming families, Manutea circled back, rendezvousing with Adanya at the mountain crossroads. They sat in comfortable silence, watching overhead as the fiery orb slide below the horizon. Later, the couple conversed in hushed, private whispers until the hour grew late.

The infatuated pair bared their inner most thoughts, engaging in a level of emotional intimacy uncommon for such a fresh, evolving relationship. They poured out their souls, speaking on everything that mattered - life, death, love, joy, and sorrow. Manutea, normally guarded and, most decidedly, reserved, uncharacteristically shared personal reflections. He spoke of family and responsibility. He spoke of dreams that, regrettably, disappear at dawn's first light. Sadly, the frothy, sea foam bubbles that marked his birth popped, forever vanishing, the day he followed his father's footsteps, paddling fishing boats to that place where the sky meets the sea.

Conversely, Manutea listened as Adanya recounted her own early childhood, a childhood that, not unlike his own, appeared tragically cut short. He compassionately wiped the single tear that trickled down her cheek as she spoke of the fire that forever altered her steps. The islander openly admired the discipline, the sheer fortitude, with which Adanya catapulted herself forward after the deaths of Elu and Mahwah.

"You are strong," Manutea commented. "Many mortals, mortals much older than you, would die by their own hand rather than face what you endured."

Adanya shook her head. "I think perhaps it was merely my path to walk," she offered. "The Creator placed each stone before my feet."

"But you could have chosen not to walk it," Manutea countered, unwilling to let Adanya summarily dismiss such courageous action. "Or you could have walked it, silent save for the sound of incessant wailing or the angry gnashing of teeth."

Adanya smiled. "There might have been a few nights where the gods slept naught as I railed against the fates. But Mahwah always taught me that all things work for good. She used to say, 'The Universe is unfolding perfectly.'"

"Mahwah was very wise," Manutea noted, quite seriously. He lowered his lips to hers. "For the Universe is, indeed, unfolding perfectly." Twilight's fading glimmer no longer shone between them.

Through it all, Running Wolf and the Winged One remained, as always, never far from the Beloved's side. Yet they did not seem unsettled by Manutea's increasing presence in Adanya's life. For Manutea's part, while he failed to comprehend why the beasts moved only at the graceful woman's command, he did not question it.

On this particular night, the couple meandered oblivious to the spirit guides' presence. Manutea led Adanya blindly through the overgrown, variegated ferns and tropical, island blooms. He expertly guided her off the well-worn mountain path into an unparalleled existence that few experienced. Her eyes grew as round as six pence as the two arrived at the uncharted destination.

Unicorns, their horns shimmering like iridescent mother of pearl, pranced proudly in a nearby field. Cherubs filled the raspberry flecked sky. Was that a fairy that flitted past on wings of spun gold? Perhaps it was only the fickle light of dusk. Adanya's blinked rapidly, unbelieving, unable to trust the visions. Were they real?

Still Manutea urged Adanya's reluctant feet to walk on. This marvelous march, though enchanting, might last forever. The Beloved sighed contentedly as she realized it mattered not. Certainly, with Manutea by her side, she did not want the journey to end. His love, as well as the sights and sounds of this place, filled her with immeasurable ecstasy.

Finally, however, Manutea pushed aside enormous feathery ferns to reveal the crown jewel – a turquoise lagoon shimmering in dusk's reflective light. At its head, water fell, tumbling from heaven itself, flowing as rippling silk to the waiting, unbroken surface below. What was this place? Was she dreaming? Willow trees, seemingly identical to ones that grew in the Valley of Lilies, ringed the lagoon. How was this possible?

"Manny," as she had come to affectionately call Manutea, "it is the most glorious vision. What is its name?"

"I cannot translate our word into one that you will understand," replied Manutea. "This is the *Garden of the Gods*. Their breath paints every creature. Their touch gives the water life. I come here when I want to be alone."

Then, looking meaningfully into Adanya's sapphire eyes, he added, "But I find that I no longer desire to be alone."

Adanya's heart swelled even as she inhaled the unimaginable beauty that sprang up all around her. Afraid to spoil the moment, she barely spoke above a whisper, "Nor do I."

From the edge of the lagoon, Adanya peered into the endless pool, mesmerized by the sparkling images. Fins of every size and shape waved up at the girl from the depths below. A cobalt blue fish, sporting vivid splashes of sun-colored spots, winked "hello" from his underwater vantage point.

A brilliant chartreuse fish tipped his head gallantly. Adanya clapped her hands, laughing, jumping up and down with delight, like a small child.

"Come," Manutea urged. "Let us join the sea creatures in their home." He pulled his giddy, playful companion towards the shallow end.

Adanya stuck her toe in the tepid water as she lifted the hem of her garb to protect it from the water's touch. "But, Manny," she cautioned, her voice unexpectedly forlorn. "My robes cannot get wet. For the sisters will surely know of our meeting."

A wicked smile formed on Manutea's lips. "Then take them off. I am certain that Poseidon himself never set eyes upon a more fetching mermaid."

Adanya, who usually felt exceedingly comfortable in her own skin, remained unconvinced. "It is not right, Manny," she stated reluctantly. "The Sisters of the Sacred Covenant would not approve." Adanya shuddered inwardly as she thought of Sister Angelica's reaction to such blatant indecency.

"Adanya," Manutea replied gently, "the gods made you for all to see. There is no shame. There is nothing to fear."

After a moment's hesitation, Adanya stepped behind the cover of a bush ablaze in purple passion flowers. Her cotton garb dropped to its sandy base. Then the flowering shrub appeared to speak. "Manny, you must turn your back until I have entered the water."

Manutea chuckled at such unnecessary modesty. "As you wish, my lady," he said, bowing low in feigned chivalry before turning his back, loosening his own wrap and letting it fall from his trim, narrow waist. He moved, without looking at Adanya, into the inviting waters.

Adanya, as amused by Manny's humor as she was confident of his integrity, eased herself from behind the shrub, walking again, somewhat self-consciously, to the lagoon. Slowly, she submerged herself, allowing sacred waters to envelop her body.

Sensing the Beloved's presence, Manutea turned and gazed upon the bedazzling woman bathed in the golden palate of the setting sun. Adanya inhaled sharply as she saw his rising manhood prompt ripples in the otherwise placid surface.

"Hush," soothed Manutea. "It matters not." Seeking to reduce Adanya's obvious discomfort, he brought her hands to his lips, gently kissing them. Then he said, "Follow me," as he dove into the mysteries of the world below.

Adanya swam with Manutea to depths never before experienced.

She silently screamed, giving rapture voice, as he took her, over and over, their bodies rising and falling like the crashing of tumultuous waves in the otherwise tranquil setting. The pair moved, one with each other - even as they were eternally one with the sea and the air itself.

Later, the young lovers rode gigantic sea turtles, laughing and playing as carefree children on never-ending holiday. The obliging animals, while slow and inept on land, provided a wild, unforgettable adventure through underwater channels and colonies. They moved in and out of coral reefs as well as exotic waterways. Adanya felt vigorously alive - happy, healthy and whole.

Eventually, energy spent, Manutea and Adanya reveled under the purifying, restorative cascade of the great waterfall, allowing heaven's touch to cleanse and rejuvenate their bodies. The couple cozily rested in the comfort of a willow tree as Adanya played a soft tune on her fiddle, Manutea's damp head cradled in her lap. Crickets chirped in perfect harmony as the warm glow of fairy wings lit the nocturnal paradise.

Manutea's soft snoring brought the impromptu concert to a close. Adanya, sleepy yet bewitched by the moon's hypnotic spell, took out her feathered quill. Opening her journal, she invited night to scatter its gifts.

### *The Fairy Dance*
*Fairies dance along my garden path,*
*Whimsical flights of fancy.*
*Moonbeams glisten off silken wings,*
*Twinkling lights in the midnight mist.*
*This world comes alive on a summer's eve.*
*The breeze breathes life in every form.*
*Cherubs, mermaids, and leprechauns -*
*Mystical creatures, magical charms.*
*Crickets sing a lullaby,*
*As the willow tree gently sways.*
*The sandman closes sleepy eyes.*
*Slumber, my soul, under starry skies.*

# CHAPTER XXV

The lovers' passion ignited with an intensity that rivaled the torrid heat of Apollo's flaring sun. Day after day, Manutea toiled with his peers on the soon to be completed temple. Adanya continued to prepare meals, teach children, and pray with the other sisters. But, though their days might unfold separately, each magnificent sunset belonged exclusively to the embracing sweethearts.

Manutea, or more specifically, the relationship with Manutea, brought forth an unbidden stream of consciousness within Adanya. The young woman previously endured a relatively solitary existence. Now she enjoyed the intimate company of another. She thrived on the sharing of thought, the union of spirits. Perhaps this was the gift that the goddess intended.

Her journal reflected these newfound feelings.

*Our love is a gift from the Creator. The heavens whisper our names with one breath. Lovers' fate, sealed by sacred contract, began before the Earth's first rotation. Two souls on a journey through this Universe. We are one.*

*The Creator's imprint on your soul, my spirit, is unmistakable. We do not own one another. Rather, we choose this dance for its unparalleled joy. Our union produces unimaginable ecstasy. For our hearts are forever intertwined, eternally connected, in Spirit.*

For the first time, Adanya seriously contemplated serving the Creator outside the perceived safety of the convent's sacred walls. Certainly the gods could use her, work through her, even though she might one day also serve as a wife and mother. The Sisters of the Sacred Covenant would understand. Why, these spiritual leaders might even teach our children, Adanya thought.

Then she cringed. Adanya always experienced an accompanying pang of guilt whenever she considered the Sisters of the Sacred Covenant. They treated her with such love and acceptance. How could she let them down? Surely she could no longer take the vow of commitment in the fall. The sisters specifically prohibited unclean women from joining their order.

Yet it felt so good to be loved, truly loved, by someone. Interestingly, neither Manutea nor Adanya discussed long-term plans for their relationship. Adanya shied away from such a sensitive topic, feeling too vulnerable, overwhelmed by the intensity of her own feelings. Undoubtedly, Manny, who also remained notably mute regarding this matter, felt the same.

Adanya did, however, broach the subject of revealing the ever-deepening bond to the kind sisters. It made sense to her, spiritually and intellectually, to share their good fortune. One evening, she proposed this very course of action to Manutea.

Manutea, sprawled on the grass under the shade of a willow tree, listened, his eyes closed. Adanya spoke quietly, suggesting that they seek Sister Angelica's wise council. "Surely everyone will be happy for the love that we share," said Adanya. "Perhaps we can even ask them to bless our union."

Her man, this man that she so deeply adored, remained momentarily quiet, as if considering Adanya's comments. "It is true," he finally said. "Our love is a glorious gift but I do not think that this is the time to unveil such news."

Adanya looked up at him in astonishment. "But Manny, why not? I think that the sisters will be surprised but, honestly, I think that they will be happy for us. Master still speaks fondly of the years that you attended this school."

"There will be time for all that," replied Manutea. He took the Beloved in his arms. "But, for now, I do not wish to share you with anyone. Let us not allow others entry into our private nirvana - not yet." With those words, he lowered his full lips to hers - silencing further discussion.

Truthfully, Adanya reveled in Manutea's unanticipated response. He thought their relationship so special that he wished to shield it, protect it, from the prying eyes of the world. It was as if other people might spoil this amazing time in their lives. And, indeed, there was a connection, a special language between them, which existed through all eternity.

Yet Adanya wondered about Manutea's family. What would they think of her? She listened, enthralled, as he recounted the siblings' escapades as well as his parents, Hori and Lelani. Long before their son's celebrated birth - before the tribal elders sanctioned their union - the two lived as star-crossed lovers. For Lelani, the daughter of a medicine man was of royal blood, too pure, according to the law, to be impregnated by the seed of a common fisherman.

But Lelani, a woman of great will, persisted, prevailing upon her father to bless the union. Initially, Ganu adamantly refused, holding fast to time honored convictions, until one day his perception of Hori changed. The medicine man witnessed Hori snatch a youngster from the horrifying jaws of death without regard for his personal well-being or protection.

It happened in the twilight hour. Hori, preparing for the next day's fishing expedition, heard the seven year old boy's faint, desperate cries for help over the ocean's incessant roar. He scanned the horizon to see the boy frantically moving about, being forcibly pulled under the water's churning surface. Shark!

Other men, drained from the day's excursion, lingered listlessly by and watched as Hori dropped his nets, grabbed a 20 inch scaling knife, and dove, mid-run, into shark invested seas. The twenty year old man swam skillfully, with powerful strokes, fending off other predators with short, aggressive jabs to their snouts, until he finally reached the victim.

Flailing wildly, the terrified child clung frantically to his heroic rescuer, accidently knocking the knife from Hori's weakening, slippery grip. Hori stared helplessly as it tumbled, gone forever, into the ocean's endless depths. Weaponless, a shark's steely bite locked on Hori's thigh, the fisherman beat the shark about the nose and head until it involuntarily released its prey.

Frenzied, sharks pursued Hori as he struggled to swim with the young boy in his weakening grasp. Battered, blood gushing with every pulsating movement, Hori stumbled to the shoreline, carrying child to his relieved mother, and collapsed on the sand.

Convinced of Hori's honor, his inherent courage, and, perhaps, weary of his daughter's unrelenting pleas, Ganu consented to the marriage - with one stipulation. Hori promised, as stipulated, to ensure that Ganu's regal bloodline endured. For the Creator entrusted children born of the medicine man's lineage with special gifts. They walked between two worlds, understood things seen and unseen. This heritage must, therefore, be preserved.

Adanya laughed. Apparently, Hori and Lelani took the stipulation quite seriously. To date, Manutea counted seventeen brothers and sisters. And, though Manutea's mother's once dark hair now shone a silvery gray, she delivered the last female child only six months earlier.

"Manny, what was it like to be a part of such a large family?" Adanya thought it wonderful to eat and play with brothers and sisters. Her childhood, though idyllic, had been notably isolated save for the creatures of the forest. Imagine what it must be like to live with a big, boisterous family!

Manutea chuckled. "It is good - unless your little brothers shoot kiwi seeds through reeds or your little sisters insist on being lifted upon your shoulders." Then he said quietly, "It is why I come to the *Garden of the Gods*. Only here can I find relief from the demands of the family."

He stopped mid-thought as a shadow obscured part of his face. Adanya grew concerned as her loved one absentmindedly rubbed the goddess on his arm.

"Manny, what is it?" implored Adanya. "Is something wrong? Please tell me."

But, if something troubled Manutea, the moment passed. He playfully swatted Adanya's enticing posterior. "Come, let us swim," he said as he turned and ran off towards the lagoon.

Adanya, after a brief hesitation, followed. Her love was so compelling, so blinding. She would, in fact, have willingly followed Manutea into the burning belly of an active, erupting volcano.

In some ways, that's exactly what the Beloved did.

# CHAPTER XXVI

The volcano erupted. It bubbled up, without warning, spewing Adanya's life out like oozing bits of molten lava - one broken piece at a time. Her beating heart lay senselessly trapped under cooling layers of hardening, unforgiving rock.

The day itself provided cause for great rejoicing, a celebration of the Creator's work through mortal endeavor. For the men, only twenty-four hours earlier, completed the temple, soundly putting the final stone and mortar in place. It stood as a gleaming monument, a physical testament to superior craftsmanship wrought through unfailing dedication to the gods.

Not surprisingly, the magnificent structure proved a sight to behold. Its bell tower rose as if to kiss heaven's gate. The humble altar, made of crushed seashells, boasted thousands of hand-dipped candles already lit in honor of the deities. The building's painted walls, its towering ceilings, displayed human interpretations of the gods and their feminine counterparts. It startled Adanya to see that the ancient symbols for male and female, when merged, make a perfect, six-pointed star - a pentacle. It suggested that the deities, neither male nor female, achieved perfection through a combination of both sexes best attributes.

The sisters conducted a dedication ceremony as the sun peaked over the mountain. They gave thanks for the ever present hand of the Creator. In ceaseless prayer, the woman offered the worship place as a refuge for all who sought comfort. Then, in appreciation of the back-breaking effort of the workers, they presented the tribal chief, adorned in flamboyant ceremonial robes, with a holy staff, intricately carved with the signs of the zodiac. Tales of old claimed that the Creator himself once held the instrument as he commanded the moon and the stars, the sea and the sky, to appear.

After the ceremony came to its climatic conclusion, the men made their way down the mountain for a brief period of well-deserved rest. The convent itself, however, remained a flurry of non-stop activity. Tonight the sisters hosted a great feast attended by all inhabitants of the tiny island. The entire covenant made haste as the men would soon return with their wives and families.

Unfortunately, Adanya missed the long-awaited dedication as well as the day's events. She awoke that morning feeling uncharacteristically ill. What was going on? This physical malady mirrored the merciless demons that tormented her on the ship. Still, she pulled herself up from her pallet. But the sudden movement caused her stomach to churn wildly and the Beloved grabbed for the porcelain wash bowl. After a prolonged period of retching, the girl stood, wiped her face and walked the halls, still cool with early morning air, to the dining area.

If anyone noticed Adanya's pale, disheveled appearance, her fatigued nature, as she slipped wearily into the kitchen, no one said anything. The girl fell into a stiff rhythm with the rest of the women, gathering grains and placing bowls out to receive their fill. Yet, as she sat with the other sisters at table, Adanya barely lifted her spoon.

Why did this have to happen - today of all days? She intended to talk to Sister Angelica, after the feast, about her relationship with Manutea, hopefully, at her side. And, while she intentionally failed to mention this planned conversation to Manny, she felt certain that he would agree to the timing. With the temple completed, there was no reason that the lovers could not move forward into their lives - together.

Adanya felt annoyance as her insides continued to wreak internal havoc. She swallowed in a futile attempt to control the rising bile and tentatively took a miniscule bite of grain, softened in chilled goat's milk, hoping that it might quell the nausea. Instead, the entire dining hall watched in collective alarm as Adanya simultaneously dropped her spoon, the instrument falling with a pronounced clatter on the stone floor, and fled the room. The sound of retching echoed in the halls.

Adanya retreated to her bed chamber, per Sister Angelica's explicit orders, tossing in and out of fitful sleep. She tracked the passing of the time by the shadows that played across her wall. It must be at least four o'clock. She heard the men returning and the sound of tables set up for the evening's long-anticipated events. Had Manny come?

The next time Adanya awoke, dusk fell. She heard the high-pitched sound of children's laughter. The families arrived. The smell of roasted pig wafted through the air. Unfortunately, that smell, an aroma she previously enjoyed, triggered untold waves of nausea. Nonetheless, it also transported her back to that memorable spring night when she stood hidden behind the grape arbor. So much had changed.

Adanya smiled as she recalled that first meeting with Manutea. He looked so incredibly handsome and self-assured. Surely he must be the gift that the goddess intended for her. Soon they would build a life together.

As she drifted off to sleep, Adanya noticed a little boy with dark hair and ruby lips. He must have been about three or four years old. He also possessed dark skin with eyes the shape of large almonds. But the color of those eyes seemed inconsistent with his obvious island heritage - robin's egg blue. Adanya wondered. How did he get away from the feast and into her room? He appeared off in the distance, waving and smiling at her.

Instinctively, Adanya knew this one to be her child. He laughed and his voice sounded like the tinkling of joyful bells.

"Child, come to me," she called out to him. She opened her arms. "Come, the time is now."

"Not yet, Mama," said the child. He turned as if to go but then stopped, looking back at her. He quizzically cocked his darling head to one side, his dancing blue eyes suddenly turning serious. "Who is my father? Who is my sacred mother?" he asked. Then, unanswered, the child disappeared into the mist.

Adanya jarred herself from slumber, disturbed by the troubling vision. It was not the first time that the question haunted her. She knew naught who her own father was. But she said nothing to no one. Instead, Adanya rose the next day feeling somewhat better, although she discovered that her belly remained intolerant of food. She performed her basic chores and attended daily prayer. Mindful thought, however, escaped her. All thoughts, as they had for so many months, drifted toward Manutea. How long before nightfall? How long before she could see him again?

As the hours passed, Adanya sometimes caught Sister Angelica's thoughtful gaze yet the older woman said nothing. Perhaps the nun was merely considering the upcoming vows for the young convert. Adanya, again, felt that familiar pang of guilt. She wanted to take the sister into her confidence but knew better. Adanya promised Manutea that they would share the news together.

But where was Manny? When the sun dropped low, Adanya, still feeling shaky, left the convent's protective walls to find him. Unable to locate the *Garden of the Gods* without her lover, she stood helplessly waiting on the mountain path where their lives first intersected. But the orb sunk below the horizon and still he did not come to her. Was he OK? Fear gripped her. If he returned to the fishing boats, unforeseen dangers might have befallen him. Still she stayed, alone at a crossroads, riveted to the spot by longing and confusion, until daybreak.

For a second day, the Beloved, after a sleepless, seemingly never-ending, night, moved soundlessly about the kitchen. The sisters, who had grown accustomed to her normally spirit-filled countenance, noticed that the novice seemed unusually quiet. Perhaps the illness visited upon her extracted a toll.

Adanya mechanically worked, her mind in a troubled haze, until the sounds of a sacred mantra interrupted her thoughts. The girl looked up to see Sister Angelica present but apart from the standard food line. The sister poured flour, sugar and eggs into a large, oversized mixing bowl. The woman hummed quietly as she combined the ingredients as if in formal prayer.

Adanya listened to the sacred, melodic flow until her curiosity piqued. Her hands continued to methodically cut papaya and star fruit as she asked, "Sister Nancia, what is Sister Angelica preparing? It does not appear to be the breakfast food that fills our plates."

Sister Nancia smiled. "No, my child, it is a cake for a celebration that we will have in honor of one of the many men who assisted us in erecting the new temple."

Adanya smiled, happy at the prospect of another's joy. "How wonderfully delightful!" she exclaimed. Despite the draining effects of her illness, she clapped her hands in excitement. "What are we celebrating?"

"There is to be a holy union between a fisherman and one of the island girls. He is young and strong and soon to take over his father's fishing nets." The older woman chuckled, "Why I can remember long ago when Manutea first came to this convent as a child."

Adanya felt brutally assaulted, forcefully punched in the stomach. All breath vacated her body as nausea again rolled over her. "Manutea? Married? What do you mean?"

"Why, Adanya, it is so exciting! Manutea is to wed his eternal flame," explained Sister Nancia. "The chief's daughter has finally come of age and a ceremony joining the two prestigious families will take place during tonight's full moon. Manutea brought her to the feast just last night. She's such a nice girl - very pretty."

If Sister Nancia spoke more news, it went unheard. For the volcano erupted, leaving death and total destruction in its wake.

# CHAPTER XXVII

*"But, Grandmother, how can that be?" said Morning Dove, the timber of her voice registered outrage. "Manutea loved Adanya. They were soul mates, eternally fated. Why did he do that to her?"*

*The Ancient One shook her head offering no answer. "Perhaps Manutea 'did' nothing to her. Adanya must decide how his choices, her perception of those choices, impact her life. Only Adanya can give his acts their meaning."*

*Morning Dove snorted. "Grandmother, why would the Creator bring Manutea into Adanya's life only to break her heart?"*

*"I cannot second guess the gods for their vision and purpose is greater than mine. But I do know that Manutea served as her wise teacher even as Adanya taught him. They gave each other the gifts of their union, gifts agreed upon long before their human births."*

*"But she loved him," said Morning Dove indignantly. "How could Manutea do this to Adanya?"*

*"Perhaps," said the old woman, "it is only important that Adanya loved him."*

On the eve of the ship's departure, Adanya visited the mountainside where Manutea once fatefully saved her life. Her mind, filled with a mix of emotion, wondered. If she again tumbled from the perilous ledge, would the island man intervene? Once certain, Adanya no longer knew the answer.

The question lingered, unanswered, as a chill swept over the girl. She shook, trembling on that treacherous cliff, staring down into the ocean below. The sea beckoned her, calling her name over and over. "Adanya . . . come," it said with the inevitable crash of each wave.

Turmoil churned within her soul. There was something inviting, even calming, about the sea. No more would Adanya's heart ache. No more would she, in anguish, cry out Manny's name during long, torturous nights. She surveyed the swirling sea, mesmerized, as loosened pebbles fell, one by one, from beneath her feet. Would the ledge soon crumble swiftly ending her unbearable pain?

Decision made, Adanya stepped forward and, lifting both arms above her head, with all her might, hurled the *Box of Intentions* into the sea. She watched as it tumbled through the air, spiraling down, gaining momentum, the amethyst crystal shining in snatches of waning moonlight. For a fleeting moment, the box appeared suspended in space and time. Then it crashed, shattering into millions of pieces, like glittering prisms upon the sea splattered rock.

Adanya felt nothing. And the emptiness, more than hate, terrified her. She stared at the box's content, laid bare on the wet, unforgiving boulders below. She knew what the parchment said. She had once written the word, *Love*, with so much hope. Now all hope dissolved as the surging water destroyed it.

The next morning, Sister Angelica met the disgraced novice at the pier prior to departure. The sister continued to extend unfailing love and kindness to Adanya. Last week, when the distraught girl confessed her alleged sin to the older woman, the religious leader simply held her tightly as the inconsolable girl sobbed.

"Please forgive me, Sister. I am so sorry for hurting and deceiving you," cried Adanya.

"Hush, child. There is no need for forgiveness. You were simply discovering your true path," said Sister Angelica.

"But now everything is ruined," replied Adanya. "You don't want me. Manutea doesn't want me."

"It is true, certain doors are, indeed, closed to you. You cannot join the Sisters of the Sacred Covenant. Nor does Manutea choose to continue on his journey with you by his side. But, make no mistake, Adanya, there is a magnificent plan for your life."

Adanya cried harder. "I cannot see anything but darkness," she said. "Is this punishment for my choices of long ago?"

The sister stroked Adanya's tear stained cheek. "How can you recognize the light except through darkness? The Creator does not punish us, Adanya. His love is unconditional. There is no hell, no devil's lair filled with fire and brimstone. We mortals merely suffer the consequences of our own acts. We create our own purgatory when we stray from alignment with the Divine's plan, his highest purpose, for our lives."

"Do not fear that which comes into your life, Adanya," continued the spiritual woman. "For all things, all circumstance, even that which you do not understand, come from the Creator. All situations forge your soul."

"But I did not find my goddess or her gift," cried the distraught girl. "How can I move forward when that which is my destiny escapes me?"

"Each sunrise lights your destiny, my child," replied Sister Angelica softly. Then she opened her hand and gave Adanya the most delicate of lotus blossoms. "To find the goddess, your goddess, you must remember the lesson of the lotus blossom." She cupped the girl's face in her hands. "Who fathered the lotus blossom? Who is its sacred mother?" Adanya remembered Elu's words under the *Tree of Life* so long ago. He spoke with such finality when he said, "I am not your father." It broke her heart, even now, to hear those words.

"Sister, I do not even know who my own father is."

"Ahh . . . but when you know, when you truly understand what is already written upon your heart, you will find the goddess."

With great sadness, Adanya boarded the ship for the long journey back to Ambilen. She knew naught why she chose to return to that particular town but she knew of no other place. It had been her home for so many years. Perhaps she could, once again, make a life there.

In some strange way, the trip was actually less painful for Adanya than her previous one. She learned many truths at the Sisters of the Sacred Covenant and this wisdom served her well even as she fully experienced the pain of Manutea's loss.

Every day Adanya wrote in her journal - pouring out her soul, working on the list of things that she knew to be true about the Universe. She struggled, yet when she revisited the early pages of her journal, she recognized her significant growth, her expanding her consciousness.

Nonetheless, Manutea's rejection consumed her. For, although Adanya searched all over the island for him, her efforts proved futile. She never saw him again before the ship set sail. He never explained his actions to her. Why hadn't he come to her?

She considered the possibilities, over and over, in her mind. Was he only using her? It was one option but his love felt so real. Could it be that he was simply caught in the chains of tradition, unable to leave an arranged marriage?

No matter how many times she went over it, analyzing the events that brought her to this place, the results were indisputable. There was no immediate answer, at least none that she understood. Perhaps if she had the opportunity to talk with Manutea . . . but she did not. Then again, she wondered. Would he even have spoken words satisfying to her soul? Maybe the truth escaped him.

No, there was no answer except, perhaps, to trust the Universe. Yet an image, a single thought, materialized in her head. She loved him. She loved him with complete intensity, a heartfelt purity, not of this earth. She loved him as best as she knew how at this time in her life. Maybe that was enough.

Something in that certainty provided immeasurable comfort. Besides, didn't the sisters teach that everything in life - each person, every experience - is her wise teacher? Over and over, Adanya wrote in her journal:

> *The journey is long and darkness surrounds me. My feet move forward yet I am unable to see the path that is before me. Shadow threatens to engulf me. Still I walk, in faith, toward the destiny that awaits me.*
>
> *I trust Spirit - even on the darkest of nights. Often, I do not understand the need to walk in darkness. Yet I know what to do. I follow the star. The star is in my heart. And its brilliance lights up the sky.*
>
> *I trust Spirit - even on the darkest of nights. The star is a sign of Creator's presence. I am never alone. I follow the star and the star leads me home.*

And, of course, the brokenhearted girl wrote of Manutea. She spoke and recorded these words daily until she embraced them as truth.

> *Thank you, Manny, for teaching me what I most needed to learn. May you also breathe the wisdom of my soul.*
>
> *I forgive you for not being who I wanted you to be. I forgive myself for expecting you to be other than who you are.*

*I release you - even as I honor you - back into the Universe. May your life be filled with the people and experiences which serve the Creator's highest purpose.*

*I release myself - even as I honor my own spirit - to live fully in the present moment. May my life also be filled with the people and experiences that serve the Creator's highest purpose.*

But, if Adanya slowly worked through her raw, jumbled emotions, other maladies plagued her. Her intense misery grew exponentially with the eternal rocking of the cargo ship. Though the vessel endured few storms, the nausea within Adayna's belly proved relentless.

Furthermore, the ever-present stench of animal and human waste left her unable to eat. She spewed the increasingly limited contents of her stomach daily - mystifying fellow travelers who knew that the girl took little fortification. When would it stop?

In the third month of the voyage, Adanya's body succumbed to a high fever. She hovered between life and death, consciousness and unconsciousness. Visions, dreams, and nightmares enveloped her. She saw Manny's face, professing his love to her on their wedding day. Suddenly, however, his handsome face, those chiseled features, melted into the form of a serpent consumed by an eternal flame. Adanya screamed in horror.

The destructive flame evolved into an eye, a wandering eye, hovering on the horizon where the sky meets the sea. "The painted one will give you your future," said a disembodied voice. Then the Goddess Lakshmi, a lotus blossom in her hair, floated down from the heavens. She tried to give Adanya something. What was it?

Before the girl could find out, the goddess vanished and the little boy from her previous dreams stood in the deity's place. He pleaded desperately with Adanya, "Who is my father? Who is my sacred mother?"

"The Universe is unfolding perfectly, Adanya," said Mahwah's voice. "Trust its benevolent flow."

Adanya tossed and turned as the fever raged.

# PART III

# THE AWAKENING

# CHAPTER XXVIII

Adanya stirred to the blurred image of a dwarfed man with a yellowish-toned, angular face offset by slanted eyes. His mustache, his long, thinning hair and beard, white as virgin snow, expertly braided into a fine chain. Refined, delicate hands with polished, carefully manicured, nails tended to something unseen.

Having never before encountered a dwarf, uncertain as to the man's intention, Adanya fought against unconsciousness. But fire-breathing dragons reared up, catching her more than a little off guard. The delirious girl watched in abject horror as the dragons transformed, shifting their form before her very eyes, into the old man. He then, without fanfare, bowed low to her, saying, "Namaste." The word conjured images of her arrival on Moricea - men parading her through the village and up the mountain atop broad shoulders. Ultimately, however, the vision, as well as the world around her, faded to black.

Adanya's heavy, sleep-laden eyes opened again. This time her once fuzzy mind appeared sharper and her thoughts far less disjointed. She blinked, adjusting to daylight as well as her surroundings. Obviously, she lay in a bed - a bed far more comfortable than anything experienced on the ship, but the location remained unknown. Down comforters covered Adanya, warding off the room's unmistakable chill.

Adanya felt confused. Her head hurt, in fact, it throbbed. It had been late summer when she departed from the tropics. Unless she was wrong, and that seemed unlikely, the ship's captain slated the journey back to Ambilen to take at least three months, perhaps more, on potentially rough seas. She didn't remember docking. Where was she? And who was that diminutive man - a man whose origins obviously stemmed from the Far East?

Attempting to ascertain her exact location, Adanya gazed 'round and, immediately, felt overwhelmed by the room's staggering appointments. Red walls, stenciled with characters in black pigment, housed shelves extending from floor to ceiling. Two of the walls displayed bottles, thousands of bottles. Glass bottles, meticulously labeled, that stored, at least from Adanya's limited vantage point, indiscernible items.

Other shelves, lining the entire surface of the two remaining walls, boasted a complete library of books and journals. Some of the titles she could actually see including *The Creator's Handbook, Healing the Soul,* and *Power & Purpose*. In fact, it appeared that this room stored more periodicals than Adanya anticipated reviewing during the course of an entire lifetime. The girl struggled to remember the last book that she had read. What was it?

Oh, yes, the *Spiritual Guide to Gods & Goddesses*. It seemed like so long ago. Her thoughts immediately shifted to Manny but, with great effort, she sadly released him, returning to the present moment. She whispered to no one in particular, "In this moment, I am safe, happy and whole. I release the past even as I celebrate this time in my life. I am loved by the Great Spirit, my Creator."

Under the window, closed tightly against bitter temperatures, sat a large, black lacquered table filled with an assortment of objects glittering in the light. They appeared to be rocks, multi-colored crystals, formed of this earth. The collection, which included stones of varying properties, proved quite extensive. Its owner, which Adanya presumed was the gentleman from the Far East, must either be quite a collector or employ the minerals as tools in his chosen profession.

Some of the crystals Adanya knew by heart. The aquamarine possessed the tranquil qualities of the sea. It lifted one's soul, promoting love and communication. It soothed one's nerves even as it helped one find his - or her - voice. The crystal proved particularly useful with ailments of the throat.

Adanya also recognized barite. Mahwah taught her that the colorless stone cleansed the body of poisonous toxins. Interestingly, a wand with a barite crystal fastened to its tip lay at the center of the elements. She wondered how her host used it.

Suddenly, a tiger cat, or was it a tabby, jumped up on the table. The animal, its fur the rich golden tone of a proud lion, displayed markings, a most impressive pattern, of tortoise swirls. Its tones suggested that an artist's brush masterfully mixed the intense variation of hues, carefully creating each unique print on the feline.

Adanya watched, fascinated, as the cat stealthily balanced along the table's narrow edge and made his way fearlessly to her bed. The unexpected visitor's pink tongue, its surface like rough sandpaper, licked her face. Then the animal lay next to her, purring contentedly. A tooled leather collar, affixing a gold bell around his neck, bore the name, "Goldwyn".

As Adanya, now secure in this new setting, surrendered to fatigue, the most unimaginable visions again materialized. She saw the cat leap off of the bed and, quite literally, take the form of the elderly man. Golden fur gone, he now sported a red silk jacket with hand embroidered dragons prominently displayed on it.

The man, as if attuned to the vibrations of the Universe, selected crystals from the table and placed them at various intervals on her body. Adanya, in a dream state, immediately registered strange, tingling sensations yet the girl felt no fear. She slept peacefully.

The periods of consciousness grew. Each day the man, her silent yet gracious host, entered the room, bowed and said, "Namaste." Then he fed her broth until Adanya regained enough strength to maneuver her own spoon. He spoke no other words until the recovering girl bravely ventured a question.

"You know how to say, 'hello' in Moricean," she said weakly. "Where did you learn it?"

"I speak many tongues," replied the old man in a soft, halting voice. "Why do you think that I speak Moricean?"

"You say, 'Namaste', when you enter the room. It means 'hello' in the land where I once lived," Adanya explained.

The old man's implacable face held no hint of surprise at her apparent knowledge. He continued to move at his own steady pace. Then he replied. "The word comes not from the island of which you speak. It is an ancient Sanskrit word that transcends all time."

"The translation," her knowledgeable host continued, "is, 'The Divine in me, honors the Divine in you.' There is more to the word but that is the simplest explanation."

Adanya, even in her depleted state, felt astonishment spread through her. The islanders, the Sisters of the Sacred Covenant, all greeted her with, "Namaste." Over and over. Again and again.

All that time - she had been wrong. They had not been saying "hello". In fact, they had been honoring her. The prospect, the idea that people would honor her, seemed incomprehensible. Why would they honor such a flawed girl?

Adanya shifted to the present moment. "Where am I?" she asked.

"You are in Ambilin."

"But," Adanya's mind reeled, "how is that possible? I don't remember the ship arriving. How did I get here?"

"You were very ill, nearing death, when the ship's captain carried you here," said her host. "I am Mikao. I am the Healer." Again, the elderly man bowed low.

Adanya thought back to the times when another healer visited Brumledi's home. He presented as a grotesquely obese man, fat cascading like thick, rolling layers of uncooked bread dough over a straining, inadequate leather belt. His breath, labored at best, harbored the antiseptic smell of grain alcohol and his hands, thick and fleshy with permanently dirt-stained nails, often roamed to areas of the body that bore no sign of either illness or injury. She shuddered at the memory.

"There was another man. I remember him from before," Adanya finally said.

Her acquaintance gave an almost unperceivable shrug. "He serves a need in some people. I serve the highest purpose of the Creator."

Adanya's thoughts wandered to her brief encounter with the dark arts. She last saw the obese healer when he attended to Brumledi's back pain - pain significantly increased by Adanya's cruel spell. The memory brought her to another place. Adanya, however, no longer knew that unhappy girl of long ago.

Still, she felt sorrow at her misguided choice to cast a spell which caused Brumledi pain - even temporary pain. But, unwilling to allow the past to hold her in its iron grip, Adanya acknowledged then released the feeling. She realized, with great relief, her own journey had taken her far. And, if presented with the same miserable set of circumstances, she would now, in this moment, handle things differently. Truthfully, the Beloved had already chosen to create a much different life for herself.

Adanya re-focused her mind as she more closely observed her host. Mikao was, indeed, a most curious fellow. Rather than common work clothes, he wore silk garments as if in the court of a great king or queen. His jacket or "ho", as she would later learn its name, was of deep red, almost a burgundy, and, as she noted before, sported embroidered dragons.

Adanya smiled as she realized that these hand-sewn images were, most probably, the dragons in her dreams. What mere mortal owned the power to transform? Certainly, it was impossible to assume the form of either a dragon or a common house cat! The very thought was really quite ludicrous. She released the silly thought and studied Mikao a bit more. His pants or "hakama" were green with red trim. He wore pointed black shoes as well as a hat that sat high on his head.

Though small in stature, certainly considerably less than five feet tall, Mikao emanated a most commanding presence. Potent energies coursed through his veins. Yet there was something calming about this mystical form. It was as if he knew the secrets of the Universe. Or, Adanya thought, considering his advanced age, perhaps he existed through all eternity.

Mikao tended to Adanya each day, providing the nourishment that her body sorely lacked on the seafaring voyage. He climbed the tall ladders with an enviable agility and pulled down a myriad of bottles. Over the course of thirty or more days, the improving patient drank a wide range of bubbling, steaming, and gurgling concoctions.

Nonetheless, the first time Adanya ventured from her bed to gaze upon her own reflection, she experienced genuine shock at the stranger staring back at her. Her cheeks appeared sunken and hollowed out, her once luxurious hair brittle. Adanya wept as she mourned the bohemian island girl who, like Manutea himself, now disappeared.

But, with each passing day, her face grew fuller, eventually wearing a slight blush. And, as her health slowly returned, Adanya regained her breathtaking beauty. In fact, some might suggest that the Beloved shone more radiantly than ever before. The young woman positively glowed.

Beauty aside, Adanya's prominent belly prompted concern. Apparently, Mikao's soup and rice agreed with her. Adanya was, without question, gaining quite a bit of weight.

"Your cooking agrees with me," laughed Adanya. "I look like an old, fat woman."

"You must nourish the one within," Mikao responded.

An uncomfortable feeling spread slowing over the Beloved. "What do you mean?" she asked Mikao, her rising apprehension apparent.

"You are with child," said Mikao gently. "Your future will arrive as the red-bellied bird sings the first song of spring."

Stunned, Adanya stared at her obviously protruding bulge. In her head, she heard a far-away voice. "The painted one will give you your future." That was what Afaitu foretold long ago. Visions of Manutea as well as the Goddess Lakshmi filled her. Manny was indeed painted. Now she carried his child - their child - in her womb.

A flood of emotion welled up in Adanya. Fear, coupled with deep shame, seized her being. People, even good people, would forever brand her as naught but a wanton woman. Furthermore, a child born out of wedlock bore a deep burden. Her son would innocently pay for the sins of the father, the indiscretion of the mother. And, to make matters worse, this little one would never know his father. How would she explain who his father was when he asked? How would he ever embrace his rich heritage?

As her mind continued to spin, more practical thoughts surfaced. How would she, a woman alone in the world, care for a child? Adanya remembered the dreams - a dark-skinned boy with eyes the color of robin's eggs. This was her son. She was responsible for his food and clothing and shelter. The prospect overwhelmed her. What will become of us? Adanya wondered.

As if reading her fearful, erratic thoughts, Mikao's words penetrated the pregnant girl's otherwise rampant brain. "There is nothing to fear. Embrace all that comes as your true destiny. This is why the painted one entered your life."

"But," Adanya sputtered, "what will happen to us? How will we survive?"

"Trust in the Creator," replied the Healer. "He will meet your every need." And, with those final words, Mikao bowed low, exiting the room. Adanya, fell to the floor and wept.

Over the next few weeks, however, Adanya grew appreciably stronger. She rose in prayer each morning, sitting on silk cushions before a special altar that Mikao housed in the parlor. She did not recognize the bald, jovial statue with the big belly positioned in a place of honor. Still, she burned incense and sought the Creator's company. Then, like her days on Moricea, Adanya performed a series of chores. Sometimes she swept floors or beat rugs. Often she cooked the meals that the two of them shared.

Dusting ranked high as one of her favorite tasks. For Mikao filled the home with all kinds of wondrous items. Adanya cautiously ascended the tall ladders and dusted the different containers of herbs and potions. There seemed to be an entire forest in the innumerable jars. It fascinated Adanya to see how the healer utilized the natural remedies.

Once, as Adanya wiped her face following yet another bout with late-stage morning sickness, Mikao asked her to join him in the treatment room.. The mother-to-be acknowledged his request, settling into a large, overstuffed chair. She watched patiently as the Healer silently pulled a conglomeration of herbs - wild yam, dandelion, ginger, vitex. He then instructed Adanya on how to use the herbs, when to ingest them.

Some woman might scoff at such nonsense. But Adanya, who learned much about the earth from Mahwah, knew better. Following the prescribed regimen, she no longer battled nausea. Her overall disposition elevated as she bid farewell to the uninvited illness that previously cursed her.

Not surprisingly, patients also left Mikao feeling appreciably better. Adanya observed, for instance, that the Widow Lockshine came to the Healer at least once a week with one fatal ailment or another.

"Healer, consumption has its grips on me," she'd say in a gravelly voice. "I won't be here to see the spring. No. The ground will still be frozen when my breath ceases." Tears trickled down deep crevices in her face.

Mikao bowed low. "I honor you, Widow Lockshine. Will you accept the life force that flows from the Creator?"

"Can't see how the Creator cares about this old woman but I'll accept anything you got, Healer," she replied.

Mikao instructed the patient to lay prone upon the exam table. Then, starting at the top of Widow Lockshine's head, he traced some symbols and placed his hands on key areas of her body. Adanya watched as the healer worked without speaking, slowly making his way down her body, respectfully, with permission, laying his hands most properly upon her.

Adanya couldn't tell what was happening inside Widow Lockshine's physical being but there was a marked change on the outside. Her rapid breathing slowed as she inhaled full breaths. The widow's hands, originally clenched at her sides, gradually opened. Her worried facial expression relaxed.

When Mikao finished, he concluded the treatment with what appeared to be a blessing spoken in unfamiliar tongue. He then, again, bowed low and said, "Namaste." The Healer immediately busied himself, turning his undivided attention to the herb gallery.

With Adanya's help, the Widow Lockshine painstakingly got up from the table, smoothed her clothes, and straightened her hat. Meanwhile, Mikao wrapped ginseng and Gotu Kola in brown paper, securing them with twine. He handed his elderly patient the package.

"This is to help you find those lost knitting needles," he said. Adanya knew that the herbs were widely recognized within healing circles as key helpers with memory loss.

Then he took some white, round balls out of an ornate, handcrafted, cloisonné jar. "You must take these for the consumption, Widow Lockshine. But be careful. They are very powerful. I can only entrust you seven, one per day. Do not take any more than that or I cannot guarantee your fate. When you have finished them, it is imperative that you return to this establishment. Heed my words. Do not forget."

"For land's sake, Healer. I'm an old woman," declared the widow. "Why I don't even know if I will remember to wake at sunrise." But her hands, exhibiting a slight tremor, accepted the pills gratefully and she left the shop with a decidedly lighter step.

When the door closed with a slight sound of the bell, Adanya straightened the room. Mikao, sensing unrest, interrupted her work. "You have questions." He said it more as a statement than a question.

"Yes," replied Adanya. "I do not understand what happened today. You work like no other healer that I have seen. There are no leeches or goat dung. Are you a magician or, as I fear, a warlock?"

"The life force - not black magic - provides what is most needed," Mikao explained. "Like you, I am merely the Creator's instrument."

"But what of the white pills that you gave Widow Lockshine? Yesterday, I saw you bring them home from Ohan's store. They were but candy, sweets for the children. Today, however, you transformed them. Now, they hold the power to cure consumption."

"Ahh . . .," said Mikao. "But, you see, the disease that consumes Widow Lockshine is not consumption but, rather, loneliness. And the sugar pills, especially the company she encounters on the return visit for more, combat it. That is why I buy them at Ohan's store."

Ohan. Adanya thought a lot about both Ohan and Brumledi - especially since Mikao restored her health. Right now, the winter winds howled up and down the streets forming ice on every surface. Adanya dared not venture outdoors due to the delicate nature of her condition. But, undoubtedly, word spread of her return to Ambilen. At some point, she would have to face them.

For now, however, Adanya concentrated on the upcoming birth of her son. Mahwah's spirit visited the Beloved, fully present, as the young woman knit blankets and crocheted booties. Mother guided daughter's hand as she fashioned infant gowns out of old, soft cloth.

There was a sense of anticipation, in worlds seen and unseen, as every entity prepared for the child's arrival. At night, the mother-to-be, in the company of angels, played endearing lullabies on her fiddle. Celestial songs dedicated to an unborn, yet uncrowned, prince.

# CHAPTER XXIX

"But, Grandmother, how can Adanya possibly heal on after the loss of Manutea's love?" Morning Dove asked. "She barely survived the unhappy parting with Brumledi and Ohan all those many years ago - and Brumledi did not treat her well."

"Make no mistake," replied the Ancient. "Adanya felt the searing pain of Manutea's rejection, she mourned his loss, grieved for the future that would never be."

"Yet," continued the Ancient, "she also grew much during her time on the island. The wisdom, the lessons learned, built on the solid foundation laid by Elu, Mahwah, and many others. Adanya developed a trust in the Universe's plan for her life - even if she did not fully understand it."

"That can't be right, Grandmother," countered Morning Dove, "Adanya and Manutea are so right for each other. It can't end there. Surely they will get back together."

The old woman smiled. "Maybe they will, maybe they won't," she said. "People are brought into each other's lives at appointed times for specific reasons. However, you are right about one thing, my granddaughter. Love never ends."

A fortnight after the red-bellied bird sang spring's first song, three women - Dagmar, Diella, and Samara - again crept into Adanya's dreams. The Beloved, rejoicing in her spirit guides' never-ending presence, offered her beautiful infant son, Temaru, to them. Dagmar, along with the others, blessed the boy, gently cocooning him in a blanket of silken cashmere.

"He is a most glorious creation," said Diella. "His life will be filled with amazing adventures."

"But it is of no surprise," interjected Samara. "Temaru is, after all, his father's son."

Adanya's heart sank a little at her guides' words. For Temaru would never know his true father. But, before she could give her thought voice, Dagmar spoke.

"The hour is late," Dagmar announced imperiously with a dramatic wave of her arm. "We must make haste."

A cock crowed, signaling the bewitching hour, as Adanya and the entire entourage, including baby Temaru, left the healer's abode. At a portal on the far side of Ambilen, where sea and land meet, Adanya watched as the three women generated thousands of light strands, like spun gold, from shared breath. Filaments, life force dancing in the moonlight, joined together to form a mystical pathway. Mother and child ascended the illuminated walkway, traversing over the sea, traveling higher and higher, in the company of night.

The path eventually stopped. Transcending space and time, Adanya and the infant, Temaru, found themselves, miles above the miraculous ocean, at the entrance to a magnificent gathering hall. Towering celestial sentries, bare-chested with wings spanning 25 feet, stood at attention, posted at the massive doors. The gatekeepers acknowledged the anticipated guests, permitting swift entry to the mother and child.

Adanya entered through the threshold, protectively holding Temaru. She literally shivered, not for cold but, rather, at the indescribable beauty surrounding them. For the room, its walls, inlaid with gold and precious gems, rose hundreds of feet into the vast, star-studded heavens. The round moon and rotating planets formed a natural, ever-changing, ceiling.

Unexpectedly, Adanya found the cashmere blanket limp, quite empty. Where was Temaru? Panic set in until as she saw Temaru, completely naked, encased in a bubble of his own breath. The baby floated, unencumbered, in this marvelous golden ball, soaring out of reach, so high Adanya feared that, unhindered, he might spend eternity adrift in the endless vacuum of the Universe. Temaru, however, only gurgled sweet laughter as the weightless bubble lifted, ever upward, in the gentle airstream.

Adanya forcibly calmed herself. For the new mother intuitively understood that neither the Creator nor her guides would allow harm to visit this child. Reassured, the Beloved's attention temporarily diverted from her son as she observed the solemn procession of elders gliding effortlessly into the room. They formed a circle in the center of the great hall with Temaru bobbing directly, quite happily, above it.

Adanya started to speak, to call out to them, but instinct silenced her. She stood at the side, seemingly unobserved, while patiently waiting for the mysteries to unfold. The group of twelve joined hands, lifting them up to the heavens, and the action, for reasons unclear to Adanya, tethered Temaru in a holding pattern above their heads.

Suddenly, the entire chamber plunged into total darkness except for the light surrounding the golden bubble. The boy shone brilliantly as if illuminated by heaven's spotlight. Adanya, watching the glowing orb, marveled at her son suspended in the life force.

Adanya, quite unexpectedly, grew increasingly aware of an omnipotent presence filling the room, almost like a collective consciousness, but visually observed only pulsating, vibrating prisms of free floating, eternally connected, lights. The energy, this being, radiated light and love and peace. It spoke, without speaking, from its intellectual core to Adanya's soul.

"Do you understand why you have been called before the sacred council, my child?" The deep voice, neither male nor female, resonated throughout the Universe.

Adanya dropped to her knees as the Being of Light addressed her. "No, Most Holy, I do not."

"You have been entrusted with the spirit you call, 'Temaru'. He is a Divine child of the Creator. And we seek to remind you of your sacred contract with Temaru. A contract agreed upon before time began."

The voice, the stream of conscious thought, continued. "You do not own this spirit in human form - rather you are entrusted with him - to teach as well as learn from him. You are to grow with this blessed child as you journey together on the physical plane called, Earth. Some travel the same path for only a short time, others for a lifetime. Your soul already knows the day and hour of your parting."

"What do you wish for me to teach him, Most Holy?" asked Adanya humbly. She did not realize that she, too, spoke in silence.

"You must teach him who is father is, who his sacred mother is. Only then can he discover who he truly is, explore his own unique gifts."

"But Great Spirit, how can I teach him what I do not know?" Adanya asked.

Without warning, Adanya found herself falling, hurtling towards earth. Farther and farther she fell, crying out - not for herself - but for her guides to save her precious son. Faster and faster she fell, until she hit the ground, ending all conscious thought.

Adanya awoke to find herself in bed cradling Temaru safely in her arms. Inside her soul, as she had many times before, the Beloved heard the answer to her own question.

"You must find the goddess."

# CHAPTER XXX

Adanya and Temaru, at Mikao's request, took up residency in the healer's comfortable, second story loft. By day, the new mother earned her keep maintaining Mikao's home and assisting him in the treatment room. At sunset, however, she ceased all labor, playing ageless songs of love for her blue eyed prince, regaling him with stories of long ago. Adanya, in what was now a bedtime ritual, held her son high, straining to reach the heavens, as she twirled Temaru around the room, in a celebration of life.

It was a joyous time of new beginnings. Mikao taught Adanya about the physical body, especially the one that her spirit had chosen as its sacred, albeit temporary, home. He instructed her on the seven chakras, descending from her crown to her third eye through her throat, heart and solar plexus. The chakras ended with her belly and feet. All energy, the life force that gives one breath, flowed through these centers.

In ministering to his patients, Mikao asked the Universe to meet each person's highest purpose. Perhaps that purpose constituted a physical healing. Many times, however, it manifested itself in a spiritual or emotional adjustment. Whatever the actual outcome, the Creator used the healer, as Mikao once told Adanya, as an instrument, providing to the patient what he or she most required.

Adanya, after receiving the attunements to provide healing, was amazed at heat radiating, coursing through her being, pouring out of her hands as she worked. Mikao assured Adanya that the energy would not harm her vessel but would, in fact, restore its own alignment, even as it flowed to the patient. Both healer and patient benefitted.

Adanya quickly cultivated her own base of clients. An eclectic following sought out Mikao's apprentice, the serene woman with the healing hands. Men and woman of all ages and social means knocked at the door for treatment. Mothers brought their children. Word spread to outlying areas that, in Ambilen, there lived a mortal who possessed the power of angels. Adanya thrived, embracing her true calling, selflessly reaching out to those in need.

She also nurtured a small network of close-knit friends, like-minded souls who shared her love of the Creator as well as Adanya's life-affirming ways. There was the boisterous Lando, a painter of some renown, and his dedicated wife, Sherlana. Wilhelmina, an eccentric, good-hearted spinster who worked in various homes throughout Ambilen, also shared the journey.

The four, this wonderfully strange surrogate family, often broke bread together. They shared in Temaru's life, delighting in the infant's overall development as well as his daily discoveries. In quiet moments, Lando passionately sketched the unassuming mother and child, eventually filling his many canvases with the most glorious images. Adanya, quite unintentionally, served as the artist's inspirational muse.

Lando sold this completed series of creative works not in Ambilen, but in the royal courts dotting the lush countryside. Art aficionados, men of wealth and privilege, marveled at canvas after canvas depicting the ethereal woman with the exotic child. The subject, this rendering of womanhood, fueled countless lustful fantasies given voice only in the lusty company of the bold, red-blooded men.

Whatever the men fancied, their royal wives were drawn, their fascination piqued, by the woman's crown of butterflies. It rivaled any jeweled tiara that their powerful, ego-driven husbands bestowed upon them. And, though these gentile ladies commissioned the finest jewelers to duplicate the gossamer crown, nothing made by mortal hand equaled its unparalleled beauty.

The women also speculated about the regal animals, winged and four-footed, at the muse's side. They stood like foot soldiers. Was this girl royalty? Was she descended from the gods themselves? Lando, in hushed, conspiratorial tones, took entire courts into his confidence, admitting nothing - save that he was sworn, by sacred oath, to the utmost secrecy.

While Lando and Sherlana traveled, Adanya spent a good portion of her time in the company of Reverend Goodheart, Ambilen's religious leader. An austere, humorless man, with long dark hair and piercing blue eyes, Goodheart dressed in impressive black robes, embossed with ornate religious symbols, proclaiming the will of the Creator and, reputedly, spending entire days fasting while in prayerful vigil. His long-winded public orations warned, repeatedly, of the gods' impending, vengeful wrath if the sinners of Ambilen failed to repent.

This message markedly differed from the teachings of the Sisters of the Sacred Covenant. For the sisters spoke only of the Creator's deep, unwavering love for all spirits. Still, Adanya, honoring the reverend as a man chosen by the Creator, tried to glean any wisdom that the good pastor might wish to impart. She desperately sought full understanding of the Universe's plan for her life.

To that end, she explored the topic of the goddess with him - surprised by both the candor and content of his answers. Reverend Goodheart listened, without interruption, as Adanya recounted key details including the pendant around her neck. She willingly revealed the ancient scroll allowing the reverend to read its missive.

Reverend Goodheart removed his reading glasses after reviewing the ancient parchment. "It is folly to search for the goddess, Mistress Adanya," he said. "For the gods would not bequest to one person at the expense of the rest. And certainly the Creator would not select a mere girl, an unwed mother, as his chosen. Surely you must know this."

"Aye, I have thought long and hard about this very thing," replied the girl in earnest. "Yet I cannot imagine that the Creator would mislead me."

The man of the cloth considered this before replying. "Perhaps the necklace and its message do not originate with the Creator." Adanya had never seriously pondered this possibility. Now she felt compelled to do so and the prospect left her feeling perplexed and empty. The words simply did not ring true in her soul. What should she do?

That unanswered question aside, Adanya was content, even happy, especially in her role of mother. She loved her son and friends without reserve. Sometimes, however, late at night, it troubled her that she no longer maintained relations with Ohan and Brumledi as well as many of the townspeople that she had once known.

But, whenever these thoughts invaded Adanya's soul, threatening to rob her of the day's gifts, she reminded herself that this was a different time and place. The past was gone. She gently released it, even as she honored then released the people involved, guiding her thoughts back to the here and now. "In this moment, I am happy, healthy and whole," she said. "I am loved by the Creator."

Then, once again, things changed. It was as simple, as uncomplicated, as that. One fall afternoon, just an hour after Adanya had gently placed

Temaru in his corner cradle, the door opened. Brumledi swept in, older, but definitely, unmistakably, Bumledi.

"It is good to see you, Brumledi," said Adanya quietly. "May I be of service?"

Brumledi, whose heart long ago grew cold, like the icy waters of a river, forever frozen by winter's merciless touch, looked up from her gnarled stance. She stared at the beautiful, peace-filled woman before her. "Do I know you?" she asked.

"Yes, Brumledi, I am Adanya who you took in as a child," she replied.

"Adanya", Brumledi spat, "was nothing more than an ungrateful girl. I opened my home and heart to her but she did nothing but vex me and cast spells upon me. I rue the day that I offered my charity to that common girl." She limped further into the room as every pore oozed contempt.

Brumledi squinted, peering over half-rimmed glasses, at Adanya, unsure as to her true identity until she spotted one of the ever-present butterflies circling the grown woman. At almost the same time, the older adult spied the wolf and bird.

"You *are* Adanya," the prematurely aged matron sneered. "How dare you return to Ambilen, you vile creature? You are naught but an evil witch!"

"Brumledi," Adanya said calmly, evenly, "I wrote of my deep regret, my sorrow, for my actions. I asked, in sincere humility, for your forgiveness. I was indeed wrong and caused great harm. Did you not get my letter?"

"Your words, that blasted letter, mean nothing. Merely the rambling of a girl gone soft in the head. May you burn in eternal damnation for your acts," said the unforgiving woman.

Adanya let silence fill the room as the two breathed in the same life force. Air filled her body as she quietly concentrated on conscious breathing. She heard the Master's voice, "Breathe in . . . 1, 2, 3 . . . Breathe out . . . 1, 2, 3 . . ." The breathing brought her back to her center, grounding her thoughts.

"I have learned better ways, Brumledi. I honor you and yours and humbly ask that we begin anew," offered Adanya.

Brumledi laughed. "Begin anew?" The cackling continued in earnest. "Are you quite daft? Why would I, someone of my position, seek the company of a witch?"

"So be it," replied Adanya with no malice. "I pray for blessings upon your house, Brumledi. Go in peace."

As Brumledi turned to go, a joyful chortle drifted from the corner of the healing room. "What was that?" demanded the woman. She peered into the shadows just as a dark, perspiring head popped out from beneath a blanket. "Whose child is this?" the woman asked imperiously. "Why is he here?"

Adanya walked to the cradle and smiled broadly at the child happily staring up at her. "This is Temaru," she said. "He is my son." She picked up the cooing infant and closed the distance between herself and Brumledi.

"Your son!" said a stunned Brumledi. She took a step backwards as she registered the child's dark skin and almond-shaped eyes. "He is but a half-breed. Who is his father?"

Without thinking, Adanya proudly replied. "My son is a glorious child of the Creator. He is like no other child in this Universe." She kissed Temaru on the top of his head on that sweet crown through which the life force flowed. "He is love and peace and light and joy."

Brumledi took one last look at mother and child. "Mark my words, Adanya," she cautioned. "You will rue the day that you and your bastard son returned to Ambilen. I will rally the villagers against you."

Then, Brumledi continued like a reckless, rolling boulder, careening with increasing speed, destroying everything in its path. "The good people of this town don't want your kind in our village. You are naught but a whore who indulges in the black arts with the high priest, Lucifer."

Running Wolf who had, until now, unobtrusively witnessed this bitter, unpleasant exchange, barred his teeth. Brumledi jumped. With a final, unintelligible sputtering, the hateful woman fled, leaving the door ajar.

Adanya sat on the floor with her infant son propped against Running Wolf, feeling the cool autumn breeze wafting through the still open door. Mother, son, and wolf, their breath in complete rhythm, dwelled as one with the Creator.

Later, long after Temaru lay in blissfully unaware, his mother opened her journal and wrote:

*Is it possible that I know what is to come ahead, even before it does? Do the Wise Ones commune with each of us in spirit form long before our birth? And is it possible that we provide input into that which we experience here on Earth? I do not know that answers to these things.*

*What I do know from my own experience is that each joy and sorrow appears especially designed for* me. Seldom do I understand this when I go through tribulations, however. But the passage of time allows me often to see the experience in a new light. And, when no such wisdom is forthcoming, I must trust that every joy and sorrow is intentionally infused with Divine light. In that, I take great comfort.

# CHAPTER XXXI

Trouble reared its ugly head the very next day. The early morning commenced quite uneventfully. Adanya traveled Ambilen's cobblestone streets with Temaru intent on the completion of several pressing errands. Initially, she enjoyed the pleasure of the fresh air, the invigorating outdoors until the Beloved noticed that each passerby discreetly averted his or her eyes, failing to offer polite, customary greetings. Some whispered unheard commentary to overly interested companions. The past repeated itself as mothers frantically grabbed their unsuspecting children, dragging them, often kicking and screaming, to the opposite side of the street.

Adanya observed this fearful, unwarranted response to her presence. But she continued her pace, without tarrying, head held high. She felt confident that her animal guides would allow no harm to befall them. The young woman's spirit, as it had for so many months, radiated peace.

Adanya counted Ohan's store as her first stop. The woman hesitated only a moment before entering the entering the mercantile. Obviously, Brumledi now knew of her residency in Ambilen so there was no reason not to relieve Mikao of his weekly shopping. The bell tinkled as she stepped into the business and, in many ways, back in time. For the shop, unaltered, remained exactly as she remembered it. Tall, functional shelves lined with flour and baking goods. Bolts of fabric to make dresses and work clothes displayed in the far corner. The candy counter gleamed, lined with hopeful, wide-eyed children longing for taffy or licorice or rock candy. The Beloved smiled as her eyes fell on Mikao's medicinal sugar pills.

Adanya remembered every sight and sound, even the musty smell of moth balls mixed with wood shavings. She felt thirteen again as she fingered damask tablecloths and traversed creaking floorboards. Petro used to know each creak by heart. He memorized every groove so that he could soundlessly, as a tiger stalking his prey, walk across them without alerting

Ohan of his intent to sneak out of the store. Adanya recalled how the young boy so precisely walked on tiptoe, shoes in hand, skillfully avoiding every age-old creak until he successfully reached the front entrance.

Back then, the massive oak door proved problematic due to the old, tarnished brass bell still fastened at the top. The bell alerted Ohan to the comings and goings of his customers. But Petro, a clever boy, merely cracked an adjacent window and, deftly, when all heads turned, slipped through it. Often, Ohan complained of a previously non-existent draft without realizing that his youngest son, not an overheated customer, opened the window. Later, Ohan discovered Petro, his pockets stuffed full of Yantri winnings, whistling, dutifully sweeping the storeroom floor.

"Adanya, what are you doing here?" The voice jarred the new mother from faraway thoughts. She looked up to see the face of Ohan. It was older, a bit thinner, but still the kind, recognizable countenance she had grown to love.

"Ohan, how good to see you! You look well," Adanya exclaimed. "How is your life? The store certainly looks prosperous."

Before Ohan could reply, a boy of about fourteen came up behind him. The youth, though shorter, pudgier than the elderly man, truthfully, he favored his mother, bore a distinct resemblance.

"Petro, you've grown! You are almost a man. Soon girls will be swooning at your feet." Adanya stepped forward to formally greet him.

Petro, however, retreated and, to Adanya's astonishment, called out to the dozen or more customers haplessly milling about the mercantile, in an amplified, unforgettable tone. "Come, my good people. Stop your work and gather 'round. We have an honored guest in our midst."

Slowly, the hesitant, perplexed customers, merchandise still in hand, gathered. Adanya experienced a gnawing discomfort, uncertain of what would transpire. Petro, however, was in rare form. All eyes upon him, he made a grand, sweeping gesture, bowing low before Adanya. His voice, thick with unmasked mocking, began to pitch like a seasoned sideshow caller.

"Come one and all and bow before Adanya, Queen of the Underworld. She practices the black arts under the light of the full moon. I, myself, live as an example of the gods' protection against her vile magic. For this jealous, imposter of a queen once sought to sacrifice me to the underworld. Yet, thanks to our benevolent Creator, I escaped."

Trepidation swept Adanya like bile rising in one's throat. She felt trapped, frozen as a yearling in a hunter's gun sight. Unfortunately, much to her dismay, the situation, though previously unclear, grew acutely unpleasant. This would not turn out well.

Besides the obvious public predicament, the possibility existed, or so Adanya thought, that she was rapidly taking leave of her senses. For a brief second, she thought she witnessed Mikao among the crowd. But, given another glance, she recognized only Goldwyn, the house cat. He wove in and out, unseen, between the legs of enthralled spectators. It made no sense. Why was the cat here?

Petro's voice droned on adopting the surreal, sing-song quality of a circus ringmaster. "And in her arms, ladies and gentlemen, is the bastard, half-breed child, Temaru. Bring gifts to the infant Temaru, good people. For Queen Adanya told my sainted mother only yesterday that he is the son of our Creator."

The expanding crowd gasped. One woman actually fainted dead away leaving her husband, already overburdened with cumbersome packages, to struggle under the weight of her substantial girth. Adanya thought she heard someone call out for smelling salts. Other fainthearted souls daintily fanned themselves to avoid similar fates.

"Yes," Petro continued. "Temaru is the powerful son of the Divine. His mother claims to have given her womanhood to the Creator himself."

Petro stopped the oration, allowing his words to take full effect on the increasingly hostile crowd. People openly bantered words like "blasphemy," "adulteress," and "whore." The inflammatory talk only bolstered outraged cries of injustice.

The young boy marveled at his ability to orchestrate this escalating scene like an expert puppet master manipulating marionettes and might have intentionally pulled even more harmful strings had fate not intervened. Simply put, Petro experienced an untimely sneezing fit. The vengeful boy sneezed again and again, startling his rapt listeners and cutting off any further discourse. The unplanned fit frustrated Petro. To his knowledge, only common alley cats evoked this uncontrollable allergic reaction. But Ohan never permitted a filthy cat to enter the mercantile.

Nonetheless, the teen, between sneezes, recognized that his work, even partially completed, was well done. He stepped out of the spotlight, secretly pleased with his keen ability to swing the masses. Petro exited, unnoticed, through a rear door.

Adanya, however, froze, rooted in place, unable to move, until she felt Running Wolf pull urgently on her sleeve. Reality struck like an unexpectedly harsh, well-placed slap to the cheek and, with a protective arm around Temaru, the Beloved lowered her head as a charging moose defending her offspring and pushed her way through the incensed, self-righteous crowd. Adanya ran, shielding her infant son, until she reached the safety of Mikao's home.

The Healer opened the door as the shaken Adanya arrived at the home. He listened to the sobbing, practically unintelligible, young woman. Gently but firmly, Mikao pried the bawling, unharmed baby from his mother's vice-like grip and, after giving comfort, placed Temaru in his cradle.

Then the Healer guided the distraught Adanya to a chair, placing a medicinal blend of strong tea in front of her. He said nothing. Yet soon the Beloved felt the soothing embrace of a serene, powerful presence. Mikao stared into her eyes and, as Adanya met his gaze, she soon found her breath slowed, ceasing its erratic pace. Eventually, she inhaled deep, full breaths. The two continued, breathing in silence, for more than an hour.

Into the stillness, came Mikao's voice. "Tell me," he said.

Calmly, Adanya recounted the morning's unsettling events. The people who refused to look or speak to her on the street as well as Petro's less than entertaining performance at Ohan's store. She left nothing out as she spoke with raw emotion, her pain overflowing.

"Is it true?" queried the Healer.

"Is what true?" asked Adanya looking up at him. It always amazed Adanya whenever she had to physically look up at Mikao since his dwarf status left him much shorter than most people including herself. This afternoon was no exception.

Mikao gestured with his hands. "The acts attributed to you, the words that they have labeled you. Are they true?"

"No," came the response but then Adanya stopped. "I mean, I don't think so. It is true that I dabbled in the black arts when I thought Aeracura was the Moon Goddess. But that's not who I am, at least, not now. I failed to listen to my inner voice. I made very poor decisions. Petro, however, either forgets or twists the facts. I saved him from the fire's spit. I never intended to sacrifice him."

"As for the other, well, I did sleep with Manny without the benefit of a commitment ceremony. But it was not done casually." Adanya looked adoringly in the direction of her sleeping son. "Temaru was conceived in love - my love for Manutea." She sighed. "I suppose I should not have told Brumledi that he was a child of the Creator."

Mikao said nothing. Instead he let Adanya's words hang in the air as he lit fine incense. The smell of sweet jasmine filled the treatment room. Finally, the Healer spoke.

"People's opinions are clouded by their own skewed perceptions of life, their own history. Sometimes they frame others in a positive light - sometimes negatively. It makes no difference. Neither judgment is necessarily true."

"You must never look outside yourself for validation - one way or another," he continued. "No matter how well-intended, others cannot give you an accurate reading of who you are. You must look within."

Adanya thought about this for several minutes. "But, can't other people sometimes see things that I cannot?"

"Sometimes," Mikao conceded, "others provide valuable feedback for us. But nothing is ever hidden from the soul - though emotion can temporarily cloud our vision. When upset prevents insight, then outside opinions might be helpful."

"But beware," the Healer cautioned, "you must always carefully consider others' words. What is true? What is false? What is the source of their opinion? Many times their source, no matter how well-intended, is not the one you call the "Creator". Regardless of what is said, you must still look within for the answer, for validation. You must know who you are - and who you are not."

Adanya looked at her teacher imploringly. "But I am flawed, Healer. Certainly my body is flawed but it is more than that. I am sometimes proud and vain. I often look to my own needs before the needs of others. How can I trust my own soul?"

Mikao stood and walked to the doorway. Before he left, he turned with a slight cock of the head and inquired, "Who gave you these flaws?"

Adanya considered Mikao's words long into the night. Who am I? What is true about me? She rolled these thoughts over and over in her mind.

"I am a loving being, comprised of light and shadow, designed by my Creator," she whispered to no one in particular as she hugged her body. Then she took out her quill.

*I am content in myself. For Spirit has revealed the many gifts contained within my soul. Oh, there are flaws. But these flaws also come from Spirit. These imperfections teach lessons not yet grasped. I am at peace. I am content in myself.*

*There is a certain freedom that flows from this understanding. No longer does self-perception sway with the ever-changing whims of other people. No longer do I crave external validation of internal gifts. I am a Child of the Universe. This is an eternal truth.*

*I am free to be me. I let go of fears and inhibitions. I sing and dance and play. Joy, coupled with carefree laughter, rises up within me.*

Adanya kissed her sweet son on his brow. "We are all, each of us, perfect in our divine imperfection."

# CHAPTER XXXII

*"That makes no sense, Grandmother," said Morning Dove. "How can we be perfect in our imperfections?"*

*"We arrive on this earth as flawed mortals," explained the Ancient. "No one is perfect. Some children limp or look at the world with eyes which do not see. The Creator, the Great Spirit, uses all of these gifts, these imperfections, to teach us, to bring us to a new understanding of both ourselves and others in this Universe."*

*"But those are physical blemishes," countered her grand-daughter. "What of vanity and selfishness? Surely our creator did not gift us with these things."*

*"Are we not born with our own unique personalities?" asked the Ancient One. "Yes, some flaws are learned on this earth. But, remember, little one, all things come to us as gifts from the Creator. All things bring us to a new awakening - even imperfections."*

An uneasy calm permeated the days that followed. Adanya, who now knew no other way, lived her life with complete authenticity. It was as simple – and as complicated - as that. She treated patients, although the number dwindled significantly after the very public, quite uncomfortable incident at Ohan's store. She spent her limited free time in the company of Lando, Sherlana and Wilhelmina. In every moment, Adanya lived in that space where her Creator dwells.

That is not to say that the villagers forgot about their bewitching neighbor. They continued to indulge in overt whispers and stolen glances. Fear resided in the town center.

Once, as Adanya and Wilhelmina strolled outside, celebrating the winter solstice, the women inadvertently found themselves surrounded by impetuous, school-age boys. The youngsters linked hands, forming an impenetrable circle, as if dancing around a gaily decorated maypole. 'Round and 'round they skipped, taunting the innocent women with verse.

*Adanya's a witch in dark of night,*
*She gives the townspeople quite a fright.*
*Who knows what evil she casts the spells for,*
*Adanya's one with the Devil ever more.*

The female companions, dizzy from the bullies' repetitive circular motion, waited patiently until their tormenters, with a final taunt, grew tired of the impromptu game, scattering like windblown snowflakes in every conceivable direction. One child, however, could not maintain pace with his older, galloping playmates. Much younger, he fell behind and, stumbling, sliced open his knee on a jagged shard of discarded glass. Blood squirted everywhere.

Adanya, without saying a word, walked over and knelt down. The boy, terrified of this witch's certain revenge, shook uncontrollably. Undaunted, the Beloved made a sacred symbol in the air and placed her steady hand over his trembling, bloodied knee. Thick, red splattering oozed out between her fingers.

Yet when Adanya removed her hand, there remained nothing - nothing but unbroken, unblemished flesh. The child's knee appeared perfect in every way. Shocked, the boy leapt to his feet and, running for his life, screamed to all who paid heed about the black magic of Satan's bride.

Adanya, listening to his high-pitched, falsetto rants, turned to Wilhelmina. With a deadpan face, she observed, "No good deed . . ." She left the rueful sentiment unfinished.

All the while, someone watched from his secret place. He watched Adanya, as he had for several months. He saw her comings and goings. He watched as she greeted patients in the morning and watched as she put her bastard son to bed at night. Nothing escaped his ever-vigilant eyes.

The Watcher knew when the temptress would draw her next breath as well as her last. Ahh . . . that sweet breath. He inhaled and closed his eyes, remembering the jasmine that anointed her body. Soon the time would be right. Soon he would make his move - but not yet. The Watcher could wait - at least for now.

Unaware that she was being watched, Adanya continued with her rewarding routine including weekly worship. In some ways, it seemed silly. For Mikao, as well as the sacred sisters, taught her that the constant condemnation, the flogging of souls, to which Reverend Goodheart seemed wholly committed, was not only unnecessary but potentially detrimental. Adanya recognized that only through understanding, embracing both the dark and light, would she find the goddess. She now accepted her flaws as pieces of an intricate puzzle, a riddle, to which her soul had the answer. And that answer, whatever form it ultimately took, came as a priceless gift from the Creator.

Nonetheless, it had always been her practice, at least since arriving in Ambilen, to participate in public worship. Certainly she thrived at the Sisters of the Sacred Covenant in the holy presence of fellow worshippers. And she had, despite her conflicted conversations with Reverend Goodheart, concluded that she needed to diligently pursue her quest for the goddess - wherever the deity might reside. Temaru's life, his happiness in this world, as well as her own, somehow depended on it.

But any effort at public worship proved increasingly futile. When Adanya arrived, walking through the town hall's pine doors, the good folk glared without comment, abruptly taking leave. Oh, not all of them. But enough that, at some point, Reverend Goodheart quietly, without fanfare, took Adanya aside and discussed the benefits of private worship. Certainly he did not directly say that she could not attend his orations but his meaning, the implication, was quite clear. The good pastor feared that he might lose an entire flock save for one wanton woman.

Sherlana, a bountiful, right-thinking sort, wanted none of this nonsense. "Why should you change your place of worship because of the nonsensical whims of an addle-brained few? They are naught but hypocrites," she practically spat, more than a little perturbed.

"No," Adanya disagreed. "Every being learns at his or her unique pace. That is why there are varying ways as well as different beliefs. They cannot sanction what their heart is not yet ready to accept. But it matters not. We will still end the journey together for we are but one." Then, upon reflection, she added quietly. "Nonetheless, if they do not welcome me, why would I seek to worship with them?"

Sherlana remained silent.

"I do not wish to cause difficulty for Reverend Goodheart," Adanya continued. "For, though our views differ greatly, he has been very good to me."

"Hrupmf," came Sherlana's stalwart response. "Why change for those who are petty and mean-spirited? Let them go out into the world and seek the fallen god who exchanged his own heart for stone," she countered.

"Did not," Adanya queried, "the Creator conjure fields alive with the color of every season? Is not the soil, laden with flowers, more beautiful than any temple? Again, why seek to worship with those who do not welcome me?" Adanya desperately wanted to avoid unnecessary conflict.

Lando and Wilhelmina listened to the two determined women banter back and forth. Finally, Wilhelmina interceded. "I will go to the mountain top to worship the one in whom all light and love dwells," she said. "Let us not argue over that which is of no consequence."

And so, traversing frozen ground the four journeyed, wolf, hawk, and baby in tow. Their silhouettes played against the setting sun as they walked across the plain into the forests of Ambilen. Finally, after following an overgrown, once well-traveled, path, the group entered a clearing. Lined with tall fir trees, the inner area appeared ideal for an outdoor sanctuary.

Lando, a towering, gentle-giant with almost 600 pounds on his 6'6" frame, carefully lowered the overfilled sack slung casually over his right shoulder. His frosty breath hung like icicles in the frigid air. Then he worked with Sherlana and Wilhelmina to erect a sacred space of solid rock. One by one, the trio gathered stone, fitting each mismatched piece with another, until the task was complete.

The finished work signaled that it was time to unpack the bag's contents. From its velvet interior Lando pulled candles of varying shapes and sizes as well as pewter holders. The women placed the arrangement of tiered luminaries, along with a rope of pine, on the upper corner of the altar. At this point, Adanya joined the group, handing a bundled, slumbering Teamru to Sherlana.

Reverently, the raven-haired woman, her cloak pulled tight around her, bent down and picked up the last item, giving thanks as she placed it squarely in the center of the altar. The artwork, a breathtaking metal sculpture crafted by Lando, appeared forged of rare metals. It consisted of two, intertwined circles.

The first circle represented the four corners of the earth - north, south, east and west. The second circle ran outside the earth at its eastern and western points, encircling the inner orb like the rings of Saturn. It represented the love of the Creator which flows around the earth as well as through it, never ending, for all eternity.

True to Wilhelmina's words, the forest glen, this original masterpiece of the Creator, proved far more exquisite than any temple erected by human hand. The friends arranged regular pilgrimages to the secluded, holy place, regardless of distance or impending weather. They came, in silent meditation. They came, in song and dance. They came, in gratitude.

Sometimes Adanya came alone. The place had a comfortable, familiar feel to it. The sun, even in the midst of winter, felt warm upon her skin. She sang to the heavens and to her blessed son even as she wrote in her journal.

*I am a powerful catalyst for change in the life flow that is this Universe. I possess a dynamic energy that sets events, intentional or not, in motion. I may or may not be aware of the lives that I have touched. I may not ever encounter some of the people that my energy has permeated. Yet the effect is not diminished. I serve as a catalyst for change.*

*I choose to act as the Spirit's instrument for positive change. For the Soul moves me to serve each being's Highest Purpose. Though I may not understand the ripples that fan out as I willingly immerse myself in life's pond, I trust that Spirit does. My life force merges with the Universe to unleash positive energy into the chain of eternally connected events. I trust that I am brought to the right moment - at the right time - for the ultimate good of all people.*

One day, as she was writing these words, Adanya consciously acknowledged a startling realization. This was the very clearing in which she invoked the Moon Goddess. This was the clearing in which she cast spells. Everything, much to her astonishment, had come full circle.

The memories, her remembered ability to cause harm, frightened her. But, with a self-deprecating laugh, Adanya realized that, as long as she fully aligned herself with the Most Holy, appropriately channeling the power within, no misfortune would befall anyone. Her true self possessed no evil. Nor was there was anything even remotely sinister about this place that once seemed so dark.

Thoughts to the contrary were but an illusion. Light flooded the holy ground even as it filled her soul. For she, like every other creature, bathed in the glory of the Creator's love. This land, the soul within her, served as the ever-changing work of the Divine. And for this, Adanya gave thanks.

All the while, the Watcher waited.

# CHAPTER XXXIII

Crocuses pushed their delicate buds upward, bursting through fertile soil, in celebration of Temaru's first mortal year. Adanya, her heart overflowing, prepared a sumptuous banquet in honor of her only child's milestone. Mikao, Lando, Sherlana, Wilhelmina and Reverend Goodheart attended the joyful festivities. They arrived dressed in their finest attire as if attending a royal ball.

Adanya greeted the guests, presenting them with a table overflowing with the earth's bounty. A rack of lamb, succulent squash, and biscuits smothered in preserves tempted the hungry lot. Potato soup, made with a rich creamy base, warmed their appetites. As the meal progressed, Lando led the others in raising their goblets, again and again, to toast their gracious hostess and her infant son.

"Here's to Temaru, son of Adanya," said Lando. "You are like no other that has come before. You are a child of this Universe. Walk this earth together, mother and child, in full awareness of the royal blood that courses through your veins." The others clapped their hands, voicing loud, hearty cheers, signifying enthusiastic agreement. The revelers clumsily clinked crystal glasses together and drank the intoxicating blood of perfectly aged, full-bodied fruits.

Adanya, overwhelmed by such generous sentiment, thanked the group for their steadfast love and support. "It means so much to me that we have walked this world together. You have all taught me more than many souls learn in a lifetime," said the humble, grateful woman. "I love you all very much." Her voice faltered and tears shone in sapphire eyes.

Not wanting to dampen an otherwise exquisite evening, Adanya hastily excused herself to retrieve dessert from the modest kitchen. There, as she regained her composure cutting the still warm shortbread into ample squares, the woman briefly contemplated Lando's verbose toast. He knew, or seemed to know, of Temaru's sovereign heritage.

But how? Adanya never spoke of either Manny or his family. In fact, she refused to reveal his name to anyone but kindly Sister Angelica. The probability that Lando knew who Temaru's father appeared, well, virtually impossible. The odds staggered her mind. How could he possibly know that Manutea, and now his son, descended from island royalty?

Something else nagged at her - something important - about the exact wording of Lando's final toast but it escaped her. What was it? Adanya racked her brain to no avail. Unable to resolve anything, she washed her hands, leaving the knife and cutting board in the sink. Then, smoothing her hair, she lifted the tray of desserts and returned to the merriment.

After dinner, Mikao invited the guests to join him in the sanctuary of his private gardens. No one, not even Adanya, had gained entry to the holy grounds prior to this unprecedented night. One by one, they crossed the step stones from the house into a different time and place. Mikao's enchanting, backyard paradise transported these residents of Ambilen into the alluring culture of the Far East.

The friends explored, in quiet awe, inhaling unspeakable beauty. Tea lights, thousands of little candles, illuminated the landscape. Aesthetic wonders, steeped in both symbolism and mysticism, covered the expansive grounds. There were nishikigoi, more commonly known as koi, ponds, and waterfalls as well as bridges. Quaint pagodas and colossal stone lanterns scattered before them.

Bonsai trees, graceful, meticulously shaped topiary, lined the stepping stones that welcomed visitors into an outdoor tearoom. Ceramic wind-bells captured the melodic sound of an otherwise imperceptible spring breeze. Shishi, a pair of enormous lion statues, and karin, a horrific mythical creature much like a dragon but possessing the physical characteristics of many other animals, surveyed the property.

Mikao led the captivated entourage mindfully through the maze of spiritual, carefully constructed, pathways until they reached an ornamental wood bridge adorning a stream at the mouth of a miniature waterfall. The serene sound of the rushing water sounded like the harmonious voice of the Great Spirit. It represented birth, growth, and death. The Healer abruptly stopped, midway, on the arched bridge. Center stage, the host addressed his enthralled audience, still lingering at the foot of the bridge.

"Tonight," Mikao spoke, his tranquil voice resonating, "we gather to rejoice in the birth and life of the eternal spirit known to all as 'Temaru'".

The Healer paused, and, with an apparent slight of hand, seemingly out of nowhere, produced a smooth, oblong pebble in his palm for all to see. Holding it high, Mikao ceremoniously released it, allowing it to fall, unhindered, into the gurgling stream. The fluid waters effortlessly swallowed, engulfing the small stone, leaving only ripples in its wake. Circles, small at first, moved outward, bigger and bigger, ever-expanding.

"His spirit," Mikao continued, "in human form, like a single pebble introduced into the conscious stream of humanity, impacts this sphere for all eternity. This infant serves as our wise teacher and we honor him."

Mikao opened his arms and Adanya ascended the bridge, entrusting her child to the diminutive man. The man placed his head on the child's soft crown. "We bring you gifts even as your own sacred breath bestows treasure upon this Universe."

Then, using ancient symbols, Mikao passed on the healing attunements to the child. This activated the intrinsic power within. Now, like this his mother before him, Temaru could reach out to those in need. He could heal through the energy of the life force.

"The power of the Universe flows within you even as it flows through you," said the Healer. "Use it only with the highest, most noble, of intentions." The Healer returned the infant to his waiting mother, crossing the bridge to the other side.

Lando, Sherlana and Wilhelmina each ascended the structure in turn. The artist presented a portrait of Temaru bathed in holy light. To Adanya, even in the low, flickering glow of candlelight, the scene looked astonishingly familiar. The painting depicted Temaru, suspended within a golden bubble. Twelve elders stood below the child in a sacred circle, their joined hands raised to the heavens. Lando titled the piece, "His Father's Son."

The gentle giant, overcome with emotion, gazed lovingly at Temaru. "May you never forget who your father is. Your heritage is the moon and the stars. All spirits bow in your presence." Moisture formed in Lando's aging eyes.

Adanya, hearing the stirring words, also felt emotion surge to the surface. It always upset her, unsettled her equilibrium, whenever she thought about her son estranged from his own father. But the moment quickly passed. Already, Lando, wiping his eyes and blowing his rather prominent nose on a billowy shirt sleeve, bounded over the flawless red planks and joined Mikao. Now Sherlana glided to the forefront, bringing a pendulum fashioned of hand-blown, art glass.

"This pendulum connects you to all the wisdom of the Universe," she said as she kissed Temaru on the forehead. "Choose your questions wisely."

Wilhelmina subsequently delivered an expansive collection of natural crystals formed in the bowels of Mother Earth. Housed in a mahogany vessel, inlaid with the twelve astrological signs, the crystals possessed enormous energies as well as special properties.

"Heal yourself, call forth the power within you, access the earth's wisdom, for your vibrations are felt throughout the Universe, little child," said the good-hearted woman. "You are the Universe in miniature." She placed the heavy box next to the other gifts then moved to join the waiting party.

Finally, Adanya displayed her own offering to Temaru. It was a crystal wand swirling with a kaleidoscope of color, adorned with gold and silver ornamentation.

"May you use the immeasurable power within for the highest purpose of all humanity," she said simply. Adanya kissed her precious son, caressing his feathery soft cheek. The child's almond-shaped eyes twinkled at his mother's familiar face, her gentle touch.

Only Reverend Goodheart remained on the one side of the bridge. The clergy member uncomfortably cleared his throat and announced in a well-modulated, most auspicious voice, "I will baptize the child at the appropriate time." Adanya, who had not necessarily expected a gift, rejoiced. The baptism, even if it occurred at another time, represented acceptance of her cherished son.

The impromptu ceremony drew to a close. Content, Adanya again felt something tug in the deep recesses of her mind. This evening, the offering of gifts to an infant, it reminded her of something long ago in the Valley of Lilies. She had neither forgotten nor consciously remembered. What was it?

For the second time that night, no answer immediately materialized. And so, the Beloved invited her friends to relax as she played the fiddle, its lilting sound weaving magically through the trees and generous plantings, over the high walls, out into the bustling town square. Villagers hurrying home for the evening meal, gave pause, wondering, now more than ever, what mysteries lay beyond the thick bamboo fence which served as a protective barrier around the exterior of Mikao's property. What unknown puzzles lay hidden in the inner sanctum of the Healer's home?

One person did not wonder. The Watcher knew. He knew what evil the witch and her devil son represented. He knew that mankind could not survive her malice, her black magic. Something had to be done - something had to be done soon.

The waiting was almost over. The Watcher stifled a silent scream as, visible only from his unique vantage point, he observed the wand and pendulum, without benefit of human hand, leave their resting place and levitate over the child's head. Untroubled, Temaru cooed, flailing his arms at the rotating objects.

The happening strengthened the Watcher's resolve. He knew what had to be done.

The time was now.

# CHAPTER XXXIV

Less than twenty-four hours later, the unrest began. It was nothing at first. Good, god-fearing people in the town square increased tense exchanges. Tavern drunkards bantered freely, a bit too loudly, about stained women and bastard, half-breed children. Nothing appreciably unusual or out of the ordinary occurred. Ill will, like a merciless, flesh-eating plague, often ran rampant, careening through Ambilen's cobbled streets.

Adanya focused on living in the space where the Creator dwells. She knew who she was - and what she was not. She continued to craft the list of spiritual truths, initiated some years back at the insistent prodding of Sister Angelica. This effort of refining, exploring her soul, assisted Adanya in embracing light even as shadow insidiously crept over the village. She rejoiced in the many blessings that the heavens showered upon her each and every day - her wonderful son, good friends, food and shelter. The list proved infinite.

In one week's time, however, the situation markedly escalated. On an otherwise blissful evening, as Mikao taught Adanya how to play mah-jongg, two players short, violence struck. The Beloved, concentrating fully on the unfamiliar game, heard a surreal crash and the subsequent, unmistakable, sound of shattering glass. Instantaneously, she felt a swish of air as a fiery object zoomed past her ear. Everything moved as if in slow motion.

Adanya instinctively shielded Temaru from danger as Mikao calmly but expeditiously smothered the flaming object and extinguished the sitting room candles. A barrage of angry voices yelled, "Death to the witch and all who follow her." The hostile, disgruntled rumblings continued for about ten minutes but, when neither Mikao nor Adanya responded, the group half-heartedly dissipated with one final, pelting of rocks. The Watcher, who witnessed the unprovoked attack, marveled at his enviable ability to control events, to create fear.

Adanya, after checking Temaru from head to toe, assisted Mikao in boarding up the windows, most of which boasted six broken panes. Then she bid her teacher good night, slowly climbing the stairs to the cozy loft. She tucked her precious son gently into his cradle and meditated. The night's incident had left her sorely in need of emotional grounding. And, while Adanya restored her soul with eyes closed and mind stilled, the porcelain mirror, originally positioned on the dresser, took flight. The Beloved, much to her surprise, discovered it the next morning in Temaru's crib.

The days to follow were peaceful - at least on the observable surface. Peaceful, that is, until one afternoon when the door to the treatment room burst open. In flew Wilhelmina, out of breath, her hair and clothing askew.

Adanya, nonplused by this explicit violation of privacy, peered at her usually thoughtful friend. "Wilhelmina, whatever is the matter? Are you alright?" The shock reflected on Adanya's face only surpassed by the incredulous expression on her elderly client's countenance.

'Adanya, I must speak with you," huffed Wilhelmina insistently, obviously short of breath. "It's a matter of great urgency." Then she looked at Mistress Longstreth who clutched her chest as if under siege, on the treatment table. "I apologize for my rude behavior but it cannot be helped."

"Wilhelmina, if you would please wait for me in the parlor," instructed Adanya. "I will be there momentarily." Wilhelmina again apologized, vacating the treatment room with decidedly less commotion than her rather unconventional arrival.

After tending to her patient, Adanya centered herself and joined Wilhelmina in parlor. Its contents shrouded in mystery, since little light filtered through the boarded up windows. The Beloved started to speak but her friend interrupted her. "Close the doors, Adanya," the woman ordered. "These words are not for prying ears."

Only after the doors, adorned with carved dragons, were pulled securely shut, did Wilhelmina proceed. She spoke cautiously, in guarded tones, frequently looking over her shoulder, as if an enemy might approach at any moment.

"I was keeping house for Mistress Marlow this early morn," she said in urgent puffs of shortened breath. "The master was home and I knew naught why because usually, before the cock crows, he is engaged in his work." Adanya knew that Marlow earned his keep as the village blacksmith.

"I was cleaning the pantry," Wilhelmina continued, "and, unaware of my presence, the master escorted a group of men into the kitchen. I could not see their faces but there were quite a few in number. I recognized one slurred tongue as belonging to that unruly brut that drinks ale long before the sun reaches its peak," Wilhelmina paused, struggling to remember his name. "Simon, I think."

"I started to come out, to make my presence known, but, suddenly, one of the men started talking about the witch who bore a warlock with Beelzebub." She looked pointedly at Adanya. "Of course, I knew who they meant."

"Of course," said Adanya, a look of disdain spreading across her face. "Go on," she impatiently urged her friend.

"Well, I tarried in the pantry, eavesdropping on their conversation. I heard one of them say, 'Something must be done to protect the women and children of this fair city.' I truly don't know who said it."

"What else? Did anyone say anything specific?" Adanya had to know if for no other reason than to protect Temaru.

Wilhelmina shook her head in frustration. "That's the problem. By then, the men finished their coffee and moved outside. I didn't hear anything else."

Adanya didn't react immediately. Instead, she sunk slowly into a chair, lost in thought. What was going on? Why was this happening? Erratic thoughts swirled around her brain.

Finally, she gave her confusion voice. "What I don't understand, Wilhelmina, is why now? Why is all this happening now when nothing of any consequence has occurred since that day in Ohan's store?"

"Oh, it's true," Adanya continued. "People stare or, in some cases, turn away as I pass, but it amounts to very little. I have done nothing to evoke such a strong reaction. Why now? Someone must be instigating this unruliness, fueling people's fears." Adanya stopped, stymied by all that transpired.

Then, as if struck by a single thought, the two friends looked at each other. Their eyes grew wide with sudden understanding. And, in the same instant, both women exclaimed, "Petro!"

Of course . . . Petro! Why hadn't she thought about him before? He had always been such a sneaky, inquisitive child. Adanya recalled how he had spied on her in the forest glen all those years ago. He followed her, watched her. And, in the passing years, Petro seemed to have developed a cold, noticeably unkind spirit. Adanya shuddered as she remembered his actions at Ohan's store just a few, short months ago.

Adanya resolved to speak with Petro in the morning when Mikao was free to watch Temaru. Relief poured through her being. Surely she could reason with Petro. It would all be alright.

By morning, however, it was too late. As the crow's call signaled midnight, armed men carrying torches descended upon the Healer's home. They stood angrily, gathered 'round the front stoop, shouting for the witch and her bastard, half-breed son to join them. Their voices, thick with menace, filled the starless, nighttime sky.

Adanya, harshly awakened from deep sleep, immediately rushed down the stairs and pulled up the rug on the parlor floor. Straining, she lifted the heavy trapdoor and, kissing him, put Temaru in the far corner of the fruit cellar. Then, ignoring the dank, musty smells and her own child's wailing, she emerged from the hiding place, carefully replacing the trapdoor and smoothing the rug which obscured the opening. Nothing must happen to Temaru . . . nothing.

Adanya nervously rubbed her bejeweled pendant, calling out for the angels to protect her son - even if tonight meant her own unavoidable demise. Her animal guides were somewhere outside and could be of no immediate help so she positioned herself in a chair and waited. For what, Adanya did not know.

The incited crowd outside grew increasingly louder, more obnoxious. Where was Mikao? She couldn't locate him. Adanya covertly, scanned the street for any sign of the Healer but, through the gap in the window boards, all she saw was that silly cat, Goldwyn. He perched on the front step, occasionally hissing, as if bravely guarding the home's occupants from intruders. The absurdity of it prompted an unbidden smile.

"Imagine that," Adanya said aloud. "My very life depends on an old alley cat." Grimly, she thought of Mikao, hoping that no harm would come to the Healer, wherever he might be.

The fevered pitch outside reached its zenith. Inside, Adanya continued to clutch her pendant and pray. She prayed for blessings upon the house and understanding throughout Ambilen and beyond. She prayed for peace in troubled hearts. She prayed in gratitude, giving thanks for her life and its many miracles.

Finally, a trembling Adanya stood, certain in her resolve. She would face her accusers. This was the only way to protect Mikao and Temaru. She must sacrifice herself for the ultimate good of others. Perhaps, the Beloved thought, ironically, only in death would she meet her evasive goddess.

But when Adanya opened the front door that blasted cat jumped at her, full-force, throwing her off balance and pitching her backwards into the house. Stunned, Adanya stumbled, her posterior landing squarely on the wide floorboards. Then she heard a voice.

"Good men, I beseech you. Go home to your wives and children. There is nothing that you can accomplish here tonight. Leave this woman in peace." Adanya could see nothing save for the speaker's long shadow.

"Go home and see your folly in the clear light of day. Go on now." The strong, reasonable voice urged the unruly crowd to take leave.

The embittered men, their spirits sagging from sound defeat in a battle never fought, limped slowly into the night. Then the remaining figure strolled towards the still open door. Adanya raised her hand to shield her face, shaking in abject terror.

"Mistress Adanya, there is nothing to fear." Out of the shadows stepped the familiar presence of Reverend Goodheart. "May I come in?"

Adanya caught her breath. "Oh, my goodness, yes. Where are my manners? Do come in. I can't thank you enough," she stammered as her pounding heart slowed.

The pastor came in and, offering her a hand up, looked around, his eyes adjusting to the dim light. "You are alone tonight? Where are the Healer and your son, Temaru?"

"Mikao appears to be out," said Adanya. "Temaru," she looked towards his cradle, attempting to gather her thoughts. "Temaru! How could I have forgotten? He's down here." Adanya rushed to pull up the rug, struggling to lift the trapdoor. Reverend Goodheart came up behind her, following closely into the murky darkness below.

A voice spoke. "Good evening, Reverend. How does this evening find you?"

Both Adanya and Reverend Goodheart, now halfway down the open cellar stairs, whirled around. Mikao, wearing his dragon outfit entered the room and bowed. Where had the Healer come from? The reverend, an indiscernible look in his eyes, made a hasty retreat up the stairs to greet the diminutive man. Soon, with the pastor and Mikao looking down into the cellar, Adanya emerged with her son.

In the cellar below, apples bobbed in mid-air like juggling red balls. Adanya, her back turned, did not see. But the Watcher, who saw all things, did.

# CHAPTER XXXV

Into Adanya's fitful slumber, hawk flew. Hawk, the messenger of Great Spirit, soared over land and sea. He swooped through the Valley of Lilies, over the tiny island of Moricea, and into the countryside surrounding Ambilen. It was as if he was searching . . . but for what?

On a grassy knoll, a playful band of kinfolk picnicked. Adanya, like a mystic gazing into a cloudy crystal ball, watched the surreal scene unfolded. Four or five friends ate together. She recognized each one. Lando, always an ageless spirit, chased Sherlana around the expansive base of a towering oak tree. The Beloved heard the couple's infectious laughter, a heartwarming symphony, played across the hills and fields. 'Round and 'round they scampered. Sherlana's false, flirtatious protests only served to further incite Lando's passionate pursuit of the bountiful wench.

Nearby, on a blanket woven of lamb's wool, sat a cross-legged Wilhelmina. She tended to Mikao, placing food - Cornish hen and pickled pigs feet - on a china plate for him. Funny, Adanya thought, she could not make out Mikao's face - it was as if he wore a featureless mask. Nonetheless, she intuitively knew the wise, eccentric dwarf. He wore vestments bearing embroidered dragons.

Off a good distance from the merrymakers sat a basket handcrafted of willowy river reeds. It stood alone in a meadow, glorious wild flowers, sprouting as sparkling jewels, growing all about it. What was inside? Curious, Adanya looked closer, mentally adjusting the focus within the foggy haze of her vision.

Why, it was a baby! Peeking through hand-knit, snow white blankets were the most beautiful almond-shaped eyes, the color of robin's eggs. Temaru! What was he doing here, so far away? Why was no one watching over him? The others frolicked, oblivious to his presence.

Sunlight radiated throughout the countryside, shining down on the joyful, impromptu party. Soon, however, even as Apollo's orb continued to burn brightly, an ominous storm cloud instantaneously formed less than ten feet above Temaru's basket. Jagged lightening, like incisive, razor sharp swords, shot down around him, imprisoning the helpless infant, drawing ever closer.

Fear gripped Adanya. Why wasn't anyone protecting Temaru? Carefree laughter continued to ride the breeze as wrath of an unknown origin threatened her only child. Adanya could hear the adults as they played a game of hide-and-seek. Lando hid his eyes and counted. "One, two, three . . . "

Increasingly, lightening menaced Temaru. Who would save him? Adanya, her legs as useless as rotted, decaying tree stumps, felt chained, rooted forever in the bowels of the earth. Frantically, the mother pulled at her useless limbs, flailing her arms. She could not scream for she had no voice. The merriment continued. Adanya was but a ghost.

Wait. Someone was coming. Someone walked with powerful, unmistakable strides towards the vulnerable basket. Hurry! Hurry! Adanya tried to call out but no sound escaped her lips. The figure drew ever closer. Now he - or she - was only a few steps away. Lightening struck the ground all around the basket. Smoke curled ever upward from singed, blackened earth.

Facial features obscured by a hooded cloak, the unknown person extended a boney hand towards the basket. Long fingers were now just inches from snatching the boy. Adanya felt a sense of relief. Temaru would be saved. Her son would live. She cried the salty tears of the undead. Hurry! Hurry!

Without warning, however, hawk swooped down from azure skies high above the storm cloud. His incessant screeches distracted Temaru's would-be rescuer. The figure looked up, startled by the bird of flight's unexpected intervention.

"No, Winged One. Stop," screamed a silent Adanya. Fear racked her body as the would-be savior, turned attention from Temaru, looking into the eye of the storm. And, the Winged One, in a horrifying display, flew with power and precision through the threatening cloud and proceeded to expertly pluck out the eyes of the cloaked being.

Before Adanya could react, a fire-breathing dragon materialized out of thin air. It stood erect, balancing on squatty hind legs as its massive, forty-foot wingspan fanned scorching, white-hot flames. The sightless, disoriented figure, despite physical agony, sensed the creature's presence.

He cowered, curling into a tight ball on the unforgiving earth, covering his bleeding, disfigured face. A single, spectacular ball of fire unceremoniously reduced the pathetic image to ash. Only a six-pointed star remained.

Adanya awoke, her mind distressed, her body shaking uncontrollably. Had Temaru been killed? Why had the Winged One, Great Spirit's messenger, attacked her son's sole protector? One thing Adanya knew for certain. Temaru was in grave, immediate danger. They must flee. They must, without fail, leave Ambilen.

Thoughts of the goddess, Adanya's long-awaited destiny, pushed to the surface. It mattered not. The goddess would have to wait. Adanya cared little if she found the deity now - or ever. Her thoughts flowed outward, beyond her own needs, centering on Temaru.

A distinct voice, neither male nor female, said, "The goddess is nigh. She lives in tranquil waters."

# CHAPTER XXXVI

In the stillness of those pre-dawn hours, Adanya discovered her voice. No longer mute, it shouted from the depths of her soul. For the vision revealed the price of silence, the absorbent toll of inaction. She must save herself. Only in saving herself could she protect Temaru. Only in saving herself could she move forward into her true destiny. For the first time, Adanya chose to consciously walk measured, intentional steps - awake and fully alive - into her future.

Early, expanding light illuminated the dervish's whirl, a choreographed dance of feverish activity. Adanya opened drawers throwing meager contents onto the feather bed. She pulled wide the oversized, hinged doors of the armoire, seeking the priceless treasures of her life. One by one, she expeditiously added them to the voluminous pile on the bed. The worn beaded skirt, her hunting knife. She bundled the fiddle and leather journal, securing these precious items in the silk butterfly scarf that Cratch once gifted her.

Temaru's possessions came next. Wand, crystals, portrait, and pendulum. In addition, all the fashions that Adanya had so lovingly crafted in anticipation of his arrival on this Earth. Hats, gowns, booties. All garments, regardless of function or origin, were unceremoniously dumped atop the growing conglomeration of possessions - all except one.

Temaru's baptismal gown. Made of shimmering satin, the snowy white cloth symbolized the eternal purity of this child's, indeed, every child's, soul. Each cuff and hem, skillfully sewn, featured delicate lace spun of angel's wings. Adanya paused, sinking into the comfortable seat of the old rocker, remembering the feel of its steady glide as she had carefully stitched each separate piece into one. She so desired that the Creator's mark be placed upon her son.

Adanya shook these thoughts from her head. There was work to be done. Eventually, however, she abandoned the loft in search of Mikao. She called out for him at the foot of the stairs but her greeting went unanswered. Adanya instinctively knew his location. She removed her shoes and entered the private, outdoor gardens, walking each path, waiting for their eternal spirits to connect. She encountered Mikao in the temple, sitting cross-legged in deep meditation. He wore the same dragon ceremonial robes that Adanya had seen in her vision. She knelt, bowed her head, and waited.

Minutes passed. Ten. Twenty. Thirty. Finally, sensing he was not alone, Mikao said, "You are leaving." It was a statement, not a question. The dwarf continued to sit with his back to her, facing the benevolent, big-bellied Buddha.

"Yes," said Adanya, her voice barely above a whisper. "It is time." The inherent finality of the situation sunk in.

"Indeed. The goddess is nigh," Mikao answered. "Her time is now."

Dumbfounded, Adanya stared at the dwarf, this man who had taken her in, served as her teacher. He remained, undisturbed, in the lotus position. "The time is past, Mikao," she responded, a definite edge to her voice. "I no longer search for the elusive deity. I must leave Ambilen at once for we are in great danger."

"Is it necessary to search for that which one already possesses?" said Mikao. "Can anything ever separate us from ourselves?"

Adanya, puzzled by the apparent riddle, the disjointed comments, said nothing more, taking her leave. She gathered Temaru in her arms, setting off to arrange their impending departure. Mother and child walked the familiar streets of Ambilen, one last time, until they arrived at their first stop - Ohan's mercantile. With an involuntary sigh, Adanya pushed open the door, again entering her past.

Her thoughts, nonetheless, remained squarely focused on the present. Cornmeal, cured bacon, blankets - one by one, Adanya efficiently placed the supplies on the counter. Ohan, fully absorbed in assisting other customers, took no notice. The goods stacked higher and higher. Adanya knew enough to secure at least a three month stock in order to meet the most basic of survival needs.

"Planning a trip, Mistress?" The query broke Adanya's concentration. She looked about, alternately juggling her son and a rather weighty sack of flour, until she found herself staring directly into Petro's beady eyes. "Does not our fair village suit you?"

"Petro, I bear you no ill will - nor do I wish for any trouble," Adanya evenly replied. "As it happens, we will be leaving Ambilen very soon."

"By 'we', I assume that you mean that you will be taking your bastard, half-breed child with you," sneered the boy. "Or do you plan to leave him with his father - the creator of this great universe?" Petro's words, laden with heavy sarcasm, oozed contempt.

Adanya, sensing that further exchange served no purpose, gave Petro a brief nod and turned her attention to the miscellaneous items on the counter. She arranged for their immediate delivery to Mikao's cottage then sought to vacate the premises without additional discord or incident. As she closed the portal to her past, however, Adanya overheard Petro's running commentary to another customer.

"You do know that the witch claims her child to be the son of the Great Spirit, the creator, the one who made each sunrise," he said. The boy's ignorant words only strengthened Adanya's resolve to leave behind these troubled, embittered people as quickly as possible.

Next, she made her way to Lando's studio, a former hay barn on the outskirts of town. Inside, she encountered a well-endowed, bare-chested Sherlana, lounging on an overstuffed settee, posing provocatively for her artist husband. Adanya stood quietly, in the shadows, secretly envious of the obvious connection the two shared. Silent, save for the occasional soft sounds of the painter's brush, their remarkable bond proved deafening.

Temaru, slightly less impressed with the intimacy of the moment, released a flatulent offering, followed by a ripe, unmistakable smell. This humorous, somewhat unexpected, occurrence prompted Adanya to step forward into the light. Sherlana immediately released her pose and, with a squeal of delight, took the infant into her arms - not to mention the generous folds of her ample bosom.

"Adanya," Lando's voice boomed. "Such a pleasant surprise! What brings you and my handsome boy out on such a glorious morn?"

Adanya shared news of her troubling vision. The two listened attentively, Lando, at times, shaking his head in disbelief, as the girl outlined her plans. When Adanya finished, Sherlana gave her friend a long hug. Then she whispered, "Are you sure about this, girl?"

Adanya looked at both of them. "Aye, for while I know naught what the dream means, Hawk is the Creator's messenger. And Temaru is definitely in danger," she explained. "I must go."

Lando nodded vigorously in obvious agreement. "You will not go alone, however. Sherlana and I will journey with you - at least until you are settled. Then, alas, we must part company. For our life is here in Ambilen. We will deliver these canvases on the return trip." He gestured to a stack of completed canvases in the corner of his work area.

"Thank you," replied the grateful woman. "Temaru and I would be most happy to share your company - if but a short time."

Sherlana was about to speak when the trio of adults heard a strange groan from high above in the structure's rafters. They looked up only to see a rope, holding multiple bales of hay. The sound, this creaking, grew louder, more pronounced, as the bales shifted, swaying in place. With but a split second to react, Lando shoved his wife, as well as the mother and child, out of harm's way, as the rope snapped, hurtling heavy, unrestrained bales of hay to the ground with a sickening thud.

Dust and grain particles rose from the barn floor, swimming in streams of sunlight. Adanya stood up, Temaru unharmed, still in her arms. The shaken women watched as Lando painstakingly climbed the rafters, an optical array of legs and arms swinging across hundred year old beams of wood, intent on examining the rope strands. After a few minutes of intense concentration, rolling the rope over and over in his calloused hands, he looked down at Sherlana and Adanya. Even from a distance the women could see his broad, bearded face lined with concern.

"This rope didn't just fray from the strain of the weight," he said. "It was intentionally cut. Someone wanted those bales to fall."

Without delay, Lando and Sherlana escorted the mother and child safely home. There was little conversation among the shocked party - although Sherlana promised to advise Wilhelmina of the upcoming travel plans. Adanya seriously doubted that Wilhelmina could afford to journey with them. Time off work robbed the working woman of both coin and customer. Adanya experienced a sense of profound loss for she would sorely miss her friend. In fact, she'd miss all of them - Mikao, Lando, Sherlana, Wilhelmina, and, of course, the Reverend Goodheart.

Reverend Goodheart! Suddenly Adanya realized that she had not yet told him of her plans. She must find him. In his own way, he had been quite good to Adanya and Temaru. He had even calmed the angry mob that threatened her life on that starless night, now just a day past.

But there was no time to tarry. Clients waited patiently for Adanya's services. She spent the afternoon hours giving treatment as well as messages of love and hope. These kind folks had become much more than professional acquaintances. They held a sacred, irreplaceable place in her heart.

With the last appointment completed, Adanya's thoughts again turned to preparing for their journey. A rap on the door, however, interrupted the effort. She answered it only to find the austere reverend standing at the threshold.

"I bid you good evening, Mistress Adanya. How does this evening find you?" The visitor carefully surveyed his surroundings as if taking personal inventory.

"I am well, Reverend Goodheart. What brings you out on this summer's eve?" inquired Adanya.

The guest did not immediately respond to her question. "Where is Mikao on this fine evening?" he asked instead.

"Why, he has gone to tend to Widow Lockshine. Her gout, the pain in her legs, makes it necessary for him to travel to her bedside." Then she added, "I'm afraid that, this time, the good widow might actually be ill."

Reverend Goodheart remained silent. The sweet summer air hung between them as they stood in the entryway. The good pastor appeared to be debating, weighing his options. In short time, though, he cleared his throat.

"I hear the townspeople talking, Adanya. They say that you are soon to leave Ambilen and travel to parts unknown," he ventured.

"Aye, for the Great Spirit has sent his Messenger, Hawk, to warn me of grave danger. We must leave the village at once or great harm will befall Temaru," explained Adanya.

The reverend searched the Beloved's face. "You believe that the Great Spirit, our Creator, speaks to you?"

"Of course, good sir. The Creator speaks to each of us, unceasing are his words of love, his sharing of eternal truths. He speaks in moments of wake and sleep. We need only listen." Adanya's spoke gently, without reproach.

Seeing the uncertain expression on Goodheart's face, Adanya continued. "Why every tree and flower speaks to me. I hear the Creator's voice in the wind. He places messages of joy, peace, and comfort before me. I ask for guidance and he writes upon the stars as well as my heart."

"But," said the reverend, his voice registering an unidentifiable emotion, "the Creator does not actually speak to you, I mean, talk directly to you."

Adanya grew quiet. "Yes. I hear my Creator speak. He speaks to all of us. As I said, we need only listen."

There was an uncomfortable energy, electricity filling the room. Adanya felt it envelop her. She fought it, struggling with an overwhelming impulse to snatch Temaru from his cradle and flee into the abyss. But the moment passed. And Adanya felt silly as she heard Reverend Goodheart's next words.

"Then we must baptize Temaru - at once. I will take him now and prepare him. You can lock up here and join us momentarily."

Adanya, while her heart leapt at the prospect of Temaru's baptism, experienced an almost paralyzing fear. She did not, under any circumstances, want to separate from her son.

The reverend, sensing her unrest, took her hand. "What is wrong, Adanya? Do you not trust me?"

Hearing Goodheart's soothing tenor, his concerned voice, Adanya immediately lowered her eyes in shame. "No, Reverend. It is not that. You have been overwhelmingly kind to Temaru as well as myself. We are humbled by your generous offer to baptize him. It is all that I could hope for, all that I have prayed for."

"Then, what, dear woman? What causes you such inner turmoil? I know that you fear for Temaru's life but have you not considered the protection that a baptism might offer him? Why, once baptized, Temaru can call upon the protection of the angels!"

The sentiment gave Adanya pause. She had not, in fact, considered this. Truthfully, she believed that Temaru - not to mention any mortal - could call out, prevail upon angels at any time. Still, there was something to be said for being sure. A little extra protection, especially now, could not hurt. Besides, her heart ached for the acceptance that the baptism of her son represented. She simply could not turn the reverend's offer down.

"You are most kind, Reverend Goodheart. I am sorry but this day has, most certainly, addled my brain. Forgive my bad manners. Of course I wish for Temaru to be baptized. Thank you for your most generous offer. We will visit you in the early morrow on our way out of town."

A shadow appeared on Reverend Goodheart's brow, creeping over his meticulously groomed features. "No!" The words flew out of his mouth with such force that Adanya stared at him in alarm.

She curiously watched as the reverend struggled for a moment to regain his trademark stoicism. He straightened his holy garb, running a hand through his dark hair. "Now I must ask for forgiveness," he said apologetically. "Forgive me, Adanya. My emotions have gotten the better of me. It is simply that you and the boy have grown to mean so much to me. The full moon is rising, even as we speak, and the sacrament really must be done tonight, before the rising of the sun."

"But, Reverend, I cannot leave - not just yet." Adanya gestured to the food and supplies that had been delivered earlier that afternoon from the mercantile. "I do not wish to leave Mikao's home in disarray. The wagon must still be loaded."

"You are right, Mistress. Let me take the boy and prepare him for the events of this night. You must come to us as soon as you have completed your duties here."

Adanya hesitated. It wasn't that she did not trust Reverend Goodheart - he was one of the few villagers that extended kindness to them. But she was reluctant to let Temaru out of her sight - at least until the immediate danger, whatever it was, passed.

"I don't know . . ." Her thoughts trailed off, interrupted by the sound of a light thud. The pair turned in the direction of the noise to witness a powdery cloud, a white haze, settling across the room. When the dust settled, the adults saw only a white mound sitting on the floor. A chortle, coupled with almond eyes, left little doubt as to its identity, however. Temaru had emptied the entire flour sack, dumping its contents on his head.

"Oh, no," wailed the already exhausted mother. "Temaru, what have you done?" Truthfully, she was also a bit perplexed. How could one so young even raise such a heavy load above his head? It didn't seem possible.

"Do not fear, Mistress Adanya." Reverend Goodheart walked over and picked up the quivering, flour-covered one year old with little regard to the state of his own dark clothing - now coated with a thin layer of white powder. "I will take your inquisitive helper with me and clean him up. You can join us after you make amends here."

This time, Adanya did not protest. It was obvious that her "little helper" hindered any possible progress. She sighed, for the second time that day, even as she reached for a broom. "Perhaps you are right, Reverend. I will attempt to bring order to chaos and, in short time, join you."

# CHAPTER XXXVII

Adanya reluctantly closed the door behind Reverend Goodheart and Temaru. Then she aggressively moved the broom about with swift, broad strokes attacking the fine grains before they took up permanent residency in the wood planks' narrow grooves. Her strokes accelerated, faster and faster, as a perplexing thought snaked its way through her brain. How had Temaru managed to hoist the bag of flour over his head? Surely one so young could not possibly lift a five pound bag. It simply wasn't possible. And, for that matter, how did the hand mirror appear in his bed that morning, not so long ago? Recently, more often than not, things seemed mysteriously out of sorts.

But more than these unexplained happenings troubled Adanya. The angry mob, for instance. What stirred them to action? Or, perhaps more importantly, *who* stirred them to action? Petro? Brumledi? Certainly no townspeople rallied without an organizer. Left to their vices, people registered dissatisfaction, voiced narrow judgment, through the open exhibition of unbridled contempt, content with a cold stare or an unkind word.

Minutes ticked away. Adanya worked efficiently, cleaning the floor as well as preparing items for impending departure. Still, something nagged at her. She couldn't get the picture of Temaru, entrenched in Reverend Goodheart's arms, out of her head. It was as if her subconscious, her higher self, screamed at her, crying out, warning her. But of what?

It was probably nothing. She experienced so much chaos in the last twenty-four hours. The mob as well as the intentionally staged "accident" in Lando's studio took their toll. These events, coupled with the previous night's vision, haunted her. Adanya's raw nerves cut her, slicing her soul like a jagged blade of a hunter's knife.

Knife. Where was that knife - her knife? Adanya dropped the broom as she walked over to the stack of possessions awaiting loading onto the bed of Lando's wagon. She hunted through the assortment of goods, as if looking for a needle in a haystack, until she found it, still in its suede sheath. For reasons unknown, she took the knife now, fastening it to her waist. Maybe that would soothe her otherwise jumbled wits.

As she returned to the task at hand, Adanya's hand brushed something - something smooth as silk. She looked down to see a flash of white. Temaru's baptismal gown! How could she have forgotten to give it to Reverend Goodheart? That must be what her subconscious was trying to tell her. Now the picture, the nagging feeling, finally made sense. Or did it?

Adanya turned on heel, almost stumbling over Mikao. She struggled, her body tipping to and fro, to maintain balance. Where had he come from? Tonight, like so many nights in recent weeks, he wore the dragon robes. Why was his wardrobe suddenly so limited? Surely he had not worn the sign of the dragon to tend to Widow Lockshine.

"Mikao, I apologize, my teacher," said Adanya hurriedly. "I neither heard your footsteps nor felt your presence."

The Healer bowed low. "Namaste." He then stood to full height, raising his eyes to meet hers. "Where is your son?" His voice possessed an eerie, commanding quality.

That feeling, that nagging feeling, swept over Adanya again. What was it? Her mind held the mental image of Goodheart carrying Temaru into the night.

"He is with Reverend Goodheart," she replied. "The good man offered to baptize him." For some reason, the speaking of those long-awaited words elicited no joy. Adanya rushed on. "I plan to join them shortly." She gestured to the infant's ceremonial gown, still draped over her arm.

"Precious moments pass like grains of sand," said the teacher. "You must go to them without delay, Mistress. You must find your son." Mikao spoke with such undiluted urgency that it frightened Adanya. He motioned towards the packed items. "What is the value of gold compared to the life of your son?"

"What is wrong, Mikao? What do you know?" Adanya tripped over her tongue as the words shot out. "You must tell me," she implored.

The dwarf's eyes bored into Adanya. "Nothing is hidden from the soul. You know the truth."

Truth? What truth? Why was this wise man speaking in riddles - again? "I know only that I cannot have my precious son blessed with the Creator's mark in naught but his diapers." Adanya attempted a nervous laugh but it fell sorely short. She then asked, "Would you like to witness the giving of the Creator's mark?"

Mikao looked at Adanya. For a moment, she thought that he might speak on matters of monumental importance. But, when he finally gave his thoughts utterance, the actual words carried little weight. "I will come," he said. "But do not wait for me. There are matters that I must attend to."

With nothing more than a quick good-bye, Adanya entered the veiled mysteries of night. Running Wolf, already yards ahead of her, maintained a rapid pace. And she knew intuitively that the Winged One flew the never ending sky. Like Mikao, these animal guides communicated a sense of imperative movement. From the open door, the dwarf watched. Then he, too, disappeared.

Adanya moved in haste, leaving the cottage far behind as she journeyed towards the heart of Ambilen. Reverend Goodheart's willingness to open the town center at this late hour surprised her yet his kindness often amazed her. Tomorrow, with the Creator's mark upon Temaru, she could readily let go of this town with its toxic, rancid atmosphere. But she would miss her cherished friends, including the reverend.

Then it happened. Out of the corner of the eye, Adanya caught a fleeting glimpse of shadow, an unexpected movement. She ceased walking, her senses heightened, as her right hand instinctively moved to the blade at her waist. The woman stood perfectly still, trying to slow her wildly beating heart. What being shared the cloak of darkness on this summer's night?

Her answer came, without further delay, in a blurred, swirling pattern of lion-like fur . . . Goldwyn. Adanya chuckled in sheer relief. That blasted cat invested a considerable amount of time, especially in recent weeks, following her. He'd shown up everywhere - in the treatment room, at the baker's. It mattered not. In fact, Goldwyn spent more time with her than he did in the company of his own master. Adanya doubted, in fact, that she had ever seen the two of them together. The feline always managed to be out, undoubtedly on the prowl, whenever Mikao spent time with her.

Mystery solved, Adanya continued to the town center. If fully alert, she might have wondered about the fact that no lights flickered in the distance. Now, however, standing at the building's pine doors, Adanya felt truly perplexed. No light emanated from the water glass window panes. Could the ancient ritual possibly dictate that the ceremony occur in total darkness?

She reached out to pull the entry doors open but they held firm. That's when Adanya first noticed the big steel chain with its links weaving in and out of the door pulls. A large metal lock held them securely in place. Dread crept over Adanya. She frantically banged, pounding her clenched fists on the doors, tugging desperately at them. The hinges refused to budge. Running Wolf circled, back and forth, trying to find an alternate way in. The Winged One sounded an alert in the nighttime sky.

Undeterred, Adanya located several discarded crates in the alley adjacent to the building. She piled them, unsteadily, one atop another, until she could stand, equal to a side window, and peer inside. But what she saw caused her heart to sink further. Nothing. She saw nothing. No light. No movement. No Temaru.

In desperation, Adanya unbuckled a shoe and, covering her hand with her skirt, smashed the window using blunt force of a sturdy heel. Clearing away broken fragments of glass, she hoisted herself over the wide sill, sliding inside to the floor. She cried out for Temaru and Reverend Goodheart, shouting their names with her new-found voice. Again and again. Nothing. Inch by inch, meandering like a sightless man, bumping into the religious altar as well as pews and candles, she searched. Nothing. Panic mounted.

But Adanya pushed the feeling away, willing herself calm. There was no time for that. She intentionally forced her breathing to slow. Breathe in . . . 1, 2, 3 . . . Breathe out . . . 1, 2, 3.

"The Universe is unfolding perfectly," she said to no one in particular. This time, however, the dread, the stone residing in her stomach, found the familiar affirmation almost impossible to embrace.

Think. This made no sense. Reverend Goodheart specifically said that he would baptize Temaru. Tonight. He said it had to be done tonight because of the full moon.

The moon! That's it! "He's doing it under the full moon." Adanya again spoke aloud. And, suddenly, she knew Temaru's location - the forest glen. Strangely, the thought failed to comfort her. Certainly Adanya felt close to the Creator in that beautiful clearing. Yet she wondered why the reverend chose to take Temaru there. She knew, better than most people, that the reverend's conservative, fairly traditional views hampered his ability to experience the Great Spirit outside the walls of town hall. This made no sense.

Still, Adanya knew it to be true. Temaru was in the forest glen. The concerned, apprehensive mother exited the building in the same manner that she previously gained entry. Then she followed the moon. She followed the moon down the well-traveled path, past the tall trees and the summer flowers. She followed the moon, trusting its translucent beams to light they way.

And, in the clearing, that round, fully formed moon shone on Temaru. Like a spotlight, it illuminated his nakedness as he lay motionless on the stone altar - oblivious to the knife clenched directly over his heart.

# CHAPTER XXXVIII

Unaware of her son's plight, Adanya crashed through the brush and tangled vines into the familiar clearing. She stopped short, however, as a surreal scene unfolded before her. The open space, encircled by a cluster of majestic fir trees, still and silent, shrouded in darkness save for the light of the moon, the elusive flickering of altar candles. Neither bird nor beast cried out.

The shimmering light, for but a fleeting moment, illuminated a mangled, discarded mass on the ground. Adanya recognized the twisted metal as the junked remains of Lando's inspirational sculpture. Intentionally flung its position of honor, the artwork rested in a crumpled, lopsided heap. Her eyes rapidly darted to its former place of honor. Atop the stone altar, rolled Temaru, her son. A menacing, shadowy figure, stripped bare to the waist, hovered over the infant, wielding a six inch blade.

"Mistress Adanya, I've been expecting you. Welcome home to your lair. Or should I call you, 'Mistress of the Underworld'? You are the Satan's lover, are you not?" Reverend Goodheart spat the words with an intense loathing, the likes of which Adanya never before experienced.

Adanya felt as if Goodheart plunged a knife through her very own heart. Confusion mixed with an almost suffocating terror threatened to paralyze her - yet she never took her eyes off her son. "Reverend Goodheart, I don't understand. What are you doing to Temaru?" She struggled to steady her voice but feared the battle lost. "That doesn't look like the sacrament of baptism."

"You are quite astute for a pagan, Adanya. Where do they teach witches such things?" Reverend Goodheart gave a throaty, almost maniacal, chuckle. "Nay, this is not the ritual that most god-fearing people seek for their children. But, when this knife rips through the flesh of your bastard, offspring, spilling the taunted fluid that courses through his veins until he gasps his last breath, he will, indeed, receive the 'mark of the Creator'. He will, most assuredly, feel the Great Spirit's wrath."

Adanya involuntarily trembled, watching the knife quiver in the light of the moon. An elusive candle reflection danced eerily off its blade. Her own weapon was bigger, longer, and, probably, sharper. But could she pull the knife from its sheath in time to rescue Temaru? It was difficult to calculate the inherent risk, the probability of success. Better, Adanya thought, to keep this stranger, this man she once considered a friend, talking, at least for now. Perhaps she could reason with him.

"Temaru is without sin, Reverend. I am the one who chose to accept Manutea's seed without the benefit of a commitment ceremony. Take me, kill me, if you must, but leave Temaru unharmed." Adanya hoped against hope that she could reason with the crazed clergy. He had obviously taken leave of his senses.

"Without sin? Did the Creator tell you that when he spoke with you last? What else does he say to you?" The reverend's cruel, ridiculing words cut Adanya to the core of her being. "You boast that he talks to you. What does the Creator confide in you?" This misguided mortal, his obvious sarcasm, openly mocked the terrified young woman.

Adanya felt as if she walked a taut circus tightrope finely stretching hundreds of feet in the air. One false move, one misstep or poorly chosen word, would cost her dear son his life. She spoke in even, cautious tones. "It is not my intention to boast, good reverend. For the Creator speaks to every spirit. Surely you have heard him call your name. A man of your stature is chosen by the Great Spirit - just as every man and woman belongs to him."

"You are a temptress, Mistress Adanya," the looming figure replied. He gazed at her as if seeing her for the first time, sweat streaking down his muscular chest, his face betraying feelings akin to lust. "How many nights have I lain awake thinking of you? Those perfect lips, round, supple breasts." Goodheart's eyes slowly, methodically, moved down Adanya's body like groping, uninvited fingers.

"The fire in my loins burns for you. Over and over, I begged the Almighty to take this curse from me, to purify my soul. I even submitted my vessel for purification to no avail." The reverend rotated into the light, ever so slightly, so that the horrified woman could witness the unmistakable scars of self-flagellation. Not once, however, did Goodheart release his hold of the weapon.

What was he talking about? Adanya's mind raced. Did Reverend

Goodheart have feelings for her? He never previously professed more than a proper, abiding friendship. What was going on?

"But you see, Adanya. How could I ever possess you when you claimed to have slept with the Creator? It is blasphemy, yes, blasphemy." He gestured to Temaru. "Here is the evidence of your wickedness, 'Temaru, son of the Creator'. I must, you see, eradicate this embodiment of evil. Only then can you be wholly mine, pure, without the stain of your past indiscretion."

Adanya stared at Goodheart, this man from whom she once sought counsel, in utter disbelief. Who was the madman before her?

"Good reverend, surely you, you of all people, must understand," Adanya implored. "We are all children of the Creator. You, me, Mikao - everyone. We all come from the father. The sacred mother gives birth to all. I am special, chosen by the Creator. But I am not exalted over another. This legacy is every person's birthright."

Goodheart laughed, raising his face to the heavens. "Oh, Adanya. You wield words turning sand into fool's gold. You wish me to believe that Temaru, this bastard, this unwanted half-breed, is the chosen son of the Creator? Nay! I will not." The man's voice now turned from loathing to an all-consuming, unimaginable rage. "I know that he is naught but the seed of Satan."

"Do you not know that power within your own son? Have you not seen the witchcraft that flows from him? Levitating pendulums, apples and flour sacks?" The reverend glared at Adanya's incredulous face with disdain. "You think I lie about events that I have seen with mine own eyes," he snarled. "You think that I am making up the events of the garden and cellar? Adanya, your son dumped a bag of flour - floating mid-air - on his own head! What mortal possesses such power?"

"I have watched this evil incrementally reveal its insidious nature. I have watched and waited, rather patiently I must say, for a long time," said the reverend. "I'd hoped that a well-placed word here and there might incite the townspeople to kill Temaru. Then you and I could be together. But on that fateful night, when they finally took up arms, those foolish boars, mindless twits that they are, sought to sacrifice you. And I couldn't let that happen. Can't you see the depths of my love for you?"

Adanya's mind raced back to that night. Wilhelmina had warned her - warned her that the townspeople plotted to act against her. Adanya knew then that someone, undoubtedly, provoked the crowd to action. But she thought that the instigator had been Petro. Could she have been wrong?

It made no sense. In the midst of crisis, the reverend actually calmed the angry mob.

"You, Reverend? You whipped the townspeople into frenzied acts? But you've always been so good to us." Yet, even as she said it, previously unacknowledged truths crept into Adanya's consciousness. The reverend never expressed support for her search for the goddess. In fact, he deemed Adanya so unworthy that he'd cast her out of the town hall worship. Or, at the very least, he'd done nothing to prevent the ouster. Could he have orchestrated other disturbances under this twisted guise of friendship?

Reverend Goodheart continued to brandish the knife but he held it carelessly now, relishing his innate ability to entertain a captive audience. How many years had he honed this skill? It fed his uncontrolled fury, his insatiable ego, to transfigure an emotionless crowd, to evoke long dormant fears with little more than vivid imagery and dramatic license. He played them, like a masterful musician, tuning their erratic thoughts into a common state of accepted discord. The dissonant sound, rising like a crescendo, spilled out into the streets from the town hall.

"I spied you in this forest glen," he said, wildly punctuating his words with reckless gestures of the blade. "You and all your pagan friends. I watched and I waited. I knew that the Almighty called upon me to vanquish the dark forces of evil. I followed you. I followed you every day. I observed this vile spirit you call, 'Temaru' discover his power. Pendulums swung in the air without benefit of human hand. Apples danced in your cellar. His powers were expanding, growing potent. I dared not delay."

"Today, with the power of the Almighty on my side, I decided to strike a decisive blow against evil. As you and that oaf, Lando, along with his meddling wife, visited, I snuck into the old barn's rafters, slicing the rope that held the hay bales aloft." Reverend Goodheart paused, sensing Adanya's intense focus on the knife in his hand. "It cuts the hair on your arm without effort," he said, momentarily digressing.

"Of course, I had no idea that the flamboyant artist also stocked a bit of altruism in his veins," snarled Goodheart, continuing the discourse with unconcealed contempt. "The free-falling bales would have broken this little bastard's neck if not for Lando's swift - quite unwelcome - intervention."

The conversation spiraled nowhere, fast. With every word, Reverend Goodheart descended further into madness. Adanya was running out of time and she knew it. She edged ever closer to her destiny as evil's manifestation ranted, enthusiastically spouting hell and damnation. She sent out a frantic, telepathic call to her animal guides.

Still, Goodheart rambled on and on. "But I love you, Adanya. I could never hurt you. I mean only to erase any evidence of your transgression," declared Goodheart.

He gestured to Temaru, his fevered pitch at its dramatic climax, and, muscles tensed, lifted the knife, grasping its bone handle with both hands, high above his head. "The time for purification is now," he proclaimed. Then, fueled by illusions of grandeur, his perceived self-importance, the delusional mortal plunged the knife irreversibly downward.

As the blade's tip touched the soft flesh of its yet unflinching target, Running Wolf materialized from the forest, lunging at the man's right arm. Goodheart screamed and turned, more enraged than seriously injured. The sheer force of the attack, however, threw the reverend off his feet as man and beast rolled over and over, a cloud of dirt obscuring merging forms, in a deadly fight to the finish. Adanya, recognizing the narrow window of opportunity, flew in the direction of Temaru, snatching her son safely from the altar.

A massive dark stain seeped into the rich soil. Still, Adanya moved forward through the billowing haze, barely skirting the raging, tumbling bodies. Had the blade penetrated her son? Would Running Wolf vanquish the madman? There was no time to think. Every determined step brought her closer to liberation. Soon they would be out of the clearing, protected by dense foliage. The blanket of fir trees offered refuge. It was their only hope.

Suddenly, however, inches from the protective shelter, Adanya's body snapped, lurching uncontrollably, as a bloodied, desperate hand grabbed her ankle, cementing it firmly in place. The sheer force, coupled with inherent momentum, catapulted Temaru into the air, landing the infant outside of his mother's immediate view. Her own body smacked the ground's hard, unforgiving surface with a sickening thud. Her head rang as her body fought waves of nausea. Even so, in a blurry moment of delirium, as her face forcefully, unintentionally kissed the earth, Adanya thought that she saw that silly cat, Goldwyn.

Wounded, holding her injured stomach, the Beloved attempted to scramble to her feet but Goodheart, who outweighed the girl by more than a hundred pounds, soon overpowered her. He lay on top of her - swearing, bleeding, and seething. "Did you think that the scraggly wolf could stop me, Adanya? How dare you thwart my purpose! What a foolish, stupid little heathen you are! And that foolishness" he roared, "has just cost you your life!"

With that hate-filled declaration, Goodheart's fists assailed Adanya. He beat her relentlessly, without mercy, over and over, about the head and face, his blood joining with hers. Punch after devastating punch brought the Beloved closer and closer to her imminent demise.

Adanya squirmed under the stone-like weight of her attacker. She strained to reach her knife still in its tight-fitting sheath. But it was no use. Finally, listening to a voice from within, Adanya ceased to struggle. And in that brief moment, before committing her body to spirit, the young woman acted upon the inner wisdom. Adanya prevailed upon the archangels.

She cried out with each precious, remaining breath, her voice rising to the heavens, invoking celestial protectors to come to her aide.

> *Archangels of the heavenly realm*
> *Fly to my side, your power at the helm.*
> *Michael, Remiel, Raguel*
> *I beseech thee.*
> *Uriel, Gabriel, Raphael*
> *Come to me!*

Fists - raging, lethal weapons - continued to pummel her. But, as she was about to surrender to death's sweet sanctuary, the brutal battery stopped. The air, the clearing's atmosphere, felt infused with an unmistakable electrifying charge. Adanya sensed Goodheart's confusion, his bewilderment, as he, sufficiently deranged, looked about.

Then it happened. A rotating whirlwind, of no conceivable origin, kicked up in the midst of the clearing. The mighty wind, this unstoppable funnel cloud, swept through the outdoor area tossing everything in its path - everything, that is, except the Beloved. Goodheart found himself torn from Adanya, hurled with excruciating force off of his intended victim. In fact, the weaving corkscrew pinned the dumfounded man against a large boulder. But, before either Adanya or Goodheart could fully comprehend what had transpired, nature's force vanished. The wind simply evaporated. Calm, invincible vibrations replaced the chaotic frenzy of the previous moment.

Adanya, blood streaming down her bruised, beaten face, forced open one swollen eye. She blinked. For before her eyes materialized a most magnificent vision. Was she hallucinating? Angels, imposing, towering angels, standing more than fifty feet in the air, filled the sacred clearing with their holy presence. Remiel, Raguel, Uirel and Raphael surrounded the four corners of the open space. Michael soared above it like an angelic ceiling as

Gabriel's form actually became the earth beneath Adanya's tortured body. The Beloved found herself cradled breathed a sigh of relief, protected in a winged embrace.

Adanya experienced the angels' majesty, their unmistakable authority. She instinctively knew that, whatever the outcome, she was forever loved, eternally protected. Serenity replaced fear.

Goodheart, however, encountered no such state of grace. This man who professed to serve the Creator viewed the celestial sighting, the presence of archangels, in abject terror. Defenseless, he cowered behind a rock, hunkering low, until nagging curiosity overtook trepidation's paralysis. The madman cautiously craned his neck upward, turning his eyes to the sky.

That was a mistake. But, by the time the misguided mortal recognized his folly, it was too late. Reverend Goodheart's final earthly image consisted, not of angels, but of a mighty hawk's talon swooping down to pluck out the offender's eyes.

Adanya, her body racked with inconceivable pain, lost consciousness. But, even as she lapsed into the comforting arms of blissful oblivion, she witnessed the most unbelievable, other-world transformation. Goldwyn, looking every bit like a majestic lion, stealthily jumped upon the stone altar. Adanya, her strength slipping away, watched, her sight blurring, images shifting, as cat became dwarf and dwarf became dragon.

The firmament shook uncontrollably. The altar crumbled, disintegrating under the excessive weight of the massive, twenty foot creature. With no more effort than a horse might swat an annoying, overly zealous fly, the ferocious dragon dispensed of the resulting debris, stepping over it, clearing a path with his mighty tail. The Earth quaked with every reverberating step as the beast closed the distance between his oversized snout and a blind, senseless mortal, still helplessly seeking refuge behind rock.

Mercifully, Goodheart, reduced to a shrinking vestige of his former self, could not envision the horror that was about to befall him. His unseeing eyes, outward symbols of an inner spirit devoid of compassion, could not see the approach. Yet he knew the hour, the very moment, his death drew near.

With a single emission of fiery breath, one final transformation occurred. Reverend Goodheart, this malevolent being, returned to the earth in a spectacular display of blazing fireballs. *Ashes to ashes, dust to dust.* Only a six-pointed star remained.

# CHAPTER XXXIX

The buttercup sun trumpeted the arrival of four road weary travelers into the magnificence of the Valley of Lilies. Adanya surveyed the familiar land with anticipation, feeling the overpowering presence of Elu and Mahwah. She witnessed Elu's form in the flaxen fields and distant mountains. Mahwah lovingly caressed the Beloved's cheek with the fleeting, feathery touch of a hummingbird's wing. Images of the past superimposed on the present.

Adanya luxuriated in the beauty of the meadow, dotted with blooms of every hue. Then, in a moment of carefree abandon, she thrust Temaru upon Sherlana's generous lap and sprang from the slow moving, ox-drawn wagon. She joyfully frolicked through the high grass, butterflies streaming in the wake of her vibration, the past, present and future melding to create this glorious moment. She spun 'round and 'round, beaded skirts twirling, as she lifted her arms to the infinite blue of heaven, becoming one with the Earth.

Adanya galloped like the fiery, wild horses that still roamed freely in the canyon, faster and faster. Her soul's passion spilled out, overflowing into the limitless Universe. Then, without warning, as quickly as it had begun, the impromptu celebration abruptly ceased.

The Beloved's demeanor changed, her spirit transformed, as she solemnly bowed low and entered the Tree *of Life's* full, leafy canopy. As her father before her, Adanya reverently knelt, offering immeasurable gratitude. For she now understood the sanctity of the tree, the sacred ground in which it grew. She humbly gave thanks for everything - all people, all experiences - that had brought her to this specific place, this critical crossroads, in her life. All the while, the Winged One circled overhead, guarding the Beloved's solitude.

Soon, as one might anticipate, Running Wolf trotted into full view with Temaru bouncing unsteadily atop him, chubby, uncoordinated fingers clumsily grasping onto the animal's fur, riding like an entitled nobleman. The wagon carrying Lando and Sherlana lumbered not far behind. Adanya welcomed the honored guests to her childhood home.

The group quickly erected a make-shift camp by the serene, azure waters of the lake. After dinner, Adanya, her stomach full on a common man's feast of corn bread and pig entrails, took out her fiddle. Woodland creatures, as they had so long ago, encircled the mortals. Their heads, their bright, shiny eyes, peeked out from behind rocks and trees, their alert ears quivering. Fox and fawn, rabbit and raccoon. They appreciatively listened to the eternal song that played throughout the valley. Somewhere a distant flute accompanied the girl in silent harmony.

That night, after tucking Temaru securely into his cradle, Adanya meditated under the *Tree of Life*, in the company of the spirits of those who had walked before her. Their lives permeated her soul. As dusk gave way to a mystical twilight, she took pen to paper.

> *I am part of all that has come before me. My spirit connects to the Universe - at a place where there is no beginning and no end. The stories of all eternity play throughout my soul. I feel the joy and sadness. I remember the peace and the struggle. It all comes together to make up that which is me - a physical, spirit-filled being, at this moment in history.*

> *Yet I am my own person. For never before has a human walked this Earth with my footprint. My connection with the past only serves to prepare me in the present. What I do with this connection, the information that extends beyond all time, is up to me. Only I can determine its interpretation for my life.*

> *I ask my Higher Self to help me as I consider the wisdom of the ages. What pieces will reach across time to touch my life? How will I use this gift for the greatest good? In the silence, I ask Spirit, my sacred father, to speak.*

Then the Beloved spoke for all beings to hear. "Creator, thank you for this story, my story, which begins before time began. I now open it to the current chapter of my life. Guide me as I ask the wisdom of the ages to help me write my own tale. Let me understand and appreciate the connection that flows between every life and every lifetime. May all thoughts, words, and deeds serve my highest purpose. Amen."

Adanya avoided the burned out cabin, the site of Elu and Mahwah's physical passing, until the next day. As morning's soft light spread sleepily over the mountains in the East, she kissed her slumbering boy and quietly departed from the campsite, careful not to wake her fellow travelers. She walked, her heart in her throat, to the place where flame once irreversibly fused endings and beginnings.

A flood of memories washed over Adanya as she surveyed the site through the early morning mist. She remembered laughing with Mahwah as they prepared the evening meal. She saw Elu's figure move to pray at the homemade altar before leaving the cabin, intent on the day's work. One by one, the visions appeared, unbidden, mixing and merging. The past, once again, superimposed on the present.

Truthfully, Adanya fully expected to find the homestead exactly as she had left it. She saw, however, that only the stone fireplace remained. A healing wind had scattered the ashes, the charred lives, beyond the four corners of the earth. Now mice and squirrels lived on the land that once bore her childhood home. They scurried in and out of obscure hiding places, content with the bounty provided. And, as Adanya gazed through dawn's pink blush, she spotted something else. There, in the center of the earthen space, a single flower grew. . . a lotus blossom.

Adanya fingered the pendant around her neck. It made no sense. She stared at the flower, alternately blinking and rubbing her eyes. Had she gone mad? Had the memories of this place overwhelmed her? No lotus blossom could grow in this soil or survive the ever-changing climate. It simply was not possible.

Yet, as she carefully brushed its soft petals, burrowing her nose deep within its fragrant flower, Adanya knew it to be real. In her soul, a voice spoke, "Who is your father? Who is your sacred mother? The goddess lives in tranquil waters."

Tranquil waters? Adanya continued to pensively finger her pendant. Something turned within her brain. Could it be? Did the goddess live within Tranquility Falls - or the peaceful waters of the lake below? Why hadn't she thought of it before? The years of searching, of preparing her soul

- were they for naught? Had the goddess resided here, all this time, in the Valley of Lilies? Did the goddess dwell within Adanya's very own home?

Lando's gravelly, unmistakable voice drifted from the campsite, interrupting her thoughts. The Beloved instinctively sensed her son's stirring. There was no time to think about these matters now. But soon, very soon. The goddess was indeed nigh.

Adanya's immediate priority - survival - necessitated the homestead's preparation for herself and Temaru. Miraculously, Elu's crops re-seeded themselves and an ample supply of corn, potatoes, squash and tomatoes continued to grow. If neither pest nor plague visited the fields, this year's anticipated harvest would yield more than enough to meet the modest needs of the young mother and son.

Meanwhile, as the mid-summer sun beat down upon them, Lando and Sherlana sought to disassemble the destroyed cabin's fireplace stones. Day after day, they employed ax and chisel to dislodge the firmly entrenched stones. Bit by bit. Piece by piece. The chimney, a product of Elu's fine craftsmanship, refused to easily yield.

Nonetheless, after a week of intensive, backbreaking labor, the stones lay, one next to another, awaiting reassembly, in the harvest barn. The three friends decided that it made sense for Adanya and Temaru to take up residency in the oversized structure. Elu originally built it of fine oak planks, masterfully connecting the boards with intricate wooden pegs, and, unless lightening struck twice, it was likely to withstand nature's fickle elements for more than one hundred years. There would be more than sufficient room within its protective walls for a mother to raise her growing boy. Later, if Adanya chose, she could section off a portion of the former barn for grains and vegetables.

As for animals, at present, Adanya's livestock consisted of one lone milk cow, a cantankerous, fairly mean-spirited bull, one cock and hen, and an amusing, mischievous goat. Lando bartered with an old farmer - surrendering one of the artist's original masterpieces in exchange for the meager grouping. It wasn't much, but it was enough to sustain them. The animals would endure winter's frigid cold alternating between the fields and a converted shed that stood on the property.

Still, both Lando and Sherlana privately anguished about their friend. How would a woman survive alone on the land? A fortnight before their departure, as the women shared a quiet moment, Sherlana, always candid, spoke to Adanya.

"Lando and I worry about leaving you here, girl," she started. "The

Valley of Lilies is beautiful, to be sure, but the land can be unforgiving. Are you certain that you want to stay here alone?"

Adanya looked over at her son, playing just a stone's throw away. "I am never alone, Sherlana," she responded.

Sherlana smiled. "The boy is indeed a gift from the gods themselves," she agreed. "But an infant, even one so precious, may not be enough. What will you do if the waters rise or a warring tribe walks upon your land?"

Adanya did not respond immediately. Instead she pointed to a brilliant star shining on the ebony canvas of night. "Do you see that star, Sherlana? I trust Spirit even on the darkest of nights. The star is a sign of the Creator's presence. No, my friend, I am never alone. I follow the star, even if my own self-created clouds of uncertainty sometimes obscure it. Its light led here to this place. Its light led me home."

"The time is near," continued Adanya. "Every moment of my life brings me back to my authentic self. I grow stronger with each passing day. Nothing - neither flood nor famine - can destroy me or those that I hold dear. We are forever connected by the energy, the love that gives us life."

"But, Adanya," Sherlana interrupted her friend. "What of those who wish you harm? What of those who do not understand your ways, who do not understand Temaru's gifts? Reverend Goodheart was not the only misguided soul on this Earth."

Adanya nodded in sad agreement. "Aye, I also fear that there are more people like Goodheart, more towns like Ambilen. But today, and in the days to come, I walk in peace. Never again will I war - as I once did with Brumledi - with those who think or look different than I do. Never again will I speak words of hate against those who I naught understand nor those who naught understand me. We are all one. We are born of the same energy, the same Creator. To hurt another is to strike my very soul."

"You are not being practical, Adanya," announced an exasperated Sherlana. "What about Goodheart? He would have killed you, murdered your only son, had it not been for the intervention of angels."

"The fact remains, we are all one," the young woman steadily replied. "It is true, some mortals are more evolved in any given moment, but we are all still learning, my friend. We will all ultimately come to the same awakening, the same end to the journey."

"My actions may confuse many people," Adanya conceded. "But there are no differences in Spirit. The truth is clear."

Lando joined the females under the *Tree of Life*, giving his wife a playful peck on the cheek. "What are my fair women speaking of in such serious tones? Is not this evening made by the hand of the gods?"

"You are true-tongued, Lando," said Adanya. She sighed, enraptured. "It is a most glorious evening. And I can hear her clearly - especially on a night as magical as this one."

Lando and Sherlana exchanged puzzled glances. What was going on with their dear friend? Secretly, they expressed concern to one another about the impact of Goodheart's treachery. Adanya seemingly healed so quickly, outwardly appearing to bear no ill effects from the traumatic events. But, perhaps, their initial assessment proved wrong.

"Who speaks to you, lass," queried the increasingly concerned artist. His eyes searched Adanya's face. "Who can you hear?"

Adanya, wrapped in a dreamy, faraway look, stared off into another time and place. Then she leaned forward, speaking excitedly. "In the silence of my sacred space, I hear the voice within. She is strong and clear and wise. Her voice lifts upon the wind like the melodic sound of carillon bells."

Sherlana listened to Adanya, increasingly uncomfortable, alarmed at the young woman's speech. Perhaps it was to be expected, however. Adanya had been through so much in the short time that she walked this Earth. Surely, Sherlana thought, Lando and I should have anticipated this break with the world and its reality - for the world's reality had been quite unkind to the girl.

Adanya recognized the overwrought looks exchanged between husband and wife. She chuckled. "Do you think me daft? Fear not, for I can indeed hear her. She guided me through that unforgettable night with Goodheart into a new dawning. She knows the way. I trust myself to follow the path that she makes before me."

The gentle faces before her registered shock. Adanya sought to reassure her dear friends. "Rejoice! For the path leads to the Creator, to my Divine self. The Creator lives in me and around me and through me. I can hear her!"

Sherlana moved to gently embrace her friend. "Who do you hear, my child? Whose voice speaks to you?"

Adanya pulled away, incredulous. "Why, the goddess, of course."

# CHAPTER XXXXI

The siren's song beckoned in the languid heat of late summer. It whispered Adanya's name in quiet, private moments. From the fathomless depths of the lake, shimmering as a flawless diamond, it called to her. Dusk to dawn, long after fireflies extinguished their ethereal glow, the voice rode the wind. It summoned the Beloved, again and again, enticing her with its seductive aria, to enter the watery world.

"Adanya, come to me," the voice urged. "Adanya, come to me." Its rapturous tone sounded like the dulcet cords of a harp.

Night after night, as celestial bodies aligned in the heavens, Adanya heard the tempting siren's song. But she ignored it. For she knew that Lando and Sherlana neither understood its pull nor her rapt fascination. It took the young mother days to assuage her friends' fears after she openly acknowledge that the goddess - in addition to the Creator - spoke to her. In fact, Lando, his face creased with extreme anxiety, insisted on temporarily postponing their long planned departure.

Yet, in too short a time, after repeated assurances, as well as more than a few tears, the artist and his wife bid Adanya farewell. The Beloved watched as her friends' larger-than-life presence disappeared over the crest of the mountain range. With them, went her past. But the couple, despite their necessary exit, left the landscape of her life forever altered.

Adanya, not surprisingly, initially experienced a deep, pervasive void. She desperately missed her eclectic, handpicked family, connected by love rather than blood. Even so, the core of her being remained firmly rooted in an underlying peace that surpassed understanding. The sense of contentment, this trust in the Universe, intensified with every hour that the Beloved walked the Earth. Adanya consciously dwelled in the place where her Creator lived.

This was her home - a home that she now shared with Temaru. Perhaps that's why the final days of Indian summer assumed a golden quality. Every morning, Adanya awoke and, after giving thanks to the Creator, dedicated her fiddler's bow to the archangels, praising them with song and dance under the *Tree of Life's* mighty limbs. Then she returned to their spacious cabin, the former harvest barn, and snuggled with her treasured son.

The mother and child spent their days together in the fields, tending the land that Elu once worked. Adanya sat Temaru on the soil with his gifts, Running Wolf keeping watch, as she pulled weeds or harvested vegetables. Often, as she wiped the sweat that seeped through her clothing, she turned to see Temaru's minerals bobbing in mid-air or the pendulum swaying without the benefit of human hand. This spectacle both amazed and amused the Beloved.

Adanya talked to the Creator while she toiled on the land. She thanked the Great Spirit for all circumstance, for everything that brought her to this time and place in her life. She thanked him for Temaru and his power, power that she, admittedly, did not understand. And she thanked him for the fact that she could now hear the goddess, even if she had not yet laid eyes upon her.

The goddess was nigh. There was no denying her. Adanya could no longer ignore the seductive call - nor did she want to. Less than a handful of sunsets after Lando and Serlana took their leave, Adanya answered the never-ending summons. She slipped from her feather bed and, after wresting Temaru from his dreams, journeyed to meet her celebrated, long-awaited, destiny.

A full moon, its circumference dominating the expansive nocturnal sky, lit the way but Adanya could have walked this familiar path even without illumination. She surveyed the lake, watching the surrounding willow trees sway in the night air. To her astonishment, fairies appeared, flying in and out of the willowy branches. Was that a unicorn? It was as if the mythical creatures were playing a spirited game of hide and seek. Adanya called out to them and the fairies, unafraid, tilted their glittering wings in acknowledgment.

These sights, the fairies' presence, reminded Adanya of the magical world that she had discovered with Manutea on the island of Moricea. Fairies. Leprechauns. Unicorns. It was a world steeped in wonder and mysticism - a world that, at the time, try as she might, she thought she was unable to enter without her lover's presence. Now, however, she conjured the delightful sprites of her own accord.

Adanya stood at the water's edge, rippling its placid, azure surface with her toes. She lifted her arms to the starry sky and spoke. "I am here, Goddess. Your humble servant Adanya has heard your voice and faithfully answered your call. Rise up from your watery kingdom. Make your presence - your power and your majesty - known."

Nothing. For a moment, the scene reminded Adanya of her disastrous, wholly ineffective attempts to summon the Moon Goddess in the forest glen. The thought unnerved her a bit. She prayed that this effort might yield a better outcome.

But this was a different time and place. The goddess, the true deity, was nigh. Adanya knew that the lake held the fortune of which the scroll foretold. The goddess was here, in this lake below Tranquility Falls.

Adanya kissed Temaru, her lips brushing his sweet brow as she entrusted his care to the fluttering fairies. Then, with Running Wolf and the Winged One by her side, she painstakingly climbed upward, ascending the rocky trail to the top of Tranquility Falls, her bare feet cushioned by a plush carpet of velvety green moss. She instinctively knew each turn, every crevice, on the stone passage to the fall's head.

The deafening crash of water as it tumbled, free-falling into the basin below, silenced all other sound at the highest point. Adanya gazed down from overhead and effortlessly slipped out of her dressing gown, letting it fall wordlessly. Naked, her glorious vessel exposed to the Universe, she walked purposefully into the rushing water, motioning for her animal guides to join her.

The Winged One perched on Adanya's extended left arm, as Running Wolf flanked her right side. Wolf. Woman. Hawk. Three spirits eternally connected, forever joined, since time began. Proud and strong, they poised on the brink of Adanya's future, their silhouettes outlined against the full moon.

Adanya took one last look at Temaru, on the Earth far below, his sleeping figure protected by fairy magic, before turning her attention back to the animals. "I know naught what my destiny holds, but you have served me well, dear friends. You are forever in my heart," she said.

A single, crystal tear fell as a lump materialized in her throat. The surging, unexpectedly raw, emotion surprised the Beloved. She hugged Running Wolf, commanding the beast to return to dry land. Then she stroked the Winged One and, with one bold flourish, released him to the heavens. Alone, Adanya inhaled the life force, expanding her lungs to full capacity, and called upon the protection of the gods. Then she dove, head first, off the cliff into the unknown.

One with the night, Adanya's form cut through the blackness as she fell, hurtling towards the water, her body accelerating to greater and greater speeds, her mind void of all thought save the deity. Her firm, supple body, descending like a projectile, parted the tepid lake waters, plunging below the previously unbroken surface. The outside world, the firmament from which she sprang, grew distant, muffled. Adanya no longer heard nocturnal sounds offering a final goodnight. For the Beloved listened to only one.

"Adanya, come to me. Come to me." The siren's song permeated the underwater kingdom even as it consumed Adanya on dry land.

"Adanya, come to me," it said again and again. The Beloved propelled herself downward into the abyss. There was no going back. Deeper and deeper, she thrust into the uncharted waters. "Adanya, come to me." Her lungs pounded. Her head throbbed. She pushed her body beyond the limits of human endurance.

Still, she observed nothing. No fish. No fauna. No goddess. Nothing but blackness. Where was she? Adanya lost all spatial orientation. Up was down. Down was up. Fear crept in at the outer parameters of consciousness. Her chest hurt. Overtaxed lungs cried out for the life force. But she couldn't give up - not now. She was so close. The goddess was within her grasp.

Where was she? She could still hear her voice. "Adanya, come to me." But the Beloved's thoughts scrambled erratically as her limited air supply depleted. Soon the voice sounded like Elu and Mahwah. Was that Sister Angelica that she heard?

Something inside Adanya told her to return to the surface. Temaru needed her. But her leaden arms and legs refused to cooperate. Finally, she called forth her last bit of strength to somersault upward. Or, at least, she thought it was upward. But, as she did so, something physically shifted. A chain grazed her skin. The pendant! Loose, it slithered farther and farther away, out of Adanya's reach, aimlessly drifting in the water's incessant pull.

Panicked, Adanya attempted to follow the necklace. She couldn't leave the lake without it. It held her destiny. Maybe she could find her prized possession in the silt on the lake's bottom. A voice from deep within said, "You will find your gifts within the goddess."

As the crow's call signaled midnight, a lifeless body floated on the surface of an otherwise placid, azure lake.

# CHAPTER XXXXII

Atop falling waters, a lone wolf howled in the pale moonlight. His plaintive cry echoed off the mountains, reverberating through the valley and beyond. A hawk, the messenger of the Great Spirit, circled in the vast expanse of night, keeping a solemn watch over the body. A baby, finding no comfort in the grim reaper's presence, cried for his mother.

Legends told 'round the fire by ancients - faces creased, memories faded - hint that the moon's spirit gave heed to the animal's anguished plea. Or perhaps the orb merely conceded death's unfavorable repercussions on generations yet unborn. No mortal knows for sure. But on that unprecedented night, as the mysterious veil between two worlds evaporated in a fine mist, a portal opened in the sky.

From its depths, an enchanting being of decidedly feminine persuasion emerged. The shapely figure glided down an opaque, unwavering moonbeam - graceful, elegant, and majestic. Adorned in a translucent gown of glittering gold with accents of spun silver, her golden hair a mass of upswept curls, this woman shone with the beauty of all eternity. She radiated love, a befitting escort for the spirit about to leave this earth.

Yet no spirit ascended. Instead, the lifeless vessel remained face down, suspended in neither heaven nor hell, adrift in a watery purgatory. The celestial visitor tarried not under the lake's surface but effortlessly strolled over it, never once breaking its glassy surface. The woman - if that is indeed what she was - gently turned the floating mass over, outlining sacred symbols in the air even as she blew stardust across the ashen, already bloated, face.

The body's shell, as if suddenly possessed by unknown entities, jumped. Eyes, the color of sapphires, opened wide. The mouth, already agape in death's frozen strangle, emitted a rattling noise, followed by desperate gasps, like a fish stranded on dry land, as it inhaled the life force. The vessel flailed both arms and legs, moving violently, slapping the water.

Extending a hand, the deity assisted Adanya to her feet. Then the two walked, again crossing the glassy surface, levitating ever upward, not to the Beloved's heavenly reward, but only as far as the uppermost peak of Tranquility Falls. There, water raging around her, Adanya cried bitter tears of surrender. She failed. Her life, which was obviously at its physical end, had been for naught.

"Why do you cry, Adanya?" the celestial visitor inquired. "What heartache, what anguish, possesses you?"

"I failed," sobbed the distraught mortal. "I failed to find the goddess. It was my life's mission." Her hands moved instinctively to her neck, now bare. "I even lost the ancient scroll."

Adanya suddenly stopped, her tear-stained face rising to meet her companion's gaze. "How did you know my name?" she asked, her eyes reflecting fear. "How did you know my name?"

"This is not the first time we have met, Beloved. We have known each other for all eternity," came the affectionate reply. "Have you forgotten? Not so long ago, we conjured spells in the forest glen outside of Ambilen."

Adanya scrambled backward, assuming a defensive posture. "You are Aeracura, Goddess of the Underworld!"

The woman smiled. "I am whatever, whoever, the Creator calls me to be. But, yes, that is what I said. Tonight, however, I am as you once named me, 'Moon Goddess'."

"But," Adanya sputtered, "why would you come to me as Aeracura? What purpose did that serve?"

"It served your highest purpose, my child. For you needed to understand the heavy toll that separation from spirit takes. You needed to explore your darker side so that you could later choose freely to walk in light."

"Then you really are the Moon Goddess?" asked Adanya.

"Yes, I am the one who rules the moon, who governs the ebb and flow of the tides," assured the deity.

Adanya instantly dropped to her knees. "I have searched for you my whole life, my goddess. I honor you and bow low before you."

The Moon Goddess placed a hand on the Beloved's back. "Rise up, Adanya. There is no need to bow low. I am not the goddess that you seek."

Adanya head moved sharply as she stared at the Moon Goddess in disbelief. Her tone reflected years of frustration. "But they said that I would find my gifts within the goddess! That the goddess lives in tranquil waters."

"There was a goddess in the lake tonight, Adanya. But it was not me.

The tranquil waters of which your teacher spoke of are not the peaceful blue of this lake but rather the color of your very own soul."

Adanya, truly confused, remained mute as her mind reeled. What was the Moon Goddess saying? Her thoughts were interrupted by the deity's next words.

"Beloved, you know the truth. You worked hard, diligently, to discover it." The Moon Goddess turned, scanning the immediate shoreline. "Where is your listing of spiritual truths, the one that Sister Angelica asked you to record at the convent?"

Adanya could not quite comprehend what this mystical feminine spirit was saying. Still, she answered her as if from rote. "It's in my journal back in the cabin. I was writing the truths, revising them, earlier tonight."

The Moon Goddess made a sweeping gesture, spoke a few unintelligible words, and the journal appeared in Adanya's lap as if it had been there all the time.

"Read your own words, Beloved. What does your heart say?"

Adanya half-heartedly flipped the book open to the last page, water lapping all around, her words illuminated by the light of eternity.

> *1. Honor the voice within. It shines light onto life's journey. It also gives warnings when we move towards people or behaviors that don't serve our highest purpose.*
> *2. We are all connected - every plant, every person, every animal. We share each others' joys. What hurts one, wounds another. A closed fist, an unkind sentiment, can be felt throughout the Universe. Never intentionally dishonor another spirit.*
> *3. Be careful what you wish for.*
> *4. Nothing is either exclusively good or bad - all things are merely opportunities to grow and learn.*
> *5. Everyone has a choice. It is possible to be a victim yet each one must decide if events victimize beyond the initial act.*
> *6. The Universe is unfolding perfectly. Trust in its benevolent flow.*
> *7. I must live in the here and now. For every breath is sacred. The past is gone. The future is yet to be. Only this glorious moment is real. And, in this moment, I am safe. I am happy. I am whole. I am loved by the Creator.*
> *8. I am connected forever to the Creator, always surrounded by love.*

*9. Do not limit the Creator. His plans, unhampered by my limited perceptions, exceed my most glorious expectations.*
*10. We all learn things at our own pace. That is why there are different opinions, different beliefs. There is no hurry. We will all finish the journey.*
*11. All situations are temporary. Nothing is permanent save the Creator's love.*

As Adanya's voice trailed off, a quill appeared in her hand. "You have learned well, Adanya," said the Moon Goddess. "Now it is time to embrace one more truth, perhaps the most important one. Do you know what it is?"

Adanya shook her head.

"I think that you do. Who is the goddess that you seek?" asked the Moon Goddess. "Tell me about her."

"That's the problem," cried Adanya as she threw down her quill in a fit of total annoyance. "I can't find her. I've searched and searched. Convents. Islands. Villages. I even sought her love through man."

Then Adanya stopped. "Maybe that's the problem."

"Mankind - or a specific man?" The Moon Goddess waited patiently as the mortal considered the issue.

"No, not Manny - or, for that matter, mankind," replied the young woman. "But I destroyed the *Box of Intentions* when Manny rejected me, discarded my love for him. In the box, I had written the word "love". When I destroyed love, when the box smashed upon the rocks, perhaps it prevented me from finding the goddess."

"Adanya," the Moon Goddess replied, "you cannot destroy love. You are love. *Love is your true nature.* Love is not an abstract destination - nor is it found exclusively in the arms of another. Your life is a journey *through* love."

"Besides," she continued, "the power never resided in the box. The box merely served as a tool to help you refine what and how you asked the Universe for things. The power to draw things - people, experiences, possessions - into your life always resided in you."

"I have the power?" Adanya sounded uncertain. "I draw people and experiences to me?"

The deity did not immediately answer. When she spoke, she intentionally created clear images in Adanya's mind. A deer crafted on ancient pottery. Beads for a young girl's skirt. One memory melted into another like the moonbeams.

Into these visions came the goddess' serene voice. "Is that not what you meant when you wrote, '*Be careful what you wish for*'?"

"I remember asking for the deer," said Adanya slowly. "But," she said, straining to remember, "I didn't remember the deer on the pottery until now." Then she added, almost accusingly, "Besides, it wasn't what I wanted."

"No?" The goddess countered. "Perhaps not. But it was exactly what you asked for. Your mind held no specific image of a deer in a forest or on a mountain top. The Universe chose to whimsically manifest your wishes on a serving dish."

"You must be very specific regarding what you ask for," instructed the deity. "Otherwise, you might get the Goddess of the Underworld instead of the Moon Goddess."

Adanya hung her head in shame.

"Nay, do not wear a badge of self-reproach, Adanya. There is no dishonor. You are still learning." The Moon Goddess cupped the Beloved's chin, lifting it. "Life is learning. Learning about love, learning about better, more enlightened ways. You will die an old woman who is still growing in spirit."

"Besides," she said referring to Adanya's list of spiritual truths, "you have learned. Did you not write, '*Do not limit the Creator. His plans, unhampered by my limited perceptions, exceed my most glorious expectations.*'? Is it not better merely to ask the Universe for those things that serve your highest purpose?"

"You are learning," explained the deity. "Yet the truth dwells within you. You know the truth. That is why you came to this physical plane - to learn *and* teach. You must teach what you know - these spiritual truths and so much more. You grow as you uncover your authentic self, as you discover your gifts within the goddess."

"But that's the point," exclaimed Adanya. "I don't know *who* the goddess is or, for that matter *where* she is."

"Answer the question that has been posed for all eternity," directed the Moon Goddess. "Who is your father, who is your sacred mother?"

"I don't know!"

"You know who the father of Temaru is."

"Well, yes, but Temaru will never know Manutea," replied Adanya flatly.

"Manutea may indeed be the earthly vessel who facilitated Temaru's arrival on this planet, even as Elu and Mahwah served as sacred instruments in your life, but who created him?" The Moon Goddess intensely prodded, probing, pushing the Beloved to new levels of greater awareness. "Who did you tell Brumledi the father was?"

Flashbacks streamed through Adanya's consciousness. She remembered Elu that final night in the field. "I have loved you like a daughter yet you are not my child," he said. Then she heard the words she herself spoke to Brumledi. "My son is a glorious child of the Creator."

Adanya cringed. "I beg the Creator's forgiveness," she offered contritely. "I spoke out of pride and arrogance."

The Moon Goddess smiled and stroked the Beloved's cheek. "I heard neither pride nor arrogance in your speech - only truth," she asserted. "The Great Spirit *did* create Temaru. And, if you indeed spoke the truth, as I assure you, you did, then what is the lesson of the lotus blossom?"

Adanya thought back to the island of Moricea, to the Sisters of the Sacred Covenant. She saw the sand and the waves. She saw the peaceful faces of the islanders. She again felt the love that permeated her life. And she clearly remembered the three or four year old boy who proclaimed, in all seriousness, "The Creator lives within the flower, Teacher."

Other students, certain that his words constituted mere folly, ridiculed the small child. But the teacher bowed low before him saying, "Namaste. You are my wise teacher and I honor you."

The Beloved strained to process, to make sense of the information. What did it mean? For years, she dissected this riddle, rolled it over in her mind, poked at it. Maybe now, with all that she had learned, the moment had come to actually answer it.

Truthfully, unbeknownst to her, she already gave the answer voice. What had she told Sherlana under the *Tree of Life*? Adanya couldn't quite remember now. The Moon Goddess awaited her answer.

"If the Creator creates all things," the Beloved began slowly, choosing her words carefully, "and we originate from his hand, then every spirit is a son or daughter of the one who created the Universe."

The Moon Goddess nodded her head encouragingly. "What else?"

"Well," Adanya continued, "if we are all spawn from the Creator, then we carry his imprint in us. He is actually within us, not just a separate figure existing on the outer parameters of our lives."

"You speak the truth," said the Moon Goddess. "But if he created us, and we all carry his imprint, then what does this mean?"

Adanya thought. Then she looked incredulously at the deity as a realization spread through her. Was it possible? It seemed almost sacrilege to give her thoughts utterance. Yet, like a newborn babe unable to return to the safety of his mother's warm womb, Adanya could not turn back.

"It means," she said, "that no one need seek the goddess in a town or a lake. For the riches of which the ancient scroll foretold are neither gold nor silver. They cannot be found in another man - or woman. For the priceless gift that awaits each of us is our own understanding, the certainty, that we are each a divine child of the Creator."

Without waiting for confirmation, Adanya picked up the discarded quill, whetted its tip, and recorded another eternal truth - perhaps the most important one of all.

> *12. I am, as is every spirit, the Creator's divine child. He is my father, she is my sacred mother. His power, his infinite love, dwells within me. I possess all wisdom. I must act according to my rightful inheritance as a child of the Universe. I honor the divinity of every soul.*

"Who is the goddess that you seek?" queried the Moon Goddess.

The Beloved, her spirit aglow, answered humbly, her voice barely above a whisper. "The goddess is . . . me."

In accordance with that celebrated, long-awaited proclamation, the starry backdrop of the nighttime sky transformed itself. Night turned to day as the heavens ignited, ablaze with a wondrous exhibition of shooting stars, their trails crisscrossing into infinity. Adanya, her bare form resplendent, again dove into the sparkling water below. And, when she emerged, defying all laws of nature, she stood suspended in mid-air like a phoenix rising out of the ashes.

A most startling change occurred. Adanya, her body draped in a rainbow of splendor, looked every bit the physical manifestation of a goddess. A bejeweled crown anointed her head while a magnificent Persian blue ring, its shank encrusted with tanzanite and blue topaz, rested regally on her right hand. Adanya, astounded by the appointments, self-consciously touched her neck only to find that her pendant, feared forever lost, graced her décolletage once more. The Beloved's outer grandeur reflected the true nature of her inner spirit.

On her back, as if one with the glorious butterflies which encircled her, luminous, gossamer wings sprouted in honor of the Beloved's spiritual metamorphosis. Lotus blossoms, symbols of mankind's divine heritage, floated on the water's surface as far as the human eye could see.

Then, as Adanya absorbed these spiritual experiences, another indescribable happening occurred. Spirits, shimmering vibrations of light, appeared. They came from sky, earth, air and fire. They came out of the Beloved's past, present, and future.

"Who are these spirits?" asked Adanya. "Why are they here in this time and place?"

'These are the spirits who journey with you through all eternity. Before time began, you entered into a sacred contract to teach and learn from one another," explained the Moon Goddess. "They now come to honor the Goddess Adanya who recognizes her rightful place as a child of the Divine."

Adanya gazed in awe of the growing assembly of spirits, now bowing, calling out, "Namaste," as they entered her presence. She cried as she saw Elu and Mahwah. Mikao and Sister Angelica arrived together. There was Cratch and Brumledi, Reverend Goodheart, and so many others. Many of the apparitions she did not recognize, at least not on a physical level, but she rejoiced in the understanding that these kindred souls consciously chose to journey with her.

At some point, however, a question tormented her. "Most Holy One," ventured Adanya. "I understand why Elu, Mahwah and some of the others came tonight. They love me. But . . ." She paused, struggling to find the right words.

The Moon Goddess smiled, understanding the Beloved's conflicted emotions. "You want to know why Reverend Goodheart and those who hurt you, even hated you, now bow low to honor of you."

Adanya nodded. "Yes," she said simply. "It makes no sense."

"Only love is real, Adanya," explained the deity. "All else is but an illusion. When spirits agree to enter the physical plane, they enter, as I alluded, into a sacred contract. The agreement is to serve one another's highest purpose."

"You needed, among other things," she continued, "to learn to love yourself, to listen to your inner voice - regardless of what society or other people thought. Divine spirits, including Brumledi and Reverend Goodheart, assumed roles to facilitate your growth. Likewise, you assumed appropriate roles in their lives to teach what their spirits most needed to learn."

Suspended in space and time, Adanya immersed herself in the love that created her, surrounded her, and lived through her. She embraced the Creator as her father, her sacred mother. She marveled in the divinity of every spirit. Then, as the moon bid adieu, fading into the birth of a new day, three spirit guides arrived to accompany one very tired goddess home.

Adanya awoke in her feather bed as the sun peeked over the mountains. She instinctively reached for Temaru only to find her son snuggled against Running Wolf. The Beloved, after giving thanks, opened the cabin door to greet the new day. The Winged One perched in his normal spot, high in the boughs of a fir tree.

Everything appeared normal. Was it all a dream? Still in her dressing gown, pendant at her throat, Adanya saw no sign, no outward indication, of the night's previous ceremony.

Yet something was different. Something in her soul stirred. Adanya hugged herself as she remembered. She *was* a divine child of the Creator. This was the gift - her gift as well as that of every man and woman. What would this divine status mean - to individuals, to families, to the world? How would the sacred nature of every soul manifest itself? The tantalizing possibilities, hampered only by the narrow limitations of the human mind, proved infinite.

Perhaps, however, it merely was a dream, an illusion of grandiose proportion – or perhaps not. For, as Adanya picked up her quill and opened her journal, she noticed a large turquoise ring, the shade of Persian blue, regally adorning her right hand. Adanya smiled a secret smile. Words danced unbidden across the page.

### Sacred Woman
*Guiding light on an eternal journey,*
*Of this world, yet spirit-filled.*
*Dancing to the Earth's rich rhythms,*
*Divine celebration of celestial love.*
*Enlightened Master - teacher to all,*
*Seeker of immortal truths.*
*Sacred, the Woman who dwells within me.*

# EPILOGUE

*Morning Dove, listened, mesmerized for hours, without interruption, but now spoke. "Grandmother, was it all a dream?"*

*The old woman did not immediately respond. Instead she moved from her position by the fireplace, pausing to steady her ancient, shaking limbs. Then she walked to where her grand-daughter reclined. Removing the pendant from her own neck, the elder leaned down and reverently placed it over Morning Dove's head, lifting the girl's curls, adjusting the necklace as it fell to her chest.*

*"Rise up, Goddess Morning Dove. This is your time. Accept your power and majesty as a divine child of the Creator. Embrace your rightful inheritance." The Ancient spoke the words slowly, solemnly, so that her granddaughter might fully understand the importance of this occasion.*

*Morning Dove, looked in amazement at the spectacular jewel. "But, Grandmother," she responded. "I cannot accept your gift. This was given to you."*

*"No, my child. You are wrong," replied Adanya. "This gift is not solely mine. For it is every man and woman's spiritual destiny. Rejoice in it. The Creator gave these treasures to you before your birth. Now is the time to accept your divine place as a daughter of the one who gives breath to all living things."*

*Morning Dove considered these words then squealed, jumping up to hug the old woman. "Oh, Grandmother, thank you!"*

*The Ancient smiled indulgently, returning the heartfelt hug. "You must not thank me, Goddess Morning Dove. Bow down before your father, your sacred mother." The old woman kissed her check then turned to take her leave.*

*"I will, Grandmother," Morning Dove assured her. "I will. But, wait, before you go, tell me the story of Temaru."*

*Sapphire eyes clouded. The Ancient's demeanor changed. "Ahh . . . so you want to know about Temaru?"*

*Morning Dove nodded. "Yes, Grandmother."*

*"That, my child," the old woman said, her voice tinged with unidentifiable emotion, "is a tale best told on another day."*

# ABOUT THE AUTHOR

Cynthia E. Kazalia admits, unabashedly, to her status as a late bloomer. She walked many paths before discovering the truths that dwelled within her very own soul. These truths, never hidden, were discovered with the guidance of the Creator and support of many wise masters. Kazalia celebrates the divine souls, human and otherwise, who help her to listen to the voice within. She consciously chooses to live where her Creator dwells. (Flawed, she is some days more successful than others in this spiritual endeavor.)

Kazalia currently lives in Grove City, Ohio with her husband, John. In addition to writing, she professionally works with diverse, vibrant women, facilitating workshops and empowering individuals to transform their lives by manifesting their passion.

www.ingramcontent.com/pod-product-compliance
Lightning Source LLC
Chambersburg PA
CBHW020838260626
47169CB00003B/1042